Busted

Gina Ciocca

Cover design by Vanessa Han
Cover images © kaisersosa67/Getty Images; Efimenko Alexander/Shutterstock

Published by Sourcebooks Fire, an imprint of Sourcebooks, Inc.
P.O. Box 4410, Naperville, Illinois 60567-4410
(630) 961-3900
Fax: (630) 961-2168
www.sourcebooks.com

Library of Congress Cataloging-in-Publication data is on file with the publisher.

Printed and bound in the United States of America.
VP 10 9 8 7 6 5 4 3 2 1

For Aunt Gloria, the reason that this story made it out of my head and onto the page.

1

SCALING THE BACK OF A HOUSE SPIDER-MAN STYLE HADN'T BEEN PART of my Saturday-night plans.

Yet there I was, clinging to the ivy-swathed lattice above the garage of a house I'd never been to, peering through the window of a rec room dominated by an oversized leather couch, which was occupied by a boy whose name I couldn't remember as he made out with a girl I'd never met. Two pints of abandoned vanilla ice cream sat on the end table next to them.

The vanilla ice cream that had started it all.

Two pints of Fudgie's ice cream were slowly turning to soup in the front seat of my car because of these two. If I hadn't been in line behind—what the hell was his name? Greg? George?—my double order of Sexual Chocolate (yes, really) and I would be on our way to Charlie's house for a Saturday movie, gossip, and anti-nutrition night like so many Saturdays before. Except, as I stood there waiting to pay, wondering, *Where do I know this kid from and why don't I like him?* it clicked. I'd met the tall, lanky blond boy once, albeit briefly, at a football game I'd gone to at Charlie's school to watch her cheer. He'd been draped over the fence, flirting with her between routines. When he saw me approaching, he'd given me a lazy once-over and sent a halfhearted nod in my direction before taking off.

It was him all right. Longish nose, small mole on his left cheek—*check, check*. But between the way I'd kept my face warm by burying it inside the collar of my winter jacket that night and his disinterested lack of eye contact, he must not have remembered me at all. Because when his eyes darted over to me as he stuffed his wallet into his back pocket after paying for his pints, they didn't show a trace of recognition.

This was Charlie's boyfriend. The guy she went out of her way to not talk about, because she insisted their relationship was no big deal. Yet we'd been dress shopping that very afternoon for a dance he'd asked her to. And she'd tried to hide the dejected look on her face as she'd held a half-zipped, sparkly blue dress around her torso and scanned his last-minute text message canceling their date tonight. I wondered if he planned to drop by with ice cream to make it up to her. Until I watched his two pints of ice cream—Vanilla Bean Dream—disappear into a brown paper bag. I whipped out my phone and sent Charlie a text: Did you change your mind about vanilla ice cream?

Her response came seconds later: **I would not waste energy swallowing ice cream w/o chocolate and you know this.**

That's what I thought.

Curiosity mixed with a bit of admittedly premature disgust and indignation welled inside me.

And just like that, I knew I had to follow him.

Ten minutes later, I'd wound up parked in front of a white colonial with carefully tended flower beds lining the walkway and pillars flanking the front door. It could've been his house for all I knew, but I'd had to circle the block while he parked, and my little detour hadn't allowed me to see how he got in. I'd hoped he lived there and that the vanilla ice creams were for him and his mother.

And maybe tomorrow, I'd wake up a monkey—or a spider, as it stood.

The diamond-shaped wood lattice serving as my foothold groaned softly as I maneuvered my cell phone out of my back pocket. There were probably bugs galore in that ivy, and I didn't even want to think about bigger, hairier creatures that might also be present. My biggest concern was whether the chipped, splintering strips could hold 116 pounds of prying teenage girl long enough for me to get what I came for.

All I could see of Greggie-George and Mystery Blond were their heads on the armrest of the couch, eyes closed, mouths sealed together, oblivious to the television and me, their captive audience.

My lips tightened and the desire to punch him, or bang on the window and give him the finger, flared up inside me. I didn't do either of those things, of course. Instead, I angled my phone toward the two of them kissing like they were going for the gold in the make-out Olympics and snapped a picture.

And realized too late that I hadn't turned off the flash.

Greggie-George's dumbfounded face shot up over the back of the couch. It was the last thing I saw before I gasped and ducked to the side of the window—and before my cell phone slipped out of my hand, landing below with a rustle and a smack.

"Shit!" I hissed.

"What was that?" Mystery Blond's muffled voice came from inside the house.

"Probably nothing," he replied. "Maybe it's your stupid cat."

"Go check. What if there's a raccoon in the yard and Mozart ends up with rabies?"

Shit! Shit! Shit!

My fingers curled around the wood diamonds until they ached and I pressed myself as flat against the house as I could, face buried in the ivy like a child in time-out, fervently hoping that if I couldn't see him, he couldn't see me.

The light shifted as his frame filled part of the window. I refused to look, but I felt his presence, like he was standing right beside me, ready to drop a bag over my head.

A second later: "There's nothing out there. If Mozart's foaming at the mouth next time you see him, just shoot him."

I went limp with relief as the window brightened with his retreat. Mystery Blond's responding giggles died down, and I could only imagine they'd picked up where they'd left off, because I sure as hell wasn't sticking around to find out. I climbed down the lattice as fast as I could, reminding myself to find secure footholds for my black flats so my breaking bones wouldn't become the next sound to pierce the night. My whole body shook with nerves and adrenaline by the time I stood on the ground, level with the garage windows. I frantically scanned the patio for remnants of my phone until a glint in one of the cement planters beneath the windows caught my eye. I made a mental note to never let Charlie make fun of my jeweled phone case ever again as I plucked my perfectly intact phone from its cushion of mums.

A smug smile crept across my face as the screen lit up with my photo. I might've done something rash and stupid, but already, it felt totally worth it. I didn't know who this guy thought he was, but he sure as hell didn't get to screw with my best friend's life.

Of course, I didn't know it then, but I'd just captured the picture that would change *my* whole life.

2

"CHAR!"

I burst into Charlie's kitchen, panting. Doggy nails clicked against the tile as Jelly, her rat terrier, ran in excited circles, as if I hadn't entered the house a million times before. That's the great thing about dogs. You're never old news to them.

"Marisa? I was about to call you! Where the hell have you been?" Charlie appeared in the doorway between the kitchen and living room wearing yoga pants and a sweatshirt that said *That's Madame Bitch to You*, cell phone in hand. Thanks to our dark hair and eyes, Charlie and I have been mistaken for sisters a few times. Granted, my hair has a natural wave to it and Charlie's is poker straight, but we're even the same height—five feet, four and a half inches. Except tonight, she looked freshly showered and ready to relax, and I looked like a train wreck who'd done battle with an overgrown shrub. She eyed the brown bag in my hand that was dotted with wet spots from the melting ice cream. "Is everything okay?"

I scooped Jelly into my arms, giving myself a second to catch my breath. "Everything is fine. I mean everything will *be* fine. I mean..." I shook my head, trying to force my adrenaline-jacked thoughts into coherence. "I have some bad news." I put the dog down and held my phone against my chest. "It's kind of a long story."

"What is? Out with it."

"It's about your boyfriend."

"Jason?"

Jason. I was a little off with the whole Greggie-George thing. And also surprised that Charlie had given up shunning use of the word *boyfriend* when we talked about him, which meant she was finally ready to admit how much she liked him. Which made my news suck all the more.

"He was at Fudgie's buying ice cream."

Charlie's left eyebrow shot up. "He's supposed to be sick in bed right now."

"Right. I thought maybe he was feeling better and bringing the ice cream here for you until I realized they were both vanilla. So... when he left the store, I followed him."

"*Followed* him? What are you getting at, Palmera?"

"He went to someone's house." I pulled up the picture on my screen and held it out to her. "Anyone you know?"

Charlie stared wordlessly, her lips pressed into a taut line. "That. Piece. Of. Shit," she growled. But her voice caught on the last word, and I wished I'd given my delivery more thought.

"I'm sorry, Char."

"No. No, it's fine." She exhaled and straightened her shoulders. "What time does the mall close? Ten?"

"I think so. Why?"

She snatched the bag from my hand, opened the cabinet beneath the kitchen sink where the trash can was located, and dumped our ice cream in it. "Change of plans. We have a dress to return."

The more I thought about it, the more I wished I'd handled breaking the news about Jason differently. It felt wrong to have told Charlie while I was on such a high, but I couldn't help it. Outing a scumbag felt more badass than anything I'd ever done—especially when I told her how I'd gotten the picture, and she looked at me like I'd parted the Red Sea.

Still, by the time Monday rolled around, I continued to worry that I'd been an insensitive jerk. I didn't think I'd *acted* excited when I told her, but knowing I'd felt that way kept eating at me, like maybe she thought I'd trailed him for me and not her. So on Monday afternoon I slipped out of my yearbook staff meeting a few minutes early.

My brother took the bus home on days when I stayed after school, so I made my way out of the building via one of the side exits, planning to head to Charlie's house to apologize.

"Marisa! Hold up!"

I paused at the mention of my name and the accompanying sound of sneakers slapping against concrete. TJ Caruso came flying down the stairs toward me. It took me a second to register that he'd called to me, because I was so unaccustomed to hearing him speak. He'd transferred to Herring Cross for senior year and didn't strike me as unfriendly, just quiet. He usually sat in the back of the yearbook classroom with his feet propped up on the chair in front of him or earnestly editing whatever interview he'd been assigned for the week. Seeing him so animated was a little weird.

"Hey," he said, coming to a stop in front of me. "This, uh, fell out of your pants."

"Excuse me?"

He opened his hand. In his palm sat the silver *M* charm from my ankle bracelet.

"Oh no," I groaned, bending down to inch up the right leg of my jeans. They were tight enough that they'd prevented my broken bracelet from falling off completely, but as I eased the limp strand into my hands, I saw that at least two other charms had slipped free—including my favorite glass poinsettia bead. "Did you happen to find any others?"

He shook his head apologetically. "Only that one." Seeing the dejected look on my face, he added, "But I can take another look when I go back."

"Thanks. I appreciate it."

He jogged up the steps as I contemplated going back inside to search for my charm. My mother had special ordered it for Christmas last year, and the thought of it getting swept into the janitor's dustpan and thrown out with the trash made me nauseous. Except I had no idea where to start looking. The clasp could've snapped this morning and been slowly leaking beads ever since. I'd have to retrace all my steps and—

"Oh, Marisa?" TJ's voice cut into my thoughts and I turned to see him on the landing, one hand poised on the door handle. "Is it all right if I send you my interview with Mr. Leroche on Tuesday? I'm working a ton of hours this weekend."

"I'd really like to get it locked into the layout on Monday, if you can."

TJ scratched his head, making a few of his dark curls dance. "Let me see what I can do. I have this other…obligation that I might be able to get out of."

"No, don't cancel your plans. It's not that important," I said, even though I got the feeling he kind of wanted to get out of whatever it was.

"It's not something I'm looking forward to anyway."

"Oh. Good luck then."

"Thanks. I'll need it." He started toward the school again. As I clutched the remains of my ankle bracelet in my palm, I thought, *You and me both*.

And as I approached my beat-up red jalopy, I realized I needed it sooner rather than later.

Because someone sat perched on the hood of the equally beat-up car that had been backed into the space next to mine, feet propped on the bumper, one hand resting on the faded gray metal as the other typed on a cell phone. Someone with wheat-colored hair, long, slender legs clad in black leggings crossed beneath a short jean skirt, and a cute, freckle-dotted button nose.

No freaking way. I made a mental note to bump up my next eye exam, because that could not be Kendall Keene, my oldest frenemy, draped across the hood of a random car in my school's parking lot.

She looked up then, as if I'd spoken her name out loud. I halted midstep as her green eyes went big. "Oh my God, *Marisa*? Marisa Palmera?"

"Kendall? What are you doing here?"

Her familiar smile, the one with the slightly crooked teeth that somehow made her even more adorable, lit her face. She hopped down from the car. "My boyfriend goes to school here and I thought he needed a ride, but I had the days confused." She waved her cell phone, and I assumed said boyfriend was the one she'd been texting a second ago.

"But I thought you moved to Arizona."

"I did! We moved back to Pennsylvania last year. We're living in Monroe now."

"That's… Wow."

Wow about covered it. Kendall and I had gone to school together and played on the same rec soccer team from third through sixth grade, before I moved to Herring Cross. We did everything together, but our friendship operated like a race run neck and neck. If I had a new pair of shoes I couldn't wait to show off, Kendall would get the same ones and wear them first. If rumors swirled that a boy she thought was cute liked me instead, suddenly I'd find myself the lone member of our circle not invited to her sleepover. Whenever we'd get assignments back, without fail, Kendall asked what grade I got. If she'd scored higher, she'd flourish her paper and show me. If she hadn't, she'd say "oh" and turn away without telling me her score.

By the time she and her family moved to Arizona at the end of sixth grade, we'd grown past most of the immature head-to-head, but our relationship had exhausted itself into friendly-but-not-friends status. So the way Kendall stood there, smiling like we were lifelong BFFs, had me wondering if I'd stepped straight into some kind of time warp.

"Right?" Kendall said, apparently oblivious to my speechlessness. "My dad's job transferred us back last fall. Arizona was amazing, and we met so many great people and did so many cool things, and

Dad got promoted, like, three times, but we really missed our family." She threw her hands up in a *ta-da* motion. "And here I am. What's new with you?"

Until she asked the question, it'd never occurred to me how little my life had changed since the last time we saw each other. Sure, my family had moved too, but two towns over, to a slightly larger house. My mom still taught kindergarten, my dad was still a manager at the Big M grocery store, and my brother had shot up to almost six feet tall but still hadn't grown a filter between his brain and his mouth. I had no life-altering experiences to gush about.

"Not much. Waiting to hear back from colleges, possibly planning a road trip across the country this summer with my best friend. Nothing terribly exciting."

That part was sort of true. Charlie and I talked about road-tripping all the time, but we never seemed to get further than what kind of food we'd need for the ride.

Her eyes lit up. "Are you kidding? A road trip across the country sounds superexciting! Your parents are cool with it?"

"Uh, yeah, so far."

"And your boyfriend?"

The corner of my mouth turned up. "Nonexistent, so definitely."

Kendall slipped her hands behind her with a sheepish expression. "Sorry, dumb question. I've been with TJ so long that I forget some people are still single."

Normally my inner fifth grader would've reared her passive-aggressive head at what felt like an obvious jab, but my interest in the other thing she'd said overshadowed my defensiveness.

"Do you mean TJ as in TJ Caruso? The new guy?" I pointed to the school like he was still standing outside, even though I knew he wasn't.

Something changed in Kendall's expression, but I couldn't quite put my finger on what. It was like a wall had gone up, though I didn't know why when she'd been the one to bring up the subject.

"So you know him?" Her words sounded as carefully measured as a cup of sugar.

"I wouldn't say I know him. He's on yearbook with me, but he's pretty quiet, and we've only talked about school stuff. I didn't even know he had a girlfriend."

She scraped the toe of her ballet flat against a loose piece of asphalt and muttered something that sounded like, "Of course not." I couldn't help but notice the braided, caramel-colored leather bracelet that wound around her ankle. If I hadn't been so busy trying to figure out if this was some sort of strange dream, I would've been salivating over it.

"So wait," I said, slipping the remnants of my own bracelet into my bag. "If he's here, then where are you going to school?"

Her sunny smile returned and she kicked the chunk of asphalt aside, leaving me to wonder if I'd imagined her momentary funk. "Templeton Hall. I applied for the Hartley honors program. All the slots were full when I transferred, but they let me in anyway. Guess I got lucky."

Color me not shocked at all.

"My friend goes there. I'm actually on my way to her house right now. Charlie, Charlotte Reiser—do you know her?"

The expression that passed over Kendall's face made me wonder if I'd said the wrong thing.

"Charlie's in a couple of my classes," she said. "I'm working with her and Mindy Kishore on a history project, so I also know she's not home. I'm meeting them at the library as soon as I leave here."

"Oh. Then can you tell her to call me when you're done?"

"No problem." I took a step forward, thinking we were about to say our goodbyes, head to our respective vehicles—hers, I realized, must be the sleek black Volkswagen parked next to the aging gray Hyundai that must've belonged to TJ—and go our separate ways. Instead, she blocked my path and pointed to my bag. "So," she said brightly, "you're still into crafts, I see."

I fingered the heart-shaped pin attached to the front pocket. A familiar pang rippled through my chest as the memory of my and Jordan's first kiss flashed through my mind. For the hundredth time, I thought about ripping off the pin and letting it rust in a smelly landfill, since I couldn't do as much to Jordan without landing myself in jail.

"It's a hobby of mine. I mess around with making jewelry—earrings and necklaces and stuff. I have a ton of these pins, so I design and decorate them for people who, um—" Who what? Whose boyfriends cheated on them? I didn't even know where to go with that thought. "—who like them." Wow. So that's what a total sentence fail sounds like. "I was on my way to give Charlie hers, but I guess it will have to wait."

"You made one for Charlie Reiser? Can I see it?"

The instinct to clutch my bag against my abdomen and refuse kicked in immediately, like I expected her to run off with the pin and somehow claim credit for it. I nearly snorted out loud, silently chiding myself for being so childish. "Uh, okay."

I fished around inside my bag and placed the pin I'd made for Charlie in Kendall's waiting hand. She held it close to her face, running her thumb over the tiny red and black crystals I'd arranged into alternating stripes down the length of the heart's surface. Without taking her eyes off it, she said, "I heard you caught her boyfriend cheating."

"You *did*?" I blurted. I had to bite back the *How?* that threatened to fly off my tongue next.

She traced a row of red crystals with a cream-painted fingernail. "Mindy mentioned it earlier today. Of course, I didn't realize that she meant Marisa as in *you*-Marisa, but now it all makes sense."

Mindy. I loved Charlie's "Templeton wife," but sometimes she seriously needed a muzzle. The last thing Charlie would've wanted was for Jason's cheating antics to be public knowledge, and I sure as hell didn't want anyone knowing that I'd stalked him by hanging from the woodwork outside the house of his side dish.

"I—well, yeah I guess you could say that. It's kind of why I'm giving her the pin."

The way Kendall's eyes snapped up toward me reminded me of a window shade that had been pulled too hard. "Do you give one to everybody you help?"

I didn't have a clue what she meant by that, and I had to make a conscious effort to keep my facial muscles out of WTF formation. But she was obviously waiting for an answer, so I plucked the pin from her palm and said, "I make them, but it's because I like to. Going all *To Catch a Cheater* isn't really a hobby of mine, so I think the 'help' part is a onetime thing."

"Wait, I can give the pin to her if you want," she protested as the heart disappeared into my bag.

"No, that's okay." I hoisted my bag behind my hip. I didn't know why I was suddenly picking up an ominous undertone in this conversation, but I was ready for it to be over. "I see her all the time."

Kendall's hands twisted near the hem of her skirt. "Then maybe we can hang out sometime? I've always hated that we drifted apart. It would be great to start with a clean slate. Like, maybe grab dinner one weekend with Mindy and Charlie? They're in some of my classes, but I don't know them very well. I'd like to change that."

I immediately felt like an ass for suspecting Kendall had an ulterior motive. We weren't in fifth grade anymore. Why did I always have to assume the worst of people?

"Sure, we could definitely get together sometime."

And really, there was no reason we couldn't. We'd had a lot of fun together when we were younger, when we weren't being petty, and we'd both grown up since then. I found myself thinking I might really like getting to know Kendall again. Everyone deserved a second chance, right?

I didn't realize I had a smile on my face until I got into my car after Kendall and I exchanged numbers. As I drove home, my mind wandered back to the time I had gone to Myrtle Beach with her family. We'd spent a week collecting shells along the shore, trying and failing to eat Popsicles before they ran down our hands and arms in sticky, melted messes, and laughing like everything we did was the funniest thing ever. The scenes were still playing in my mind like old movies when I walked into the house.

"Hey, Mom."

I kissed my mother hello as she stood at the stove making soup.

"Hi, sweetheart." She kissed me back, then cocked her head and studied me. "Everything all right?"

Mom Vision. Never failed.

"I'm fine."

She narrowed her eyes. "Are you sure? Did something happen at school?"

"Remember Kendall Keene?"

"Of course I do. What about her?"

"She's back from Arizona and she goes to school with Charlie. I saw her today."

My mother's eyes widened and she blinked a couple times. "Oh," she said. "That's…nice?"

I smiled and shook my head and headed toward the stairs. "Yes, Mom. It's nice."

I threw my bag on the bed and walked over to my closet. On the top shelf sat a beat-up shoe box of keepsakes: awards, trinkets, my earliest attempts at sketches and crafts, one of which was a necklace I'd made from the shells I'd scavenged in Myrtle Beach with the Keenes. I lifted it from the box with a wistful smile, memories hitting me like the ocean waves. Sure, the trip had started with Kendall opening her suitcase and brandishing an exact copy of my brand-new bathing suit, but when I looked at that necklace with its pearlescent pinks and stark-white swirls, I remembered all the happy memories we'd made on that vacation and how much fun we'd had.

As I replaced the lid and hoisted the box back into my closet, I was suddenly glad for the random turn of events that had brought us face-to-face again.

Maybe they hadn't been so random at all.

3

ABOUT AN HOUR LATER, MY BROTHER AND I WERE SPRAWLED ON THE sectional couch doing homework in our sweats when Charlie and Mindy walked in.

They wore matching Templeton Varsity sweatshirts, a testament to their cheerleader status, not to mention the awesomeness of Charlie's parents. Technically, she belonged at Herring Cross High with me, at least according to planning and zoning in Herring Cross, Pennsylvania. But she'd been one of the few students from our region to test into Templeton's elite Hartley Honors program, and even though they had to pay to send her to an out-of-district school, Mr. and Mrs. Reiser had ponied up without hesitation.

When I'd broached the subject of attending Templeton to my parents, strictly out of curiosity, my dad had belly laughed and said, "Repeat after me: free is the way to be." That had been the end of that discussion, even though I applied to the honors program anyway and got accepted.

Four years in a row.

"Hey, *Charlotte*," Nick said, propping himself up on his elbow and flashing a grin. Then, because he loved to give Mindy a hard time, grumbled a cursory, "Kishore."

"*Nicholas*," Charlie drawled back. "You're looking dreamy today."

Nick's crush on Charlie was the most obvious thing in the world, but I could never tell if Charlie actually enjoyed flirting with my brother or if she got a rise out of seeing the giant dope it turned him into. I opted to believe the latter, because thinking about my best friend coming on to my younger sibling kind of grossed me out.

I reached over and pushed Nick's head. "He looks like an ape, same as every other day."

Nick shoved me back. "You look like a dog-faced beast and have the breath to match."

"Hey, don't talk that way about my hero." Charlie flopped onto a free cushion while Mindy squeezed in next to her. "Your sister saved me from making a whale-sized ass out of myself, or didn't she tell you?"

"The only one who's a whale-sized ass is a guy who'd cheat on you."

Mindy groaned and I rolled my eyes. "Nice one, Slick."

"Um, speaking of asses?" Mindy said, sitting up straighter and fixing a razor-sharp stare on me. "You know Kendall Keene?"

I pushed my books aside and sat cross-legged on the cushion. "We were friends a long time ago. I take it you're not a fan?" So much for the idea of all of us hanging out sometime.

"How could you be *friends* with her?" The pitch of Mindy's voice rose so fast that I half expected my mom's china to start shattering in the dining room hutch. "I almost died when she got put in the group with us. I don't think she knows other people are even in the room half the time because she's so in love with herself."

I opened my mouth to divert, my normal course of action when Mindy's snobby switch flipped to activate—especially since it seemed to feed an ugly side of Charlie's personality that I hadn't thought existed and was more than happy to keep dormant. Except I wasn't fast enough, and Charlie chimed in before I got the chance.

"She eats lunch with a mirror propped up on the table in case she gets crumbs on her face. Like that's not why napkins were invented."

"And she threw the *hugest* tantrum when she thought there was no room for her in the honors program," Mindy added.

"Wait a minute. Are you talking about Kendall as in Kendall's-a-Shitty-Friendall?" Nick asked incredulously.

Charlie burst out laughing. "Is that what you call her?"

"She's back," I confirmed, shooting Nick a look. "And that's what *he* calls her. But she seemed perfectly nice when I talked to her today."

Mindy snorted. "Yeah, she's fine until you beat her on a test. And don't bother trying to hide your grade; you have a better chance of smuggling the freaking Precious past Mordor."

"I know, I know, she has a competitive streak. But think of it this way—you're pretty much guaranteed an A on your history project."

"Forget history." Mindy collapsed against the backrest and started swiping through her cell phone. "I need all the help I can get with chem. Mrs. Pace is such a bitch."

"Anyone thirsty?" Charlie asked, shooting off the couch. "I'll get some root beers."

I appreciated her effort, but it didn't stop me from wincing. Mrs. Pace, the chemistry teacher at Templeton High, also happened to be my ex-boyfriend Jordan's mother. It was hard enough to keep my mind off him without direct mention of his name, but Charlie's disappointment in Jason had hit a very familiar nerve in me, and my brain was taking way too many detours into Jordanville as a result. And Charlie knew it.

"I'll get them." Nick stood up. "Sit down, Char."

"Aw, you're sweet."

She threw a pillow at his butt as he left the room and Mindy teasingly called, "I could go for a sandwich!"

I eyed Charlie. She'd slumped into the couch as soon as Nick was out of sight, and the corners of her mouth had settled into a frown. Mentioning Jordan must've reminded her of her own cheater. As the bearer of bad news, I felt guilty all over again.

"How are you today, Char?"

One shoulder lifted slightly. "Eh, I'm okay. I'm so over it. Sort of."

Total lie. Cue another rush of guilt. "Are you mad at me?"

Charlie's dark eyebrows drew together. "Why would I be mad at you? You did me a favor."

"A favor you never asked for. You know I never wanted to hurt you, right?"

"Of course she knows!" Mindy squawked. "If you really wanted to ruin her life, you could've kept your mouth shut and let her sleep with the asshole."

I gasped. "Oh my God. Were you going to?" Charlie had never been the kiss-and-tell type, but since she'd barely copped to dating the guy, this was news. To say the least.

"Were you going to?" Mindy echoed. "More like, *did* you?"

"No!" Charlie tucked a strand of hair behind her reddened ear and shrank against her seat. "Jesus, Min, way to give everyone a coronary."

"Speaking of coronaries." A heart problem reference was a weak segue at best, but Charlie was withering in the heat of the sex spotlight, so it would have to do. I pulled my book bag off the floor and dug around inside. "I have something for you."

Charlie gave me a quizzical look as I reached out, extending the heart pin I'd made in my open palm. A smile pulled at the corners of her lips as she took it, running her thumb over the sparkling red and black stripes. "I love it. Thank you." Her fist closed around the pin. "For everything."

"Hey," Mindy said, poking Charlie's arm. "We have something for her too, remember?"

"Oh, right!" Charlie bent to retrieve her own bag on the floor, then handed me a photocopied piece of paper from inside it. "Our English teacher gave this out today. You were the first person we thought of."

"*Story Break* Magazine's High School Essay Contest," I read aloud. "Topic: For Love of the News: How Far Would You Go to Get the Story?"

"They want nonfiction," Mindy said, twirling her black hair around her finger. "You scaled a freaking house to catch a cheater. You'd be a shoo-in for an award."

"Are you kidding?" I held up the piece of paper. "This is a *journalism* contest—"

"The subject you're going to study in college," Charlie cut in.

"They're looking for kids who went to foreign countries and did relief work or…or stopped a bank from getting robbed," I sputtered, ignoring her comment. "Not tales from Marisa Palmera's Idiot Files."

Mindy raised an eyebrow, unfazed. "Did you see the prizes?"

I scanned the paper again, and my mouth dropped. First, second, and third prize were all scholarships—for $2,500, $1,000, and $500.

"We thought you'd like that part," Charlie said smugly.

Hell yeah I liked that part. Shopping for a college education on my parents' budget was proving to be way more torturous than trying to barter for my choice of high school had ever been.

"I'll think about it," I mumbled.

"Think about what?" Nick asked as he reentered the room with an armful of soda cans and—to my surprise—a peanut butter and jelly sandwich on a paper plate.

"About changing her name to Marisa Palmera, Private Eye," Charlie answered, helping him pass out the drinks. "It has a pretty badass ring to it. Don't you think?"

Nick peered over my shoulder and snatched the flyer from my hand. "What would you write about? How you once took a job in the school cafeteria to see if they were putting pink slime in the food?"

"Did *you* want to eat that shit?" I grabbed for the paper, but he held it out of reach.

"Or maybe you could tell them about how you hid outside Mr. Hastings's classroom for two hours to find out if he was having an affair with Miss O'Donnell," Nick added.

"Mrs. Hastings used to babysit us! I had to know!"

"No way," Mindy garbled through a mouthful of peanut butter. "She's totally writing about how she busted creepo Jason."

Nick snorted. "Funny how Lois Lane Junior never felt the need to check up on Jordan Pace, or she might've dumped him instead of the other way around."

I jabbed at his stomach and snatched the paper from him when he doubled over. "Or maybe I won't write anything for the contest, because my days of channeling Nancy Drew are definitely over."

My phone started to ring in my bag, and I took the opportunity to shove the flyer inside while I pulled my cell out. When I saw the screen lit up with Kendall's name, my stomach fluttered a little. When a smile tugged at the corner of my mouth, I was shocked to realize the feeling was excitement.

I threw a "be right back" over my shoulder and darted up the stairs to my bedroom. As soon as I closed my door, I connected the call.

"Hey," I said. "You'll never guess what I was looking at earlier." The contents of my memory box from our trip were still scattered across my bed. I sat down and picked up a smooth, fan-shaped shell, eager to share my nostalgia.

But before I could say another word, Kendall cut in. "Marisa, I'm sorry to bother you while Charlie and Mindy are over, but do you think you can get away for a second?"

"I'm already alone in my roo—wait, how did you know they're here?"

"I really need your help. Can you come outside? I'll explain everything."

I shot off my bed. "You're at my house?" I hurried to my parents' room, the closest spot with a view of the street. Sure enough, a black

Volkswagen sat at the curb in front of our house. "Kendall, what kind of help are we talking about here?"

Kendall sighed. "The same kind you gave Charlie."

And that's when the bubble of positivity I'd been floating in since reconnecting with Kendall Keene in the parking lot burst like a microwaved marshmallow all over the room.

I STEPPED UP TO MY LOCKER, STILL MULLING OVER EVERYTHING THAT HAD happened the day before. I didn't notice Jordan approaching until his arm nearly touched my shoulder. When your last name is Palmera and your ex-boyfriend's is Pace, it's a bit of a problem to have lockers assigned in alphabetical order. I used to make excuses to stop at my locker, but that was when he'd smile and we'd chat and flirt as we switched out our textbooks. Now my book bag weighed fifty pounds at any given point specifically so I could avoid the anxiety that coiled my muscles in moments like this.

"Hey," I said stiffly.

"Hey."

He didn't even look at me, barely moved his stupid, beautiful lips when he spoke. A few short months ago, we could've given Greggie-George and Mystery Blond a run for their money with the way we made use of his lips, and now forming actual words was too much effort to waste on me. It burned me like crazy.

Nick's Lois Lane comment was still on my mind too, so I slammed my locker shut with an aggravated huff and said, "So is today the day I finally get to find out what I did?"

He inhaled through his nose, like he could gather the patience he needed for my petulant question from the air particles around him, and looked at me with those blue eyes that used to drive up my pulse rate faster than gym class—that still did, as much as I hated him for it.

"Look, when will you drop it already?"

"When you give me an answer."

"I told you. It wasn't you. It was me."

"Is there a planet where people *don't* recognize that as the biggest line of bullshit ever? You won't even look at me anymore!"

He spread his arms and his eyes widened with incredulity. "You said you didn't want to be friends!"

"I meant I didn't want to be dumped, Jordan, not that I wanted you to treat me like a leper."

He sighed, a resigned sound that made me feel bothersome and insignificant. "Look, I'll be nice from now on if it's what you want." His eyes skimmed over me, unreadable and yet the final nail in my coffin of inferiority. "But every time we talk, I start to think maybe it's better if we don't."

He turned and walked away, his books tucked against his hip, before I could respond, though I imagined he'd seen response enough in my face. I went to slam my locker, angry at myself for letting a two-second conversation get me so riled, only to get even more annoyed when I found I'd already shut it.

Damn Nick. Why did he have to remind me of the one time I'd failed to sniff out an answer? I'd told myself that the way I'd handled things with Jordan was called "giving him the benefit of the doubt."

In reality, it was the one time I'd needed the dirt on a situation but didn't really want to know the truth.

I yanked my bag around my hip and dug out a tube of Chap Stick, smearing it over my lips while I berated myself into calming down. When I threw it back into the bag, my homemade heart pin caught my eye.

I'd made that pin, with its bursts of sparkle and bright, bold colors, the night Jordan kissed me for the first time. The elation in every crystal and bead could probably ward off evil.

And if I had to look at it one more time, I'd vom my guts all over the place.

I plucked the pin off my bag and hesitated in front of Jordan's locker before turning the combination and shoving it inside. He'd probably throw it away, but I didn't care. He'd been equally careless with my real heart, so what did it matter? If the pin represented us, then it represented something that had never been real anyway.

"SOMETHING WRONG, MARISA?"

I jolted when I realized I'd been caught staring. TJ's confused eyes met mine and I squirmed in my chair and drummed my pen against the desk, searching for a way to make my gratuitous eye-boring seem casual.

It was weird to think of TJ as Kendall's boyfriend. I hadn't made any promises during my conversation with her, but I'd been thinking about her request nonstop. Probably because it still creeped me out that she'd called from outside my house. I assumed she'd followed Charlie after their meeting at the library, because I didn't know how else she'd know where I lived. Still, making a phone call and a house call at the same time was a hundred percent Kendall's brand of weird, so it's not like I was totally bowled over. Nor was I surprised that she wouldn't come inside. She and Nick had never been particularly chummy. So I'd sat in her front seat, watching her peel and push the skin around her nails as she explained that something about TJ had been off lately.

"He's so distant," she'd said. "At first I thought he was upset about switching schools, but now he's not even happy when we're together. It's like his mind is somewhere else and I'm stuck with this moody shell of my boyfriend. I can't stand it anymore."

"You mean he's not like that all the time?" slipped out before I could stop it.

Her eyes widened. "No! He actually had a sense of humor before. He liked being with me, or at least I thought he did. He keeps saying nothing is wrong, but Fall Ball was the last straw."

"The dance? Isn't that this weekend?"

"Saturday. And we're not going. He told me yesterday that he doesn't have time between work and schoolwork. I bought a dress, shoes—everything. I mean, I know he's not a people person, but these are all people he knows. And I'm his *girlfriend*." She folded her arms, her mouth a line of worry. "Something is up, Marisa, and I need to know what it is."

Her gaze turned pleading and I felt myself cracking like dried-out cement.

As I watched her, unsure of what to say, it occurred to me that Fall Ball was the "obligation" TJ hadn't been looking forward to when he'd chased me down with my broken ankle bracelet. But was it because he didn't care for crowds, like Kendall had said, or because he had something to hide?

Damn it. Why did I even have to care?

I was still asking myself that question as I sat in yearbook, sizing up TJ, trying to decide if I cared enough to do something about it. And trying to cover up my stare as he waited expectantly for an answer to his question.

My eyes darted from TJ's dark, furrowed eyebrows to the logo on the left breast of his shirt, and I sat up straighter.

"Um, where'd you get the Maple Acres shirt?"

His expression didn't change. "Maple Acres."

I fought the urge to roll my eyes. "Right. I meant, do you work there?"

"Yup." He sat back in his chair and pulled at the logo, stretching the white cotton away from his chest before turning his attention back to the computer screen. "Long time now."

As soon as he said it, my memory was triggered. I'd always thought he looked familiar but could never quite place where I'd seen him. As I thought back to every trip I'd taken to Maple Acres, twice a year since I was two years old, the image of a boy with dark curls stuffed beneath a knit cap and a heavy flannel coat that made him look like Paul Bunyan clicked into place. The farm stretched over two hundred and fifty acres, selling pumpkins and cider and offering hayrides and a corn maze in a fall, then Christmas trees that you cut down yourself in the winter. The place had a storybook quality to it that I loved, and I couldn't believe it had taken me so long to figure out TJ was a part of it.

"We go there for our tree every year. I think I've seen you."

TJ kept his eyes on the screen. "Probably. I'm usually bundling the trees or in the checkout area. Sometimes I drive the tractor for the hayrides." He glanced over long enough to shoot me a half smile. "Maybe you've seen the back of my head."

That would've been an occasion I definitely hadn't noticed him. The one and only time I'd taken a hayride had been the lone trip I'd made without Charlie or my dad, both of whom are allergic to hay. I'd gone with Jordan. Superman himself could've been driving the tractor and I would've been too busy drooling over Jordan in his plaid button-down with the sleeves rolled up around his gorgeous forearms to notice.

Vom, vom, vom. I pushed the chunks down and forged ahead. "So, that thing you didn't want to do the last time we talked, is that… still an issue?"

"Uh, no. That fell through, so my article should be good to go on Monday."

He's not making this easy for me, that's for sure.

"Take your time, really. I hope you didn't cancel your plans because of me."

He glanced over and gave me a wry smile. "No."

"So, um, the tree farm. I go all the time." I mentally slapped myself. *Twice a year is all the time?* "Do you live nearby?"

"You know the green colonial across the street behind the barn?"

"Uh-huh."

He smiled again. "That's my house."

"Wait, I thought the owners lived there."

"They do. We have for my whole life."

"Your family owns Maple Acres?" I blinked a few times, dumbfounded by my own dumbness.

"Well, co-owns. Have you seen the guy with the white hair who sneaks free gourds to all the little kids at Halloween? That's my uncle Roger. He's there all the time, but my dad does more of the financial stuff."

My face lit up. "That's awesome! I love that place! I took a picture of the white barn from the top of the hill once and tried to sketch it. All the trees had snow on them, the sky was this amazing gray color, and the pond was reflecting it"—I remembered midbabble that I'd veered off course and reined myself back in—"anyway, let's just say it was magical, but drawing isn't my strong suit. So, um, if you didn't move, then why did you switch schools?"

TJ's eyes slid back to the computer screen and his shoulders tensed ever so slightly, as if I'd brought up something he didn't really want to talk about. Now I was getting somewhere.

"Our property is right at the intersection of three town lines. Technically, I could've gone to any one of the high schools." He stabbed a few keys with his pointer finger, eliciting three clipped clicks. Maybe my eyes were playing tricks on me, but I could've sworn his jaw tightened. "I left Templeton because it was time for a change of scenery."

"It must've been hard though, transferring for your senior year." And pretty odd, in my opinion. "I'm sure you had a lot of ties there."

TJ's fingers paused in midair over the keyboard and he looked at me. "Not that many."

This time when he turned his attention back to the screen, I knew our conversation had ended. He ran a hand through his hair in a gesture that had a definite undertone of irritation. Whether it related to my question or some memory pertaining to the school, I couldn't tell. But when I caught sight of the leather bracelet on his wrist, my desire to exclaim *OMG THAT'S GORGEOUS WHERE DID YOU GET IT* almost overruled my desire to ask what the hell his comment was supposed to mean. I'd been baiting him to say, "Yeah, my girlfriend goes there." He hadn't. What did that mean?

Maybe nothing.

But damn it all to hell, I suddenly had to know for sure.

6

"I DON'T KNOW, KENDALL." I SIGHED INTO MY CELL PHONE. "THIS IS different from what I've done before. You're not asking me to follow him for a night or two. You're basically asking me to stalk him. This feels…sneaky."

"How is it any sneakier than trespassing on private property and aiming a camera inside someone's living room?"

She had a point. Still, I didn't feel quite right about this "assignment" to trail TJ, if that's what we were calling it now. I'd phoned her after school to confirm that I'd gleaned an inkling of what she'd described in her car that day and to find out how she wanted me to prove something was amiss. I'd expected her to give me a day and time when she thought I might snag him, oh, having pizza with another girl. Instead, she wanted me to watch him. Like, all the time.

"You don't understand, Marisa," she said, desperation creeping into her voice. "TJ is different. You're not going to catch him sneaking off at a party with some drunk girl. It's not *how* he's spending his time. It's how he's acting when he's finally spending time with *me*."

"Are we sure this is a cheating issue?" Because it sounded a lot more like a communication problem, and I wasn't a relationship counselor. Then again, I wasn't really a private investigator either.

"I don't know." Her voice shrank into weary resignation. "I don't know anything anymore. Maybe he is chasing drunk girls at parties. The TJ I know would rather be holed up in that shitty old barn than do something like that, but who am I to say? I'm only his girlfriend."

I flopped into the purple papasan chair at the foot of my bed. "So let's go over this one more time. You want me to drive over to the tree farm this Saturday night, park between his house and the white barn, turn off my car, and watch."

"I told you I'll pay you."

"I don't want your money. I want to make sure I understand your request."

"Then yes."

"Do I need binoculars?"

"I don't know. Do you have a pair?"

I balked. "I was kidding! Geez, do you want me to wear camouflage and paint my face too?"

"Ha-freaking-ha, Marisa. Are you going to do it or not?" And there was the bossy, impatient Kendall I knew and loved. Sort of.

I stopped myself from making a joke about designing a special camo line of jewelry called PI Jane, knowing I'd be the only one amused. Instead I asked, "Why aren't you coming with me again?"

She sighed. "Now that I'm not going to the dance, I have to go to New York with my mom for my cousin's bridal shower. No sense in letting a two-hundred-dollar dress go to waste, I guess."

I almost dropped the phone. I could tally the cost of all the jeans in my closet and not come close to two hundred dollars.

"What if he leaves?"

"Then follow him."

"What if he doesn't leave?"

Kendall paused. "Then make sure no one goes to him."

It occurred to me as I sat in my car at the edge of the tree farm that I really needed to get a life.

As if she'd read my mind, Charlie said, "We're either the coolest people ever for doing this, or the world's biggest losers. I haven't decided which one yet." She pulled her corduroy jacket tighter around her torso. It hadn't taken long for the chill of the early November night to find its way into my jalopy.

"Well, let's see. We're hanging out on the side of a tree farm on a Saturday night, ready to freeze our butts off for an unspecified amount of time, while alternately staring at a house and a barn that a guy we barely know may or may not come out of, all for a girl who can't be here because she's breaking in a new dress. What does that tell you?"

Charlie grimaced. "That you should've let her pay you."

"Come on. How can I take money for this? 'Hey, I'm sorry your heart is broken, but go ahead and make the check out to Marisa—one *s*, please—Palmera.' That's so tacky!"

"It's not tacky! Not only are you giving up your free time *for free*, but you're also probably giving her gifts like she wasn't the one who asked for your help in the first place. Tell me you're not making a pin for this girl too?"

Yup. Pink, yellow, and ocean blue, all the colors I associated with Kendall.

"Sort of."

Charlie shook her head. "You're a lost cause, Palmera. But at least it's interesting fodder for your scholarship essay."

"Do you think TJ's cheating?" I asked, steering away from the essay comment. "You know him, right?"

"He was in one or two of my classes last year, but I only knew him as the quiet dude in the back of the room." No sooner had the words left her mouth than she jerked in her seat and pointed. "TJ's walking out the front door!"

I swiveled and ducked behind my steering wheel, even though we were parked at least thirty yards from TJ's house.

"Is he getting in his car?" I hissed back, readying my hand to start the engine in case we were about to go on pursuit.

"No, he's..." Charlie's nose wrinkled. "He's walking across the street?"

We watched in silence as TJ's shadowed form headed away from the softly lit windows of his evergreen-colored house, hands jammed in the pockets of his pants, shoulders hunched against the cold, and trotted in the direction of the aging white barn set about fifty feet into the property on the other side of the road. A moment later, the cloudy windows were illuminated from within.

"Are you kidding me?" Charlie's head whipped back and forth between her window and me. "Is he really about to hang out in his barn all night?"

I shrugged. "I guess we'll find out."

"What's he doing in there?"

"How the hell do I know?"

She squinted, leaning so close to the glass that it fogged with her breath. "We're too far away. I can't see inside. How long are we supposed to wait here?"

"Cool your jets. I'm not staying all night." I reached for my keys. "At least now we can turn on the car and get some heat going—" I stopped short as the glare of headlights approached on the other side of the road.

Charlie ducked behind the dashboard. "Who is that?"

"You know I'm not actually psychic, right?"

She stuck her tongue out at me and we both fell silent as the car parked facing us, in front of the Carusos' house, and the driver's door opened. A moment ago, I'd been grateful for the remote location and lack of street lamps lighting the road, but now it made it almost impossible to see the person getting out of the car. But I could see enough in the moonlight to be sure of one thing—the person who emerged from the driver's seat and headed in the direction of the barn definitely wasn't a girl.

"Is that a friend of his?" Charlie whispered.

"Actually, it's his cousin, Aloysius."

"I hate you."

We stifled giggles as the tall, hooded frame of the mystery guy disappeared around the corner of the barn. When a few minutes passed and nothing else happened, Charlie squinted out the window.

"Did Kendall say anything about him ditching her to hang out with friends?"

"No, she said he's been distant. She doesn't know if he's cheating, but if he is, I'm pretty sure she thinks it's with a girl."

Charlie's eyebrows collided with the brim of her knit cap. "Oh my God, do you think he's into dudes?"

"That's not what I meant! Holy hell, Char, that's how rumors start. That guy could be anyone."

"Anyone sneaking into a barn with a cute guy smack in the middle of a Saturday night, when said guy should be with his girlfriend but isn't. I smell a red flag."

"Red flags come in scents now?"

"And with a free pair of camouflage earrings."

We were so busy laughing we almost didn't notice Hood Boy jogging back through the clearing toward his car. His headlights flashed as he unlocked it, and we crouched in our seats again.

"If he's gay and they're already done," Charlie said, "then that explains a lot right there."

"Geez, you're on a roll tonight. I can't take you anywhere."

Charlie grinned. "And yet, you take me everywhere."

Hood Boy jumped into his car, and Charlie and I scrunched even lower as his headlights flooded the street. He didn't seem to notice us as he threw his car in reverse, made a three-point turn, and sped off in the same direction he'd come from. I knew Charlie had seen what I'd spotted on his back windshield when she grabbed my arm and said, "Whoa, did you see that?"

I sure had. A Templeton decal centered at the bottom of his rear window. I sank against my seat. "It must be one of TJ's old friends from Templeton. Whoop-dee-doo."

"No, not the sticker, dumbass. The thing hanging from his rearview mirror. It looked like one of your heart pendants."

"Huh? What would some random Templeton guy be doing with

one of my hearts?" I wrinkled my nose. "Are you sure you're not seeing things? It's pretty dark out here."

Charlie's lips twisted into a sarcastic pout. "Normal vehicle function dictates that the overhead light turns on when one of the doors opens." She patted the dashboard. "Not flicker like it's trying to induce a seizure. I definitely saw butt cheeks with a peak, a.k.a. a heart."

"Point taken. But that doesn't mean it was one of mine."

She shook her head. "Jesus, Palmera, if you're going to be a spy, you need to sharpen your powers of observation."

I stared at the spot where the car had been parked, attempting to conjure a re-creation in my mind.

Nada.

"I was too busy trying to see his face," I said dejectedly.

But I hadn't. The sour feeling of failure curdled in my gut. What other details had I missed? And more important, why would TJ's friend have one of my heart pins hanging inside his car?

7

BY THE NEXT DAY, THE ENIGMA OF THE HOODED TEMPLETON BOY DIDN'T seem like such a big deal. Just because he had a heart hanging in his car didn't mean it was one of mine—or that it had actually been a heart, no matter what Charlie said. If it was, those pins were mass-produced, and the stash Jordan had given me had come from his older sister, who probably knew plenty of people at Templeton on account of their mother teaching there. And Charlie had pointed out that Hood Boy could've been driving someone else's car. My heap had been purchased used, and I'd had to scrape a Jesus Loves Me bumper sticker off the rear fender. Not that I didn't think Jesus loved me, but I much preferred the Swarovski snowflake ornament dangling from my rearview mirror in the way of car deco. Maybe Hood Boy's car had come with a complimentary heart, and he'd decided not to scrap it.

My point: I'd been right when I'd said Hood Boy could be

anyone. Sunday morning had completely rationalized away any need I'd felt to tell Kendall about him. Especially since he hadn't been there long enough to do anything. My official report: an uneventful Saturday night.

Not good enough for Kendall.

"She basically wants me to befriend him," I told my brother through a mouthful of cereal. "I know I'm not exactly in the business of honesty here, but that feels like fraud."

Nick ran a hand over his head, failing at fluffing his dark, flattened tufts of bedhead before slurping his own spoonful of cornflakes. "Aren't you friends already?"

"Not really. He's on my editorial team for yearbook, but it's not like we eat lunch together or hang out after school."

"Do you not like him?"

"I might like him if I got to know him, but the problem is, I feel like getting to know him while spying for Kendall makes me a big phony. I don't want to be a fake friend."

The corner of Nick's mouth quirked up, bringing out the dimple in his cheek. "Like Kendall?"

I couldn't help but smile back. Nick remembered the days of my and Kendall's frenemyship well. When we were on the outs, he called her Kendall's-Not-Your-Friendall or Kendall's-a-Shitty-Friendall. When we got along, she was Kendall-Your-Best-Friendall. He thought he was hilarious. Most of the time, I had to agree.

My father flicked his newspaper and cleared his throat. "No teenage drama at the breakfast table, please. No one is to be anyone's fake friend."

"Think of it this way," Nick said through copious crunching, ignoring Dad. "It's a good way to get back at that asshole, Pace." My spoon stilled in my bowl. Nick's mouth widened into a grin. "Oh, snap, I think I'm onto something." He elbowed Dad's arm and my father rolled his eyes.

I stabbed through a clump of cereal and tried to appear unaffected. "Jordan wouldn't even notice if I started hanging out with TJ. He'd have to care in order to be jealous."

"He'll care. Guys always care when girls get over them. It's the best way to make us notice you."

"Because you're pigs."

"Hey," my father warned.

Nick pressed his pointer finger to the tip of his nose and pushed it up until I had a way better view of his nostrils than I ever wanted or needed. "Oink, oink, baby."

"You're gross."

"And you're so gonna do it."

"Like you're so gonna go to the Templeton football game with me on Friday night?"

Nick might've known me better than I cared to admit, but I knew his Achilles' heel too.

His eyes dropped to his bowl and he stirred his cereal instead of chomping on it like a dog at a bone. "Why would I do that?"

An evil smirk spread across my face. "Because Charlie is single now and she'll be there. In a cheerleading uniform."

A grin stretched across Dad's face. "What's that saying, Nick? Oh, snap?"

I turned to my father. "Should I give him the chance to use it again by bringing up the fact that I should be a Templeton student anyway?"

Note to self: attempts at humor about a sensitive topic will come out far more bitter than they sound in your head.

"Marisa Ann," Dad said sternly. "Keep that up and Lehigh is going from your short list to your bucket list."

My lips pressed together and it took all my willpower to turn back to Nick without responding. "Anyway, you're coming, right?"

Nick made figure eights with his spoon for another moment before resuming his crunchfest. "Maybe if I have nothing better to do," he mumbled.

Miraculously, Nick's schedule was clear by Friday night. He and I bundled up in our knit caps and mittens, and headed up the hill to the Templeton football field to watch the game. Charlie's squad had been working on a new halftime routine for weeks, and she had asked a thousand times if we'd watch them perform that night. Kendall had let me off my leash for the evening, since she and TJ were actually hanging out, and it felt good to do something for me for a change.

"Where's your unsuspecting new bestie?" Nick asked as we approached the field where the game was already in progress.

"With his girlfriend, where he should be," I replied.

"Are you guys passing notes and complimenting each other's shoes yet?"

"I didn't even see him this week. He skipped yearbook for work, so I haven't had a chance to do any digging."

"Ooh, maybe we should search the eight million cars in this lot with Templeton decals and see if we can find the one you saw at the farm," Nick said with mock fascination.

I gave him a playful shove. "I'm off duty tonight."

I spotted Mindy sitting on the track in a Templeton warm-up suit and waved when she looked over. She promptly got to her feet and motioned for a couple of the other cheerleaders to boost her over the chain-link fence. As she started toward us, the sound of cheers erupted and the scoreboard flashed a new point for the home team.

"Hey," I said. "Not cheering tonight?"

"Getting over a stomach bug. Apparently yakking at the top of a human pyramid is frowned upon."

We watched as a sea of black-and-silver pom-poms shook like mad on the sidelines, and then Charlie was hoisted into the air, tossed, and expertly caught by her squad members. When they set her down, she faced the crowd and did a high kick, then shook her pom-poms and clapped. Nick's face immediately took on that dazed expression—the Charlie Face, as I liked to call it—wherein he looked like he was trying to smile through massive amounts of Novocain. When Charlie spotted us, she flashed a huge grin, then waved a pom-pom in our direction.

Mindy's head turned from the field to my paralyzed brother. "In my country, it's customary to wave back when someone says hello," she said.

"You're Indian. Don't you guys bow or something?"

"My country is America, ass."

"You guys suck," Nick grumbled as Mindy and I doubled over laughing.

Mindy fished some money out of her coat pocket. "Here, stud, go fetch us some hot chocolate. Charlie loves a gentleman." She smiled as he trudged toward the concession stand, griping under his breath. "I love that he's a foot taller than me and still does whatever I say."

"I don't know why he doesn't make a move. If he crushes any harder, he's going to start bursting capillaries."

We reached the fence, where Charlie stood with her pompoms dangling over the top. She barely got out the word "hi" before her smile morphed into a look somewhere between disgust and nausea, and I half wondered if she'd caught Mindy's virus.

"Are you shitting me?" she mumbled.

I turned my head and followed her stare. "Oh my God. That guy is wearing *shorts*." My jaw dropped as a boy with long, sandy hair strutted past us in a bright-blue windbreaker and khaki cargo shorts. He looked like he'd teleported straight from the California surf and hadn't yet registered that it was freaking freezing here.

My gawking, however, registered just fine. Our eyes met, and I cursed silently as he stopped walking and gave me a "what's up" nod.

"Not him." Charlie cupped my face and moved my head a few degrees left. In my periphery, surfer dude retreated.

Now I was looking at a tall, lanky guy in a ski headband, who was heading in our direction. The last time I'd seen him, he'd been on top of some blond. The same blond who was now at his side, holding his hand.

"Ugh!" Mindy's face contorted. "He brought his little Stanton Prep tramp with him!" She raised her voice as they passed us. "How tacky can you get?"

Only then did I notice the shorter-than-Jason-but-still-tall person behind them, trailing reluctantly with his hands in his pockets and shoulders hunched around his ears against the cold. He looked over at Mindy, his eyes the only feature visible between the knit cap pulled down around his forehead and the collar zipped all the way up to his nose.

"Keep walking, Eli. I'm not talking to you!" Mindy barked. Under her breath she added, "For once."

"Who is that?" I asked as the boy scowled and stormed off in the opposite direction of Jason and Mystery Blond.

Mindy tossed her hair with a vengeance. "A slimy, little vandalizing perv." She turned her glare back to Jason. "They're a family reunion of losers."

Charlie shook her pompom in Mindy's face. "Aw, my Templeton wifey loves and defends me." She turned to me and nudged my arm. "Aren't exes great?" she said with a sarcastic roll of her eyes.

I looked down at the wool blanket folded over my arm and rolled a fuzz ball between my thumb and the bulk of my mitten. "Speaking of that. Do you think Jordan will be suspicious if I start talking to TJ? I mean, do you think it's obvious that something's up if I'm hanging out with someone I never really talked to before?"

Charlie side-eyed me and raised an eyebrow. "Suspicious or *jealous*?"

Damn her. Years of friendship had totally given her the same X-ray vision my mom had when it came to my feeble attempts at being sly.

"Either, I guess."

Charlie shrugged. "Honestly, I think the only time that ass feels anything is when he's admiring his own reflection. The way he ended things sucked, but if you're gonna hang out with TJ because you're hoping Jordan will notice, *don't*. Especially not if you want TJ to trust you."

I sighed. She was right, of course, but I pouted anyway. When

Jordan broke it off, he told me it had been fun, but we weren't working anymore. He'd actually used those words—*it's been fun*. Like we'd gone on a ride together at Disney and he'd enjoyed it, but not enough to keep him from trying every other godforsaken ride in the park. It killed me that every time I turned around he'd be flirting with another girl like he couldn't be happier to be free, and I went to bed every night wondering what I'd done wrong and how I could make him feel even half of my hurt.

"Gotta run," Charlie said as the cheerleading squad clapped their way into formation. She threw an arm around my neck and gave me a quick squeeze. "My parents have to bounce at halftime. Can I bum a ride home with you?"

"Of course."

"Let me go check on your brother," Mindy said. "I think he got lost."

My mind stayed on our conversation as I scooted into the bleachers and unfolded the blanket across my lap. Nick had said the best way to make someone care about you is to get over them, but Nick talked a big game for someone who practically wet himself every time he got within ten feet of a cute cheerleader.

And then there was the problem of faking being over someone not being the same as actually getting over them. So why waste my energy on another lie?

Before I could answer my own question, a lidded Styrofoam cup appeared under my nose, and I looked up to see Nick smirking and shaking his head. "I think some guy just tried to sell me drugs," he said.

I took the hot chocolate from him. "What? What happened?"

He scooted onto the bleacher next to me and took a sip of his drink, then sputtered. "Shit, that's hot." He wiped his mouth with the back of his hand. "Anyway, I got a text message, so I went around to the side of the Snack Shack to put my stuff down on one of the picnic benches and answer it. I'm standing there, minding my own business, and this kid says 'I have the stuff here if you want it.' I didn't see anyone so I'm like, 'What the fuck? Are you talking to me?' Then I see this shadow around the corner and he goes, 'Do you have the money?' So I start walking toward him to see what the hell he's talking about and he says, 'My bad' and freaking bolts—like, climbed over the fence and *bolted*. Fucking weird."

A finger tapped Nick's shoulder. "Um, did he bolt before or after you traded my cocoa for some crack?" Mindy asked.

Nick bent forward, searching the area around his seat. "Shit. I must've left yours at the Snack Shack. Be right back." Mindy scooted in next to me while he trotted down the bleachers.

The next time he came back, he wasn't alone.

"What's she doing here?" Mindy asked.

I followed her gaze. Nick was walking toward us, holding Mindy's hot chocolate in one hand and pointing in our direction with the other. Next to him stood a frantic-looking Kendall Keene.

"What the…" I murmured. "She's supposed to be with TJ."

Kendall broke away from Nick's side the moment she spotted us and made a mad dash toward me. She literally tossed the blanket off my lap and almost pulled my arm out of its socket.

"Marisa, you have to come with me right now!"

"Holy—Jesus, Kendall, what's going on?"

I barely had time to scoop my purse off the ground before she had me half sitting, half standing with my arm jutting out like a broken marionette.

"I'll explain in a minute. Please hurry!"

I threw a confused glance at Mindy as Kendall whisked me away, briefly registering my brother pointing at Kendall while making Norman Bates–esque stabbing motions.

"What's going on? I thought you were with TJ tonight," I said as we scurried down the hill toward the parking lot.

"I was. We had dinner and I *thought* we were hanging out afterward, but he said something he ate didn't agree with him. He's full of shit, I know it, and I don't mean that kind of shit." She yanked at my coat sleeve, pulling both of us off the sidewalk alongside the school and behind a tree, and pointed into the distance. "I made him drop me off because I knew everyone was here. He didn't even wait for me to get out of sight before he called someone on his cell phone. And look—he's still sitting there! He's going to leave and we have to follow him!"

I looked at her like she'd fully lost her shit, because no other reaction was appropriate. "Are you kidding me? I brought my brother with me, and I'm Charlie's ride home. I can't leave them here! And what's this 'we' business? TJ can't see you with me."

She shook her head like she didn't have time to worry about petty details. "Then you go, and I'll think of something. Charlie's parents are here, right? Maybe we can bum a ride with them."

"They're leaving at half—"

"Then give me your keys and I'll follow him myself. He's going to leave any minute!"

She'd gone from desperate to ragey in a hot second. Her voice had turned shrill and even in the shadows of the tree, I could see her cheeks flaming and her chest puffing as she held out her palm for my keys. One more second, and her eyes began to well. I couldn't have her crying. This was the girl who, in third grade, had pushed Heather Upchurch's face into the dirt for knocking me off my swing at recess. How could I let her cry?

"I'll go, I'll go. Get out of here before he sees you."

Kendall exhaled with relief and sniffled. "Thank you."

"Seriously, go. I'll take care of it."

"I'll make it up to you, I promise," she called over her shoulder as she jogged toward the field.

I turned away, mumbling under my breath that I couldn't imagine how. Pulling my coat tighter around me, I slipped into

Marisa Palmera, Private Eye mode and ducked between a row of cars. TJ had parked about ten spaces away from mine, and getting to my car unnoticed would be like making my way through the corn maze at his farm. I hoped he hadn't seen or recognized my jalopy. A blinged-out rusty red heap isn't exactly subtle. I made a mental note to put my Swarovski snowflake in the glove box for future stakeouts.

Future stakeouts? How many times did I plan on doing this?

Pushing the question to the back of my mind, I concentrated on closing the distance to my car. That is, until I became distinctly aware of the sound of footsteps behind me. I cursed under my breath as I realized this was probably the first trickle of the halftime exodus, and ducked against the tire of a huge black Hummer, trying to hide both the sound of my breathing and the frosty mist it made in the air. The scuffle of shoes continued past my hiding spot and I started to maneuver my way to the front of the vehicle to peek around the bumper, only to scurry back a second later when the sound of giddy giggling and shuffling feet sent my heart rate through the roof.

I called the three girls every name in the book, in my head of course, as they took their sweet time getting into the car on the opposite side of the Hummer, cackling away as they argued about whether or not one of the football players had been flirting with them.

"Did you see him take his helmet off and smile? OMG, I wanted to die!"

I could arrange for that.

"He was totally looking at Flora James when he did that. Get your head out of your ass, Mel."

Excellent advice, Mel. Get a jump on that.

I crouched lower, contemplating whether I'd get myself killed if I tried to crawl around their car, when I heard something that made me stop cold.

"He's such a player anyway. What do you expect when he hangs out with Mrs. Pace's son? Jordan doesn't even go to school here and he's hooked up with half the student body. Did you see him? Who was that girl with him?"

Mrs. Pace's son. Jordan was at the game, and I hadn't even been there long enough to spot him because I was too busy squatting behind the wheel of someone's Hummer. Not only that, he was at the game with a girl. My heart stopped midbeat.

"Who knows?" Mel answered. "If you've seen one bimbo with Jordan Pace, you've seen them all."

My butt hit the ground with a despondent thump as the slamming of car doors muted the rest of their blathering.

I knew Jordan had been around before he and I got together. He was a flirt, and despite the way my whole body took flight when he turned his attention to me, I'd told myself not to fall into his trap.

I had no intention of being a forgotten conquest. But then, after weeks of playful banter at our lockers, he'd pulled me aside at last year's homecoming game and asked me to follow him. He'd led me by the hand to his car and opened up his trunk, where a box of heart pins sat open inside.

"My sister works at Prints Charming," he'd said. I didn't know it then, but she'd eventually hook me up with my job there. He poked the side of the box containing the pins. "They kept marking down the inventory on these, but they still had a ton. I thought you could make something nice out of them." Then he hooked his fingers around mine and pulled me a little closer. His other hand moved to my waist. Our eyes locked. His voice was low when he spoke again. "I'm pretty sure you could make anything look good."

He kissed me then, the most mind-melting kiss I'd experienced in my life. That was the night I went home and created the pin that captured every explosion of color I'd seen behind my eyes in the sheer rapture of that moment. The same pin that was probably still sitting at the bottom of his locker, forgotten and unappreciated. Like the girl he'd stayed with longer than any other girl ever. The girl he'd still dumped once the "fun" was over. Me.

I had wanted to believe I'd changed him. I wanted to believe that he'd had the decency to not cheat on me. Both notions seemed all the more ridiculous now.

The sound of another car door slamming reminded me that I

hadn't plopped down on cold asphalt for the fun of it, and I forced myself back into action. Jordan sure as hell wasn't losing sleep over me, and I had a job to do. A job I realized I'd probably botched big-time as soon as I peeked around the hood of the Hummer.

TJ stood beside his car, leaning through the window of the vehicle next to him. One of his hands moved from inside the car to his back pocket, like he was slipping something inside.

But had the person in the car given it to him? And if so, what was that about?

I remembered Nick recounting his run-in at the Snack Shack. Had the boy in the shadows mistaken him for TJ? Could Snack Shack Guy and Hood Boy be one and the same? And if so, what was he selling? Was it drugs? Or was TJ's hand cold and my imagination was working overtime for nothing?

TJ's fingers had barely left his pocket before he got into his own driver's seat and started the engine. I jumped up and dashed to my car as the other vehicle peeled out of its parking space. I couldn't see the driver, or even the color of the car, but I saw the Templeton decal on the back windshield as clear as day. Whether it was the same car that had parked in front of TJ's house the other night, I couldn't be sure, and I didn't have time to worry about it. The car I needed to follow would get away if I didn't move fast.

Somehow, even with my bumbling mitten hands, I managed to shove my key into the ignition and get onto the street before I lost sight of TJ. We wound through road after road, and when the surroundings became increasingly familiar, my breathing finally started to slow down. We were headed toward Maple Acres.

He was going home.

When TJ pulled into his driveway, I kept driving and looped back around, so I could park in the same spot that had served as my and Charlie's observatory. TJ's car still sat outside, as dark and lifeless as the starless sky above the barn. I turned off my car and waited.

And kept on waiting.

As the minutes stretched, I found myself rationalizing again. So what if TJ had called someone from the car after he dropped off Kendall? He'd said he felt sick—maybe he hadn't felt well enough to drive and had been trying to get a ride. Or maybe his mother called, for crying out loud. Kendall always assumed the worst. As for the person he'd been talking to in the flesh, it very well could've been the same guy who'd visited the barn last time. If he was a Templeton student and a friend of TJ's, it made perfect sense that they'd be talking. And the connection to Nick and the Snack Shack… Well, I was reaching, at best.

The crickets chirped, the minutes stretched, and I still had absolutely nothing worth reporting to Kendall.

I picked up my phone and typed in a text: Any chance TJ's a druggie?

The phone started to ring, sounding extra loud in the stillness of the night.

"Kendall?"

The sound of muffled laughter met my ears.

"Marisa? Want to tell me why you're using 'TJ' and 'druggie' in the same sentence?"

I sighed and slumped in my seat. "I don't know. I saw him talking to someone in the parking lot after some guy tried to sell Nick drugs at the game tonight."

This time she full-out belly laughed. "I'm sorry. I'm not laughing at you, but there's no way Mr. My-Body-Is-a-Temple-Save-the-Freaking-Whales was buying drugs. And no offense, sometimes your brother is whacked. Someone probably tried to offer him a damn hot dog."

I brushed off her comment about Nick. She was no fonder of him than he was of her. "Thought so. I'm not staying much longer but I'll call you if anything happens."

I drummed my fingers against the base of the window and started my car as my thoughts turned back to the other conversation I'd witnessed tonight, the one between that girl Mel and her friends. When the last window in TJ's house went dark, I drove away with no evidence that Kendall had been played for a fool. Me, on the other hand…that was a different story.

8

AS IF THE NIGHT HADN'T BEEN DEGRADING ENOUGH, I HAD TO GO BACK to Templeton to pick up everyone after the game. Apparently I'd become a spy service and a chauffeur service, all wrapped up in one big, loser package.

To make matters worse, Kendall spent the entire car ride making Nick and Charlie swear they wouldn't tell a soul about the "work" she had me doing for her.

"It doesn't matter that we're at different schools. You never know who's talking to who." She motioned to Charlie and me to illustrate her point, then looked from Charlie to Nick and back again. "You guys swear you won't say anything, right?" It had to be the eightieth time she'd asked since we'd started driving.

From the way Charlie's fists were clenched in her lap, she was ready to seal her oath with a backhand.

Kendall unbuckled her seat belt and scooted forward,

sticking her head between the driver's and passenger's seat. "Pull up there, Marisa. It's the one at the end of the cul-de-sac with the Corvette in the driveway." She slid back. "Anyway. You guys promise, right?"

"You know she's not finding the hidden city of frigging Atlantis for you, right?" Charlie snapped.

Kendall shrank. "Just making sure we're clear," she replied through gritted teeth. She told me again that she'd make it up to me as she got out of the car, to which Charlie yelled, "Fudgie's gift card!" as the door slammed, trapping a breeze of almond-and-anise perfume in its wake. Before I could pull out of the Keene's circular driveway, Charlie looked at me in disbelief.

"Seriously, how were you ever friends with her?"

In the back seat, Nick fake choked and fanned his hand in front of his nose. "I think I'm high from her ten gallons of eau de spaz. No wonder her boyfriend won't go near her. She's hot but you need a damn gas mask."

"Come on, guys," I said. "Kendall's a drama queen, but she's not a bad person. She's going through a tough time."

"Be a dear and pull up to my mansion," Charlie said in a high, mimicking voice. "Farther up, please, my quarters are in the east wing. And careful not to sideswipe Daddy's 'Vette on your way out."

"Her dad refurbishes cars as a hobby. Having fancy sports cars in the driveway is the norm for the Keenes."

Kendall's dad used to take us for rides around town in his latest projects, and we thought we were the coolest kids on wheels.

Charlie rolled her eyes. "One, that was *not* a refurb. Two, no one does that for a hobby without some serious cash to spare. And three, holy God complex living in a house like that! It had turrets, for Christ's sake!"

My hands tightened around the wheel. "You know it's her parents' house, not hers, right?"

Charlie might've had her reasons for disliking Kendall, but she was being downright unfair. I was half tempted to ask if hating people because their parents had more money was something she'd learned in her fancy honors program. Because if Charlie's parents had paid to send her to Templeton when mine couldn't, did that mean I was supposed to despise her for it?

She ignored the question I'd asked out loud. "Damn, I should've told her to get you a gift card to Prints Charming. That's way more you, but she probably wouldn't be caught dead in there." Prints Charming, in addition to being my summer job, was also my favorite craft and fabric store, one I'd dragged Charlie to on many an occasion. I usually made it up to her by letting her pick out beads and charms for her next Marisa specialty. She gave me a pointed look. "If she's really your friend, she'll figure out the best way to say thank you herself."

Nick scoffed. "Fat chance, Char. Don't you know this is Planet Kendall? The rest of us are just taking up space."

I started to open my mouth, ready to defend Kendall again, but it seemed pointless. Once upon a time, I'd felt the same way. And I still wasn't entirely sure I'd been wrong.

~

My eyes felt like someone had switched out my contact solution for sulfuric acid when my alarm went off on Monday morning. I knew little red threads branched out from the brown of my irises like tiny tree roots without even looking in the mirror.

As I fumbled with my alarm clock, I shot a dirty look in the direction of my makeshift craft table in the opposite corner. The top was strewn with sketch pads, pencils, strands and boxes of beads in all sizes, bottles of colored glitter, and a handful of heart pins, most undecorated or half-decorated. Those pins used to represent how much Jordan cared, how well he knew me.

Now they'd become sorry-your-boyfriend-sucks consolation prizes. Ironic and appropriate at the same time.

I'd stayed up way too late the night before finishing Kendall's pin. I must've felt guilty about the whole car-ride experience, and maybe I felt a little guilty that I hadn't turned up anything on TJ too. Not that it was my fault or for lack of trying. And maybe it was that guilt that nagged me to talk to him, though it might've been me just itching to know what his deal was. He still hadn't mentioned having a girlfriend, and I still didn't understand his bitterness toward his old school. Nor did I know if I needed to be concerned with the decaled car that kept popping up wherever he was.

Not that I was being nosy. My curiosity was strictly professional, of course.

My interest in his gorgeous leather jewelry, however, was all my own. I'd been eyeing his pieces ever since I noticed the bracelet he had on the first time I'd semi-grilled him. He had it on again today, a thick band of deep, rich color, like burned wood, lined with silver studs. It gave me the perfect excuse to pull up a chair next to his computer.

"So I'm dying to know where you got that." I pointed to his wrist as I sat down.

TJ lifted his forearm from the keyboard and looked at the bracelet. "This?" He smiled. "I made it."

My jaw almost unhinged it dropped so fast. "You *made* that?"

"Sure did." He undid the closure and handed the bracelet to me. "I make all my own stuff. Well, most of it. I tan the leather and everything."

I turned the bracelet over in my hand. I didn't see a single indication that it had been made by anyone other than a seasoned professional. The studs weren't glued on; they were punched, neatly and evenly, into the leather, which felt strong and pliable at the same time. And that *color*—like butterscotch and coffee and smoke all mixed together in some glorious cowhide potion.

"This is phenomenal. Really, really phenomenal. I've never

made something this nice. I mean, I made these"—I pushed my hair behind my ear and angled my head to give him a better view of my earring, a Murano glass charm I'd flanked with silver beads—"and I make other jewelry and sew a bit, but this is real craftsmanship. You have some serious talent."

TJ flushed at my babbling and looked down at his keyboard. "Thanks. Your stuff is nice too."

I handed him his bracelet, embarrassed that he'd deign to compliment my trinkety creations. "Not like this. I'd love to know how you made it."

A light came on in his eyes as he snapped the bracelet around his wrist. He looked like a new father talking about his baby. "I have a workshop set up in the barn. My uncle taught me some of what I know, but I mostly taught myself. I buy my own materials and create all my own designs. I'm working on setting up a website so I can take orders too."

The corners of his mouth twitched in an odd sort of grimace, like he'd said something he shouldn't have.

I eyeballed the bracelet again. "I'd definitely be interested in buying some of your stuff. Hell, I'd love to learn how to do it so I can make my own."

The bell rang and TJ stood up, slinging his bag over his shoulder. "The next time you're at the farm, come find me." I froze, then flashed a stiff smile as I realized he meant the next time I went to the farm for a Christmas tree or a hayride, not the next time I went stalking him. "I'll give you a tour of my shop."

I stood up too. "Sounds great. I'd really like that."

As he waved over his shoulder on his way out, I could barely refrain from slapping myself. In the midst of my gushing, I hadn't brought up a single topic that might've prompted him to mention Kendall or Templeton. He'd given me the perfect segue too, since I'd made the connection that the ankle bracelet Kendall had been wearing the day we'd crossed paths in the school parking lot had to have been one of TJ's creations. I totally could've worked it into the conversation to see if he'd bite, and instead, I hadn't been able to see past the silver-studded stars in my eyes.

Oops.

Still, I had a safety net. Because if he'd meant it when he told me to come find him at the farm, I'd given myself a guaranteed in.

9

JORDAN'S LOCKER SLAMMED SHUT SO HARD, I COULD HAVE SWORN the wall vibrated.

"Um, are you okay?" I asked.

"Sorry," he spat. "My car got broken into and I just got the estimate to fix it. Goddamn rip-off."

"Yikes, that sucks." It was a much more sensitive response than the first one that popped into my head, which involved calling him out on the fact that his parents would probably pay for it anyway. "Where did it happen?"

His hands slid into his pockets and he looked everywhere but at me. "At a friend's house."

A friend's house—a.k.a. the Bang du Jour.

"Sorry to hear that," I said without much sympathy. I slammed my locker. "See you later."

"So are you going to Kevin Davidson's party Saturday night?"

I looked over my shoulder to make sure Jordan, not a passing ventriloquist, had asked me the question. Had he actually said something conversational to me? I blinked to make sure I wasn't dreaming.

"Are you?" he prompted.

"Are *you*?"

"Probably."

"Then why do you care?"

Jordan rolled his eyes and gave a soft grunt of annoyance. "You don't have to give me attitude. It's only a question."

"Are you trying to make sure I'm not going so I don't ruin your night?"

Jordan threw up his hands. "For fuck's sake, forget it. Sorry I asked."

He started to walk away, but I called him back. "Wait, Jordan. I'm sorry. You never talk to me anymore and I don't know how to react. Bitch is my first line of defense."

He smiled a little and I cursed the way my insides fluttered. "I remember," he said with a laugh.

Wait—what the…? Was that a look of fondness? If I didn't know better, I'd say Jordan was getting nostalgic. Dear God, please let him get nostalgic.

I leaned against my locker and tried to sound casual. "So, what about this party?"

"Nothing important. Kevin is having a bonfire again. I remember a while ago you were working on that fire collection, and it made me think of you."

Oh my God, he *was* getting nostalgic. My fire collection had resulted from my fascination with the different hues visible inside flames. And, if I'm being honest, the way they'd reflected in Jordan's eyes the last time we were at Kevin's bonfire together. I'd spawned a whole line of bracelets and necklaces in brilliant oranges and yellows and reds with black and sapphire accents. I'd even sold a bunch of the pieces at Prints Charming and made enough money for half the down payment on my jalopy.

Why would he bring that up now, after giving me the cold shoulder for so long?

I tried to act unaffected. "So I guess you're going?"

"I'll be there." He looked around and took a step closer. "It would be nice if you were too. It's stupid that we can't be friends."

With that, he turned and headed down the hall, leaving me a human tornado of questions and emotions. Could it possibly be that, after all this time, Jordan had started missing me?

I wandered off to class in a daze. I never ever planned to get caught in Jordan's web of hotness and hypocrisy again, but I needed to know what had brought on this change of heart. Even letting the tiniest part of me believe that he regretted our breakup made me feel powerful, like I'd gained the upper hand. And hadn't I earned the right to toy with him a little?

I stopped short in the doorway to the classroom, nearly causing a pileup as I remembered a very important detail: Kevin Davidson's property bordered Maple Acres Tree Farm. Last time I'd watched in awe as the flames silhouetted the treetops in the darkness, never imagining I'd be spending so much time at that farm a mere year later…or why. If TJ was going to be at the party this year, and if he planned to bring Kendall, we could have a problem on our hands.

Or not, I thought as I took my seat. Kendall and I could pretend not to know each other, and TJ would be none the wiser to our plan. I had been pretty adamant that the three of us should avoid being in the same place at the same time, but for one night, I didn't see the harm. It wasn't like my friends hung out with TJ's friends anyway. Besides, Kendall said TJ didn't like parties, so maybe he wouldn't even go.

All I knew was that whatever TJ's plans were for Saturday evening, I hoped they involved Kendall. Because Kevin Davidson's party was suddenly the only place I wanted to be that night, and I didn't need her love life ruining it for me.

For the rest of the week, I jumped every time my cell phone chimed with a text. I kept waiting for Kendall's panicked message that TJ had blown her off again and she needed me to be on call. I'd already planned my lie to get out of being her Girl Friday, though I knew I'd feel guilty doing it. So far TJ hadn't done anything wrong, but if he was cheating, there would be plenty of opportunities to catch him. One night off wouldn't kill anyone.

Even as Charlie and I were in my room getting ready for the party, I couldn't breathe a sigh of relief. As if he'd read my mind, Nick leaned against the frame of my bedroom door and looked in, bewildered.

"Are you putting on makeup? Did Kendall give you the key to the handcuffs?"

"We're going to Kevin Davidson's bonfire. Wanna come?"

"Nah, that guy's a douche nugget."

"You mean nobody wants a junior there?" Charlie teased.

Nick looked past me, to where Charlie stood applying lip gloss in front of my mirror. "What's the matter, Charlotte, your school too swanky to throw a decent party?"

Charlie stuck out her tongue. "Listen, I went to school in Herring Cross until eighth grade. I have friends here. Besides"—she turned back to the mirror and ran her fingers through her bangs—"Templeton guys suck." She must've missed the doofy grin that appeared on Nick's face, because she zipped the tube of lip gloss into her clutch and turned to me. "So Kendall and TJ made up, or what? I'm shocked that you're free tonight. Almost as shocked as I am that you want to go to this party."

I ignored the last part of her comment and tossed her my cell phone. "She sent me a text on Wednesday, but I haven't heard from her since. I'm not about to check in either."

Charlie scrolled through my phone. "'TJ came over after school today, smiley face.'" She looked up at me in disgust. "You realize this is code for 'he threw me down on my twenty-four-carat gold bed with its diamond-encrusted headboard and had fourteen different kinds of sex with me,' right?" She tossed the phone back and shuddered like it had cooties.

My expression soured and I said, "Thanks for the visual" at the same time Nick said, "Nice."

Charlie turned to my brother. "Are you sure you don't want to come? I may need help restraining your sister from dry humping Jordan Pace on sight."

Nick looked me dead in the eye. "I'll kill you."

"Jesus, I'm not going to do anything with Jordan! You guys really think I'm that stupid? Don't answer that."

I turned back to my closet and rifled through my shirts for the hundredth time, mostly so I didn't have to see the looks I knew they exchanged. After the way Jordan had broken my heart, wanting him to secretly pine for me made me human, not weak. At least in my opinion.

Now I just had to pray I was as strong as I pretended to be.

A BUNCH OF GUYS WERE PUTTING THE FINISHING TOUCHES ON THE bonfire as Charlie and I crunched through dead, fallen leaves into Kevin's backyard. It was freezing, and when our friends offered us beer, I shook my head, wishing someone would hand me a steaming cup of hot chocolate instead.

The Davidsons had a fan-shaped yard, spreading outward as it moved away from the house with its bi-level deck. Beyond the tree line that marked the edge of their property, the shadows of Maple Acres' rolling hills and pointed treetops were visible in every direction. The tall, narrow fire sat dead center in the lawn, and I spotted Jordan even before we pulled folding chairs up around it. He stood against the railing of the top deck, a cup of beer in one hand, the other balled in the pocket of his hoodie, talking to Sara Mendez. She twirled the end of her long black hair, threw her head back, and laughed at something he said. Jordan's eyes darted straight to her ample chest when she did.

"What's that crotch monger doing here?" Charlie muttered.

"You knew he was coming."

Charlie snorted. "I meant Sara. She's a junior. Why would she be here? Oh, right. Probably because she'll need knee replacement surgery by age twenty-five from all the time she supposedly spends on them. No wonder they invite her every year."

"Charlie, what is *wrong* with you?" I exploded. I'd had enough. It was one thing to have an off moment every now and then, but moments where my best friend felt like a stranger were a hard pass, thank you very much.

She blinked, appearing genuinely surprised by my outburst. "It was a joke, Marisa."

"It was mean. And so was what you said about Kendall in the car the other night. What's going on with you lately?"

Her head dropped and she traced the rim of her cup. "My Templeton is showing, isn't it?" she said quietly.

"I'm not gonna lie. You've been…different since you started going to school there. Not all the time, but…"

"Enough that you had to call me out for being a total bitchface." She sighed. "I'm sorry, Marisa. It's a different world over there. There's so much pressure to 'not only succeed, but excel.'" She rolled her eyes as she quoted the school's motto. "Competition is so cutthroat and it's like you have to kill or be killed. I guess I let myself get sucked into the vortex sometimes."

It was the first time Charlie had ever spoken disparagingly about Templeton, and it surprised me. "Do you regret not staying at Herring Cross?"

She shook her head. "I'm happy where I am, but it doesn't mean the school isn't ridiculous. I think people forget that it's an education, not a status symbol. Including the students. Consider this conversation my mental slap back to reality."

"Good. Because I'm not above actually slapping you."

We both laughed, but when my eyes darted back to the deck, Charlie pinched my arm. "Go get a beer. If you're going to convince me that you're here to socialize, you need to do way better than this."

I resisted the urge to stick my tongue out and headed toward the keg, which sat at the base of the deck steps. I had gotten three quarters of the way there when Jordan noticed me. He nodded in my direction and raised his cup in a wave. Before I had even finished wiggling my mittened fingers in return, he turned back to his conversation with Sara.

Okay then.

I lowered my hand, feeling ridiculous. He'd asked me to be here and that was the best hello he could muster?

I took my drink back to the fire and tried to join in the chatter, tried to care about the game of beer pong in progress, tried to keep myself from wondering if Jordan had really brushed me off or if I'd read too much into his lack of greeting. It's not like I could expect our relationship to be perfect overnight after months of cold shoulders and death glares. So when my eyes kept panning the yard like sprinklers on a timer and located Jordan alone at the keg, I stood up to prove to myself that I was overthinking things.

My cup still held half of my original beer, and it had grown warm and skunky, but I clutched it like a security blanket and forced myself to take sip of the putrid liquid as I closed in on Jordan.

"Hey," I said.

"What's up?" He glanced at me and then looked down at the tap again, giving me a twitchy smile like he couldn't decide on an appropriate level of friendly. The greeting felt lukewarm at best, but again, I told myself to stop letting my imagination work overtime.

I wrapped my free hand around my arm and rubbed briskly. "I don't remember it being this cold last year."

Probably because I'd had Jordan's arms around me all night. I shivered, but not from the weather.

"It's pretty raw out here." He scooped a second cup up from the ground. "Hey, can I catch up with you later? I have to bring this to someone." He indicated the other cup he'd picked up.

Nope, not my imagination at all. He was definitely blowing me off. The last shred of hope I'd been clinging to withered inside me and died as I realized I'd been had yet again.

"I—yeah. No problem. Later."

His smirk had enough condescension and self-righteousness to make me want to hurl my beer at his head and then barf the portion I'd drank all over Kevin's crunchy lawn. He turned and walked away to bring "someone" her beer, like I didn't know damn well who that "someone" was.

I tossed my cup in the garbage hard enough to make the beer slosh out and took a deep breath of chilly air to loosen the knot of disappointment in my chest. Disappointment in myself, that is. I'd spent an hour choosing my outfit, blow-drying my hair, and putting on makeup, all to watch Jordan flirt with another girl. What was it about him that turned me into a brainless, spineless moron?

"Never again," I said out loud.

"Is it that bad?"

I jumped and spun to see who'd responded to my chat with myself. To my surprise, TJ stood a foot away from me, his hands buried deep in the pockets of his plaid coat. I opened my mouth, but only a croaking sound came out.

"The beer," he said, nodding toward the garbage. "Is it that bad?"

"It's...not really beer weather, I guess. Too cold." I laughed, a wimpy little sound that made TJ narrow his eyes at me.

"Are you okay?"

I shrugged. "Sure. So what are you doing here? Where's K—" I almost choked swallowing the word *Kendall*. "Kevin? Have you seen Kevin yet? It's his party and he's barely been out here."

Nice one, Marisa. You suck.

TJ took a look around the yard and shook his head. "I haven't seen him. Last year, after this party, there were beer cans and crap all over our property. I really only came over to make sure no one does anything stupid."

Too late. I'm the biggest idiot in this place.

TJ grabbed a cup, looked at it, and put it back. "On second thought, maybe I should go say hi. I've gotta be social if I'm gonna make friends. At least that's what my parents tell me." He smiled. "Be right back."

He bounded up the stairs to the deck and I wasted no time yanking off my mitten and whipping my phone out of my pocket to text Kendall.

Where are you?

A few seconds later her response came: Cousin's bachelorette party. Why?

At a party. TJ is here. Thought he was w/ you tonight.

Kendall had to have dislocated her thumbs typing her response, because that was how quickly it had arrived. What party?? With who?? What's he doing??

Oh Lord. I should've kept my mouth shut.

Bonfire near his farm. Not with anyone. Doing nothing as usual.

Another almost instantaneous reply: Don't let him out of your sight.

"Geez, obsessed much?" I murmured.

"Do you always talk to yourself?" TJ stood behind me on the

deck stairs. I shoved my phone in my pocket and jammed my mitten back over my hand.

"Did you find Kevin?"

"I did, but I think he was too wasted to care." He did a double take in the direction of the fire. "Is that Charlie Reiser? I thought she went to Templeton. What's she doing here?"

"She came with me."

"Oh, right. I forgot. She's a Herring Cross defector." He squinted. "Is it me, or is she giving you the evil eye?"

I didn't have to look at Charlie to know that she was telepathically demanding to be briefed on my encounter with Jordan. Waiting for her chance to say *I told you so*. When we made eye contact, she spread her hands in front of her as if to say *So?* I played dumb and waved at her before turning back to TJ.

"How long can I convince you to stand here and talk to me so I can avoid her lecture?"

TJ raised an eyebrow. "What's wrong? She doesn't want you drinking?"

"No, if anything she probably wishes I'd drink more. A lot more. Long story."

"The fire in the middle of the Arctic tundra is lovely, but it doesn't put me in the mood for beer either." He rocked on his heels and hunched his shoulders. "If you're still interested, we could take a walk over to my shop, a.k.a. the big white barn. I'll show you where I make my stuff." He looked down like he was embarrassed at his own invitation. "If you're interested."

I brightened instantly. "I'd love to! Are you working on anything right now?"

He smiled and his shoulders relaxed. "Always. I made this belt last week." He lifted the hem of his coat to reveal a black leather belt threaded around the waist of his jeans with silver-ringed holes and a big, square buckle. I gasped and started to lift my hand to touch it, until I remembered (a) I couldn't feel the leather through my mitten and (b) it would be entirely inappropriate to put my hand that close to his crotch. Which automatically made my eyes drop to that area, which made me flush furious red and want to die on the spot.

"It's, um, really nice. Let me tell Charlie where I'm going."

I turned on my heels and prayed he hadn't noticed either my red face or my accidental ogling of his goods, and sped over to where Charlie sat cross-legged on her chair. Her eyes widened as I approached.

"What happened?"

I shook my head. "I—nothing. I'm going for a walk with TJ, okay?"

I turned before she could pry for more information, but she caught my hand. When I looked back, I only saw concern in her face. "Are you all right?"

I gave her hand a squeeze. "I'm fine. I just need to get out of here for a bit. I won't be long."

She nodded and gave me a reassuring smile. One of the many differences between my friendship with Kendall and my friendship with Charlie was that Charlie always knew when to stop talking. I'd have to hug her later when there weren't drunk doofuses around to catcall or make perverted remarks.

I shoved my hands in my pockets and joined TJ across the lawn, falling into step at his side. The Marisa who'd walked into Kevin's yard earlier tonight definitely would've looked over her shoulder to check if Jordan was watching. The Marisa who left the party with TJ didn't even bother.

MY PHONE VIBRATED IN MY POCKET AS TJ AND I TRUDGED DOWN THE frozen dirt path that wound through the farm, branching off into different areas where every type of Christmas tree imaginable grew.

I pretended I didn't feel it, knowing I'd awakened Kendall's inner obsessive beast, and 99.9 percent sure it was her, already checking in.

Too bad, I thought. I'd been dying to see TJ's workshop ever since he'd told me about it, and going there with him was strictly for me. Tonight was supposed to be a night off from investigating, and I planned to keep it that way. We had reached the spot at the top of the hill where the Douglas firs grew, the section of the farm that backed up to Kevin's yard. It gave almost a bird's-eye view of the white barn and the pond in front of it, a breathtaking sight in the daylight, especially during sunset.

"This is the spot where I took that picture I told you about, the one I tried to draw," I said. "It's so pretty here."

TJ paused alongside me. "Not many people see beauty in a rickety old barn, but I think so too. It's really peaceful."

"Peaceful is the perfect word. The pumpkin patch is fun, but the tree farm… It's like Narnia."

He chuckled. It was more of an appreciative sound than a wow-that-was-stupid laugh. "What was it about your drawing that you didn't like?"

"I don't know. Everything was in the right place and it looked like a barn and a pond, but that was the problem. It was just a barn and a pond. It felt so—flat. I couldn't capture it the way I saw it."

"Maybe it needed a centaur or a talking goat. That would've added some life."

We both laughed, and I almost forgot I had any reason to hang out with TJ other than the fact that he was a pretty nice guy. Almost, except that my pocket vibrated yet again as we continued down the hill.

Fine, Kendall. I'll do some digging while I have him alone.

"So how do you like Herring Cross?"

TJ shrugged. "So far, so good. It's like any other high school: jocks, cheerleaders, geeks, rule breakers. People like you and me who are somewhere in the middle. The usual fare."

"Uh, judging by what you said the last time we talked, I think you forgot a category."

"And what's that?"

"Assholes? You tell me. You're the one who needed a change of scenery."

He ducked into his shoulders and chuckled. "Oh that. It's funny how one bad experience can tar whatever came before it, huh? Anyway, welcome to my workshop." We'd come to a stop in front of the tall double doors that served as the entrance to the barn, and I got the feeling TJ couldn't have been more grateful to end the school conversation. Again.

He pulled a key out of his pocket and opened the padlock holding the two doors together. Then he swung one open, flipped on a light, and made a sweeping motion with his arm, as if to say *after you*. I stepped inside. My gawking was immediate and intense.

Off to the left were empty stables, some of which had neatly stacked bales of hay on the floor and saddles and reins tacked to the stall walls. They reminded me of the bedroom of a kid who'd gone off to college: unoccupied for the time being but ready and waiting for someone's return.

A room with a high, beamed ceiling spread out before us. In its center sat a long table. It was made of thick, sturdy wood and looked like it belonged in the banquet hall of an ancient castle. The walls on either side of it were lined with plywood shelves and cabinetry, and they housed bottles of dye, cutting blades, mallets and other medieval-looking tools, and rolls of rawhide, some dyed and some not. At the far end, an old-fashioned sewing machine and a cup-by-cup instant coffee machine sat side by side like old friends.

“Where did you get all this stuff?”

He smiled, sheepish and proud at the same time. “Some of it we had. Some of it I ordered online.” He must’ve seen me eyeing the coffee machine, because he added, “Do you want some coffee or hot chocolate to chase that beer?”

“Hot chocolate sounds *perfect*.”

“Great.” He walked over to the machine and busied himself. “I special order this awesome organic Aztec hot cocoa with real dark chocolate in it. Did you know the Aztecs used cacao as currency? They thought it brought wisdom and even offered it to the dead for their journey into the afterlife—” I was listening intently, but TJ cut himself off with a wince. “Sorry, sometimes my dork flag flies out of control.” He motioned toward the table, looking embarrassed. “Have a look around.”

As much as I liked the impromptu lesson on Aztecs and chocolate, I was itching to explore. The room, his shop, was amazing. And the whipped cream atop the sundae of awesome? The staircase at the opposite end that spiraled up to a loft, where smaller versions of the barn doors were closed over a window that must’ve overlooked the farm. A telescope sat perched on a tripod in front of it. I could almost hear Nick saying *I bet that’s really a bong*, but I pushed his voice out of my mind. I wanted to run up the stairs, fling open the doors, and ogle the view and everything else in the barn. Hell, I wanted to pack my suitcase and move in.

"This is the coolest place I have ever seen." I turned in circles, taking in my surroundings. I realized the temperature was much more comfortable inside the barn, and I put my mittens inside my pockets. "So much warmer than outside too."

"I had the space heaters running for a while before I went up to the party. Once they get going, they do a pretty good job of warming it up in here." He motioned toward tall, narrow heaters tucked in each corner of the room as he handed me a delicious-smelling, steaming cup of cocoa.

I almost melted into the floor at the first sip. "Mmm. Oh my *God*, this is amazing."

TJ grinned. "Good, right?"

"If more people knew about this, Montezuma wouldn't get such a bad rap." I closed my eyes and let the chocolatey steam warm my face. When I opened them again, my gaze fell on the empty stables. "What happened to your horses?"

"We had two when I was younger, but they both died. One was my dad's and the other was my uncle's. They'd had them since they were kids, but this hasn't been an animal farm in years. Uncle Roger keeps saying he's gonna buy another horse, but I think my dad would flip. They're expensive and a lot of work, but I think it would be awesome to have horses around again. Then they could do the hayrides instead of me."

I smiled and started to walk the length of the table, running my fingers along the smooth edge as I went. A large strip of black leather lay stretched across the tabletop, and a cutting blade rested on top of it. "Is this what you're working on now?"

"That's actually the piece I made my belt from." He walked over to the table. "I can make one for you, if you want, since you seemed to like it."

I blushed again at the memory of my eye contact with his fly. "I would love that, but I don't want you to go through any trouble. I'll order one once your website is up."

He shook his head and waved off my comment. "It's no trouble at all. I can start it right now. Besides, if you wait for my website, you might be waiting forever."

TJ didn't give me time to concede. Instead, he stood at the head of the table, centered the leather on a square black board, and grabbed the cutting blade. He leaned over it with the same intensity as a billiard player lining up a shot in a game of pool. It was a little intimidating to watch his brow furrow and the veins appear in his hand as he drove the blade down the swatch.

And, if I'm being honest, it was also kind of hot.

"Open up your coat," he said, bringing the newly cut strip over to me. "I have to make sure it's the right size."

I reluctantly relinquished the warmth of the hot chocolate and started working open my buttons. It was odd enough to have him hovering so close while I more or less undressed, but when he slipped his hands inside the open halves of my coat and around my waist, things went to a whole new level of awkward. How could they not, when we were so close that I could feel the heat coming off his skin?

"Maybe I should do six holes," he murmured, more to himself than me. I couldn't help but watch the intense, no-nonsense expression on his face as he wrapped the strip around me and studied it. "You have a small waist."

"And you smell nice."

Tell me I did not say that out loud.

"Thanks." TJ chuckled, and whether his grip on the leather faltered or he adjusted the drape, I couldn't tell. But his hands settled on my hips. And for a second, I forgot that his touch was supposed to feel weird, because it just felt…nice.

Until I full-out jumped, because my phone vibrated in my pocket again.

"Geez, I'm sorry. That's—it's probably Charlie," I lied, stepping out of his personal space and back into my sanity. "Do you mind if I go up there and call her quickly?" I nodded in the direction of the loft.

"Go ahead. Let her know I didn't kidnap you."

I managed a smile that turned into an annoyed grimace the minute I turned away. Kendall either had to trust me or not. I couldn't get anything done with her constantly harassing me. I stomped up the steps, almost forgetting to be angry when I saw how cozy the loft was. A worn-looking plaid couch and a long, rectangular coffee table that reminded me of the one my grandmother had for decades sat in the center of the space. In the corner, a small TV stood angled on a stand. Handmade bookshelves piled with paperbacks and hardcovers leaned against one of the walls, and an open book lay pages down across the arm of the couch, waiting for TJ to pick up where he'd left off.

Kendall really didn't understand why he spent so much time here? How could you not?

I flopped onto the couch and pulled out my phone. Sure enough, all three buzzes had come from the same source:

Whose party is it?

Is he drinking?

Is he talking to anyone?

I touched her name on the screen and took a few calming breaths as the phone rang. When she answered, I had to hold it away from my ear.

"HELLO? MARISA?" Loud music, hoots, hollers, and a cacophony of voices blared through my phone.

"Holy hell, where are you?"

"MARISA? WHAT'S GOING ON? I CAN'T HEAR YOU. YOU HAVE TO TEXT ME."

With that, the line went dead and I threw my head back in exasperation. Gritting my teeth, I punched out a reply:

He left the party. Still haven't seen him do anything wrong.

Might be wasting our time.

I shoved the phone back in my pocket with a sigh and walked over to the wood railing, where the loft overlooked the barn. To my surprise, TJ stood at the door, holding it slightly ajar. His knuckles were white, like he was prepared to slam it in the face of whoever stood on the other side. His posture was rigid. I pressed myself where the railing met the wall and tried to listen in.

Amid a hiss of whispers, I heard TJ say, "I know, okay? I forgot." I couldn't hear or see the person who stood outside, but I wasn't about to move. Then he added, "You need to get out of here. Got it?" The door shut, and he turned back to his table like nothing had happened.

I leaned against the wall and exhaled the breath I'd been holding. Just as I was thinking I might've spoken too soon when I told Kendall we were wasting our time, my phone buzzed with another text from her.

Trust me. We're not.

12

BY THE TIME MONDAY MORNING CAME, I FELT BAD FOR KENDALL. Something was going on with TJ, but I still hadn't figured out what. It wasn't like I'd found drug paraphernalia or homemade sex tapes in his barn, but he'd ushered me out and escorted me back to Kevin's party moments after his unwanted visitor left, and he'd steered clear of any attempts I made to bring the conversation to his old school or friends on the walk back.

I hadn't told Kendall what happened after we hung up, only because I still needed another day or so to mentally prepare myself for her inevitable fretting frenzy that would follow. I didn't know if she'd spent Sunday hungover or with TJ or whatever, but she hadn't bothered me and I'd rather enjoyed it. Once she knew about the mystery visitor, it would be a long time until I had a free night or weekend again.

"Hey, Marisa."

I slammed my locker a little harder than I meant to at the sound of TJ's voice. Who knew being a stalker would make me so jumpy? I pasted a smile on my face.

"Hey, what's up?"

TJ flashed a huge grin. "I finished it this weekend." He moved his hand from behind his back and held out a black leather belt dotted with silver studs. It was totally gorgeous, and one hundred percent badass at the same time.

"I love it!" I cried, instantly forgetting to regard him as Shady McShadeballs. I took the belt and slid it through the loops of my jeans, loving that it complemented my green shirt, matching flats, and silver jewelry. "What do I owe you?"

TJ scoffed. "You don't owe me anything."

"No! I can't take this for nothing. I have to give you something for it, please?"

The corner of his mouth turned up. "You can take my place interviewing Mr. Crossley about the Math League after school today if you want. I'll even let you write my article."

I smiled back. "Nice try. How about this—I'll take the belt, but only if you let me order some more of your stuff for the holidays and pay you for it. Deal?"

The locker behind me slammed and the skin on my neck crawled. I whipped around, knowing exactly who would be standing there, and the daggers were already shooting from my eyes before I'd even completed my rotation. The ice in my glare could've turned the hallway into a skating rink. TJ must've sensed it, because he said, "Fair enough. Um, I'll catch up with you later," and walked away.

Jordan's stare stayed fixed on his locker. "Don't give me that look, Marisa."

I folded my arms across my chest. "What the hell was that about on Saturday? You told me you wanted me at the bonfire, then totally blew me off. How am I supposed to look at you?"

He slung his bag over his shoulder and threw his other hand in the air. "It's not that I changed my mind about wanting to be friends, okay? It's like you said—I didn't know how to react. Things have been shitty for so long that I forgot how to be normal around you. I'm sorry, all right?"

My comeback, "Sorry is a good word for you," would've been awesome—if I'd had a chance to deliver it. But at that exact moment, my cell phone rang. And since a phone rarely rings with good news at 7:30 a.m., my attention was instantly diverted to the screen flashing Charlie's name.

I stepped into the exit alcove and barely got a hello out before she said, "Sorry to bother you, but we need to talk. You're *advertising* now?"

"Advertising what?"

"I'm hanging up to text you something. Call me as soon as you see it."

The call clicked off before I could say another word. I was still staring confusedly at the screen when it flashed with a text message. Charlie had sent me a link to a website. When I clicked on it, my heart went dead inside my chest.

A website loaded onto the screen. The word BUSTED splashed across the top of the page in bold, fat letters, glinting in red and black stripes, almost identical to the pin I'd made for Charlie. The pin Kendall had specifically mentioned liking. A squat exclamation point punctuated the word, and a jagged split between the *S* and *T* made it—along with the heart around it—appear broken in half.

Beneath the heading, in smaller print, it said *Don't hate the player...bust his ass!*

This had to be a joke. Only one person could've been responsible for this, and I knew exactly who it was.

I called Charlie back, crushing the phone against my ear as I dashed toward the computer lab. My phone was too old and too slow, and the school's cell service was too spotty to mess around.

"You're shitting me," I said when she picked up. I didn't so much sit as crash-land in one of the lab's plastic blue chairs, and my book bag skidded across the floor and toppled over.

"So you didn't know?"

I pulled the website up on the computer and scanned the page as fast as my brain could process it. "'Suspect your guy has a roaming eye? Our services are discreet, anonymous, and affordable.'" I almost dropped the phone. "She's advertising me for a fee?!"

"Keep reading. It gets worse."

"Oh my God!" I moaned. "Fake testimonials? Is she on cra—oh my God. Oh. My. God."

"Told you."

I had reached the spot where Kendall provided contact information for my quote-unquote "services." She'd listed the email address as OnTheMAP17@yahoo.com.

MAP. Marisa Ann Palmera. Not only had she used my initials, but she'd followed them with my freaking birth date. Who the hell had taught her the definition of *anonymous*? To think, earlier this morning I'd felt bad for her. Not anymore.

"Do you want me to throw a bag over her head and take her out behind the bleachers? Teach her a little lesson?" I could practically hear Charlie's knuckles cracking.

"Don't bother," I said. "I'm going to kill her myself."

"I told you I'd make it up to you!" Kendall chirped when she picked up the phone. "Not to toot my own horn, but I rock at web design."

"Are you *crazy*?"

A second of silence followed. "You don't like it?"

I slapped my forehead in disbelief and paced the courtyard. There were three minutes until the first bell, and I wanted that site down before it rang. "You used my initials! Kendall, I do not spy on people for fun! I helped a few people out. That's it! Catching cheaters is not something I want to do all the time. At least I don't think it is." I heard myself and stopped short. "No, no, it's not. And I especially don't want to charge people for it! How would I even get the money?"

"I guess a middleman or something?"

I took a deep breath and resumed walking, a little slower this time. "Listen, I appreciate the trouble you went to designing a site, but you have to take it down. Helping you and Charlie was one thing, but I can't be 'Monroe County Schools' Ace in the Hole for Girls Dating Guys with No Self-Control.'" I rolled my eyes as I quoted her ridiculous slogan.

"Wow," Kendall said softly. "I'm sorry, Marisa. I guess I should've asked before I went ahead and put it up. I thought I was doing something nice for you."

Ugh. Guilt pierced through me at the dejection in her voice.

"It was a nice gesture, Kendall. It was. I appreciate the time it must've taken, and honestly, the design is awesome. I loved the way you made the heart in the background look sparkly and broken." Might as well butter her up with the truth if I had to do it at all.

She let out a small, forced laugh. "That was my favorite part."

"Mine too, for sure. Maybe you can print that out for me or send me the image before you take it down? I bet I could design a necklace out of it." Not that I needed a picture to help me redesign something I'd technically created, but flattery seemed to be softening the blow of my rebuff.

"Um, Marisa, I guess I can take down the site if you really want me to, but it might not be that easy."

"Why not?"

"Because you already have emails from girls who want you to help them."

I froze midpace. "I what? How long has that site been up?"

"Since midnight, but I sort of sent the link to everyone at Templeton."

My knees went weak. "Everyone?"

I could practically hear her biting her lip. "All the girls anyway. I'm on student council and I have a directory of email addresses. I'm really sorry. I sent out a blast this morning, and since you're calling me, I'm guessing word already traveled outside the school."

The bell rang, but I couldn't move. I stood in the middle of the courtyard with my mouth hanging open, frozen wisps of my breath floating off into the air.

"Marisa? Are you still there?"

I croaked out a yes.

"Listen, I'm so sorry. I'm going to text you the password to the email account so you can check it out. If you want, you can ignore all of the messages and I'll shut down the site. But you never know. One of them might spark your interest. If not, say the word and I'll take it down as soon as I get home, okay?"

I closed my eyes. "Fine."

"I'm really sorry."

"So you've mentioned."

"I have to get to class, but call me later."

We hung up and I shoved open the glass door to go back inside, pounding out a text message to Charlie as I burst into the warm, fluorescent-lit hallway.

For real. I'm going to kill her.

13

I SAT WITH THE PALM OF MY HAND PRESSED AGAINST MY FOREHEAD as I scrolled through Kendall's OnTheMAP17 emails. There were already sixteen of them.

Six. Effing. Teen. Did anyone *not* suspect her boyfriend of cheating?

Most of the messages were immediate throwaways, with some outright ludicrous requests like, *Can you get a picture of my boyfriend looking at another girl so I can use it as blackmail?* One girl wanted me to key her boyfriend's car and the car of the girl he had already cheated with. Instant delete.

I had a handful left to go when one of the emails at the bottom of the screen caught my attention. It had the subject line "Dating a Player" and the username was SaraCat42. I scanned the computer lab one more time for creepers before clicking on it.

Hey,

My name is Sara and I am talking to one of the hottest guys at my school. I think he likes me, but I know he's a player, and let's put it this way, I don't share. His ex is still in his face all the time and I want to make sure she's not in his pants too. I really like him and I need to know if he feels the same or if I'm being played. Can you help?

SaraCat42

Sara Cat?

A Sara who'd recently started seeing one of the hottest guys in school. The image of Jordan checking out Sara Mendez's cleavage flashed through my mind. What were the odds that she and SaraCat42 were the same person?

I looked at the clock. I'd cut out of lunch early to use the computer lab, and I still had a few minutes to test out my theory. Part of me hoped I was way off base, because if SaraCat42 was Sara Mendez and the guy in question was Jordan, then that made *me* the ex who was supposedly in his face all the time. What a load of crap. I wondered if he'd told her that or if she'd jumped to her own conclusions after one stupid wave at Kevin's party.

I gathered my stuff and triple-checked that I'd logged out of the Busted account before heading over to the yearbook room. When I slid into place in front of my computer, I pulled up the layout for the junior class pictures and scrolled through to the *M*'s. Sara looked amazing in her picture—perfect smile, fabulous hair. Exactly the kind of girl Jordan loved to chase.

Next to the picture was her name: Sara Catarina Mendez.

I couldn't help but smirk. Not wanting to get ahead of myself, I clicked on a few more files until I found the one I wanted: girls' field hockey. I opened up the team photo and found Sara right away. She stood at the end, all the way to the right, smiling that perfect smile. Her long black hair hung in a high ponytail, and her hands were behind her, emphasizing her generous chest. And the number forty-two was splayed across it.

I sat back in my chair, too satisfied with myself to be properly indignant over her email.

Gotcha, SaraCat.

Busted indeed.

"Mom, I'm going to meet Charlie at Fudgie's!" I called on my way to the door.

I was supposed to be studying, but with all the Busted drama,

I was having a hard time concentrating on the properties of igneous rocks. So I'd called Charlie, and she was more than happy to ditch homework for a snack break.

"Wait a minute, Marisa." Mom's head poked out from the kitchen, and I didn't like the look on her face. Especially when she followed it with, "Your father and I need to talk to you."

She disappeared into the kitchen again, and I approached the room like something might jump out and scream at me. Whatever they were about to tell me, I was sure I didn't want to hear it.

Sure enough, my father sat at the kitchen table with my spreadsheet of colleges in front of him. We'd made it together. I'd listed out my top choices, and Dad had itemized the cost to attend each one. The very first school on my list was Lehigh University. Even with grants and financial aid, it pulled at the seams of our budget, but Dad had seemed confident that we could make it work.

At one point anyway.

"Marisa," he said, his lips frowning beneath his thick mustache. "I've been looking at the numbers for these schools again. I was joking the other day when I said we might have to cut Lehigh from the list, but—"

He ground his thumb and middle fingers into his temples and Mom swooped in to finish. "They're talking about closing the store where Daddy works."

"Again?" There had been rumors about the Herring Cross Big

M closing before, but the rumblings had eventually died off and the store stayed open.

Mom eyed my dad, nervously giving the floor back to him.

"It's not looking good, honey. Corporate says they'll place our employees at other branches, but until I know for sure, we can't take any chances." He shifted in his seat. "We're not trying to make your life difficult," he said.

I felt a lump rising in my throat, more because of the stress and worry and defeat that were rolling off him in waves, rather than the news he was giving me. That part hadn't quite sunk in yet. "I know how badly you want to go to Lehigh and how hard you've worked, but…I think we might need to consider your other options."

I dropped my gaze to the floor, unable to look at either of my parents, and nodded. If they couldn't afford the tuition and financial aid wouldn't be enough to close the gap, there wasn't much I could do. What could I really say?

So, without saying anything, I walked out the door.

When I got in my car, I threw my bag on the passenger seat. And of course, because I needed more annoyance when my nerves were already fraying like an old pair of jeans, my bag toppled over and spilled. I plucked up the folded piece of paper I'd almost forgotten about and opened it.

How Far Would You Go to Get the Story?

In a heartbeat, I knew the answer. I picked up my phone and clicked on Kendall's name.

Leave the website up.

"I can't believe you told her to leave up the site," Charlie said for the hundredth time since we'd arrived at Fudgie's. She licked the back of her spoon and shook her head. Kendall had texted back right as Charlie and I had slid into the cushy blue booth.

"Only for a couple of days. It's not like I have to take every case that comes along."

Charlie flailed in disbelief. "Are you hearing yourself? 'Every case that comes along'? You're not really a private investigator, Palmera, and doing this so you can keep an eye on Jordan is a bad, bad, *bad* idea."

I sat back against the booth and sighed. "It's not that I want to keep an eye on him. I don't even want him anymore." I hurried to finish before Charlie could challenge me with words in addition to her raised eyebrows. "I swear, I don't. There's only so much abuse a person can take before she should be forced to wear a dunce cap. A bedazzled, jeweled dunce cap, but you get the point." I rubbed at my temples. "I can't explain it. It's like I want to catch him hurting someone else so I know I wasn't the problem."

Charlie's face softened. "Marisa, anyone can see that Jordan was way less of a craphead when the two of you were together. Unfortunately, he's also a huge chickenshit, and I think it scared him to care about someone that much. So he did what any chickenshit would do and went back to what he knew. I wish he would've done it before he let you have such high expectations of him."

"The higher the expectations, the harder the letdown. I have a feeling Sara Cat is going to find that out the hard way."

Charlie snorted. "Well, she doesn't share, so I feel bad for any other girl you find him with. That email made it sound like she'd dismember anyone who went near him and then feed her limbs through a wood chipper."

"Maybe we'll find out."

Her face fell. "I can't talk you out of this, can I?"

I watched my spoon tunnel through my ice cream. "It'll make an interesting essay for Story Break, right?"

"Now suddenly that's a good idea too?"

I set the spoon against the side of the bowl and twisted my hands in my lap. "My parents took Lehigh off the table. Too expensive."

Charlie's shoulders fell and she swore softly. "I'm sorry, Marisa. That's the worst."

"I know. So the scholarship's worth a shot, right? I mean, Sara will never even know it's me doing the investigating. The nice thing about Kendall's website is that all of the correspondence can be done through email. I still wish she hadn't used my initials and my freaking birthday, but I doubt anyone will make the connection. And the money...working at Prints Charming three months a year and random weekends doesn't exactly put me in the running to buy a Ferrari."

"You mean a Corvette?"

I pursed my lips at her Kendall jab. "Come on. How bad could it be?"

"Famous last words. I hope you at least changed the password to the email."

"Give me some credit. Of course I did."

When it came down to it, I knew turning down this mission would eat me alive. Padding my wallet while sending Sara photos of Jordan caught in the act of cheating would give me boatloads of pleasure. If I couldn't catch him... Well, there was always the possibility that he wasn't cheating. I hadn't stopped to think about how I'd feel if Sara wound up being the next Marisa in Jordan's life. And I wasn't about to start.

BY THE NEXT AFTERNOON, SHIT WAS HITTING THE FAN FROM EVERY direction.

Nick had taken the bus home so I could stay after for a yearbook interview. When my cell phone rang with a call from him not two seconds after I'd jotted down the last of my notes, I was surprised—but not nearly as surprised as when he told me why he was calling.

"Um, Charlie's here," he said. "And she's pretty upset. I think you should come home."

He, Charlie, and Mindy were sitting at my dining room table when I got there. If I hadn't been so concerned, I would've laughed at the way my brother had his arm wrapped around Charlie as she sniffled into his shoulder. Holy opportunist.

"What happened?" I rushed to the table and took the seat Mindy vacated for me.

"I wish I knew." Charlie gulped. "I'm going to be expelled."

"For what?!" I said in disbelief.

"Because Mrs. Pace is a douchette, just like I said," Mindy piped up.

I cringed. Nick must've noticed, because he said, "Mom's grocery shopping." My mother hated "unladylike" language.

"A couple weeks ago, I stayed after class for extra help," Charlie explained, dabbing her eyes with a tissue. "Mrs. Pace had a virus on her laptop, the one where she keeps all her lesson plans and school stuff, and I helped her fix it. Then today I got called down to the principal's office. They told me the grades on our last class exams were 'unusually high.'" She stopped to wipe her nose and I jumped in like a lion on a gazelle.

"Mrs. Pace and your principal think you *cheated*?"

Charlie's face contorted and she nodded. "Pace thinks I stole answer keys and all this other stuff from her computer when I had access to it. Marisa, she was there the entire time! I didn't take anything!" She buried her face in her hands, and my brother rubbed her arm as he squeezed her against his side, murmuring words of comfort.

"Supposedly kids with failing averages scored ninety percent or better on their last assignments," Mindy added. "The school's doing a whole investigation. They told Char they'd knock her punishment down from expulsion to suspension if she came clean."

"But there's nothing to come clean about!" Charlie exploded.

"This is ridiculous." I shot out of my chair and started to pace the room. "They can't ruin your entire life over something they can't prove. You've never had less than a 3.8 GPA, ever. How dare they accuse you of cheating?"

"I got into the honors program by the skin of my teeth, Marisa. You know that. A few more points and I would've been rejected."

"That's bullshit. Even on an off day, you got in fair and square, and no one is kicking you out." I sat down hard. "Don't worry. We'll figure this out. Whatever really happened, we'll get to the bottom of it. You are not getting expelled. Understand?"

Charlie nodded and looked me in the eye. "Please don't tell anyone," she said. "Not a word."

I knew she was thinking of Kendall. "You know I won't," I said. "But news like this travels fast, and Kendall is in the same program. I can't stop her from hearing it through the grapevine."

"Fine. But don't be the grape that spills the beans."

Normally I'd crack up at one of Charlie's crazy sayings, but I didn't feel much like laughing. Mindy gathered Charlie's hair in her hands while Nick rubbed her shoulder. I leaned back in my chair and blew out a long breath. This was huge. If Charlie got expelled, she could kiss college and her reputation goodbye. Years of hard work and good grades would be down the drain.

Suddenly Jordan and TJ and all the other cheating boyfriends of the world seemed very unimportant. I'd thought I was helping people by doing my private-eye routine, but now it seemed stupid.

Because when my best friend needed it most, I couldn't be any use to her at all.

"I really like this one." I pointed to a photo of a purple bracelet with thin strips of turquoise woven through its center.

TJ and I sat in the empty yearbook classroom, looking through his portfolio of leatherwork. He had a binder full of photos in lieu of a website, and he'd brought it in so I could choose Christmas gifts for Charlie and Nick. I knew Charlie would swoon over that purple bracelet, since I'd started drooling at the sight of it.

TJ looked over my shoulder. "That's one of my favorites. I made it for my mother."

"Charlie would die for this. Purple is her favorite color."

"Did you know purple dye was once so expensive that only royals could afford it? It was made from sea snails and it took tens of thousands of them to dye one garment. That's why purple is called the imperial color." He stopped and cleared his throat, and I wished he'd stop being embarrassed by his own intelligence. "Plus, you know, purple looks great on girls with dark hair." His eyes darted to my own purple shirt. Then he coughed and looked away, his face reddening. "Um, Charlie didn't mind me borrowing you at the bonfire, right?"

"Not at all." As much as I enjoyed making him blush, I fought the urge to tack on, "Nice recovery."

"She's not still mad at you, is she?"

I waved off the comment. "No. She has way bigger things to worry about right now."

"Oh?"

I turned back to the pictures, not sure if I should open my mouth about Charlie's situation. I'd thought that the less I said about my ties to Templeton the better, but maybe discussing it openly would give me room to pry into his own connections. If he had nothing to hide, doing so shouldn't be an issue.

"Charlie might be expelled for something she didn't do. She's devastated, and her only option is a bogus plea bargain for suspension that will still be on her permanent record."

TJ leaned back in his chair and rubbed his chin, his eyes dark and pensive. "That's rough."

"I know. I feel terrible."

"It's not your fault." He continued to rub at his chin and stare at the far wall of the classroom, like his mind had gone elsewhere.

"It's not my fault, but the person accusing her is my ex-boyfriend's mother. I'm embarrassed that I ever associated with them."

TJ's eyes snapped into focus and he leaned forward in his chair. "Jordan Pace's mother?"

Damn it, damn it, damn it.

"How did you know Jordan and I dated?"

"After the way you looked at him when I gave you your belt the other day"—a smirk pulled at the corner of his mouth—"I took an educated guess."

"That obvious, huh?" My lips twisted. "God, I don't know how I ever went out with him."

"No offense, but I'm pretty surprised myself. You have such a level head and his head is jammed up his own ass."

I snorted. "Believe it or not, he wasn't like that when we dated—he mellowed out. But he seems to have reverted to his old ways with a vengeance."

TJ fiddled with a loose screw in the chair next to his. "So your friend. Why did she decide to go to Templeton?"

"She got into the Hartley program. Very hoity-toity, or so I hear."

"You hear correctly," he said tightly. "I used to be in it." I straightened in my chair but before I could press him further, he added, "What's she being accused of?"

He disappeared into his thoughts again as I explained about Jordan's mother and her laptop.

"Can't you talk to him about it?" TJ asked when I'd finished.

"Talk to who? Jordan?" I laughed. "I could try, but it won't get Charlie anywhere."

"And there's no way it could've been her?"

"No way. If you knew Charlie, it wouldn't even be a question." I paused. "Don't you know her?"

His eyebrows knitted together. "I know *of* her."

"Do you have friends on the football team?"

"Why do you ask?"

Hmm...did I detect a trace of defensiveness?

I looked down at his portfolio and casually flipped the page. "I thought I saw you at one of the Templeton football games a couple weeks ago. I was surprised because it seemed like you wanted to burn your bridges there. But it was dark, and there were a lot of people." I looked at him. "Maybe it was someone else?" I held his gaze, challenging him. Daring him to lie to me.

He slouched against the chair, folded his arms across his chest, and looked out the window. "Yeah," he muttered. "That must've been it."

I CLENCHED AND UNCLENCHED MY FIST WHILE THE OTHER HAND squeezed the strap of my book bag on my shoulder. I'd been thinking about talking to Jordan on Charlie's behalf ever since TJ had brought it up, and now that I'd decided to do it, I couldn't seem to make myself cover the ten feet between where I stood in the hallway and where he stood at his locker.

Despite his declaration that he wanted to be friends, it hadn't been any less awkward between us. But if he'd meant what he said at all, this was my opportunity to use it to my advantage. Well, Charlie's advantage.

"Hey," I said. "Can I talk to you for a second?" I cocked my head in the direction of the exit alcove.

Jordan gave me a curious look but shut his locker and followed me. He leaned against the wall, one sneakered foot pressed up against it, one hand on the strap of his bag, the other in his pocket, like he was posing for a freaking J.Crew catalog. I fought the sudden and intense urge to kick the back of his knee and watch him topple over.

"So I'm sure you heard about the situation with Charlie and your mother."

"I heard. That's too bad."

I gawked at him. "Too bad? Jordan, you know Charlie wouldn't cheat, let alone steal information and give it to other people. Isn't there something you can do to help her?"

"How, Marisa? Sure, Reiser's a nice kid, but what's my mom supposed to think? No other student has touched her laptop except Charlie, and then all of a sudden every moron she teaches starts acing their tests? Maybe it doesn't make sense, but it adds up."

My fist curled at my side. "It doesn't add up, and you know it. You went to school with her long before I did. Charlie's grades didn't need a boost and she'd never do something so stupid. You need to defend her. You need to at least *try*. If you're really my friend, then please, do that much for me."

He glanced into the hallway, like he wanted to make sure we weren't being watched, dropped his bag, and put his hands on my arms, pulling me farther into the niche.

"Listen, Marisa," he said quietly. "I can try to talk to my mother, but don't expect miracles. She's as upset about this as Charlie is."

"I doubt that."

"I swear to you, she is. She never would've expected Charlie to do something like this—"

"Because she didn't."

"Damn it, listen!" He shook me, not hard, but enough to make me raise a warning eyebrow. He let go and leaned against the wall, his jaw set in frustration. "I'm sorry. Like I said, I'll try." He picked up his bag. "But I think the best thing for you to do is accept that sometimes when you think you know someone, you really don't."

He walked away, leaving me gaping after him. What in the actual freaking hell did he mean by that?

It took me a few beats to gather my bearings and head off to class. But when I should've turned left to go to math, I veered to the right and dropped into a seat in the computer lab. I logged into the Busted account and clicked on Sara's email.

Dear SaraCat42,

I'm very interested in learning more about your case. Please email me details on who you'd like me to investigate and how I'll need to do it. If we can agree on a plan, we'll talk.

Reverse Cupid

I signed off using one of Kendall's corny euphemisms from the website, not sure how else to do it.

By third period, my phone chimed with a response.

Hi RC,

The guy I'm seeing is Jordan Pace and he goes to Herring Cross High. If he's anything like I've heard, you've probably hooked up with him already. I don't care if he looks, but prove to me that he's touching and shit's going down. Let's make that plan A-Sap.

Sara Cat

I sunk in my chair and covered my mouth with my hand. There were so many cringeworthy things in that letter, I couldn't even. The fact that she'd spelled ASAP phonetically, the fact that she'd used the phrase "go down" after the comment Charlie made about her knees. But when I read it again, one line kept jumping out at me: *you've probably hooked up with him already*.

Could she really know that?

I threw my phone in my bag and tried to pay attention to the teacher before I got in trouble. Of course, it had to be a coincidence that she'd worded it that way. She probably thought she was being cute. Gag. Sara Cat had no way of knowing she was right on the money.

At least that's what I kept telling myself.

16

WHILE I WAITED FOR SARA TO TELL ME MORE ABOUT HOW TO GET WHAT she wanted from me regarding Jordan, I decided it was time to really put the smackdown on TJ. My sleuthing had led me nowhere for long enough. I needed a new plan of attack.

When I'd called Kendall to talk over strategies, she moaned about being bored out of her skull so many times that I wound up asking her to meet me for Chinese. She agreed, but only if we got takeout and ate in my car so we wouldn't be seen together. A healthy dose of eye rolls preceded my order of spring rolls. The good thing was that she gave no indication of having heard about Charlie's cheating scandal, which must've meant she hadn't. Kendall loved gossip—unless it was about her.

"Doesn't this remind you of that time in third grade?" she said, shimmying the plastic wrapper off her fork in my passenger seat. "When we ate peanut butter cups in the janitor's closet?"

"I almost forgot about that!" I laughed, nearly choking on the smell of grease permeating the car's interior. "The whole school was peanut free because Cory Anderson and Sandy Reyes were allergic. We thought we were such rebels, sneaking in those peanut butter cups."

"I swear, everything's better when you're not supposed to have it."

And there it was, the whole reason we were even together again.

"I have a question for you," I said as I lifted a mass of wiggly udon noodles to my mouth. It was a stall tactic, but I didn't want to start with bad news. "How were you able to make the Busted website so quickly and TJ still doesn't have one for his leatherwork?"

Kendall rolled her eyes. "It's not like I haven't tried, but he's so picky. He keeps telling me he wants it to look less flashy and more *organic*, like it's a bag of carrots and not a damn website. Besides, with the way he's been acting lately, it's not high on my list of priorities."

"Right. Speaking of that—I don't have bad news, per se, but I definitely think TJ is up to something." I proceeded to tell her about his strange visitor at the barn the night of Kevin's party. She sat for a few seconds, not saying a word, poking at her container of brown rice. "Kendall?" I touched her shoulder. "Are you still okay with all this?"

She frowned. "You couldn't see or hear anything from their conversation?"

"No. And whenever I ask him about anything personal, he clams up and changes the subject."

"Sounds familiar." She rested the container on her knee and stared out the window.

"Are you sure you're okay? We don't have to do this anymore if you don't want to."

Kendall shook her head. "No, I need answers. If we stop now, I either have to break up with him for no good reason, or pretend ignorance is bliss. Ignorance isn't bliss, Marisa. It's fucking idiocy. And I don't want to break up with him." She sighed and her eyes welled up. Before any tears dared to fall, she gave each eye an angry swipe and sat up straighter, a look of determination replacing the crestfallen expression from a nanosecond ago. "I have an idea."

"Oh boy. Now I'm scared."

"Do you have any plans this weekend?" Despite the voice in my head saying *This chick is cuckoo*, I admitted I didn't. "Perfect. I'll ask him to hang out on Friday, and if he accepts, awesome. If he turns me down, then you ask him to make plans that same day and see if he blows you off too."

I almost gagged on my noodles. "You want me to hit on him now? No way. No, no, no way. I'm willing to follow him. I'm willing to chat him up. I am willing to hang out in his barn and wait for strange people to show up. I am not willing to use myself as bait."

Kendall scooted so close so quickly I thought she might land in my lap. "No, you've got it all wrong. We already know he's avoiding me and that there's someone else in the picture who's not you *or* me. I need to test his priorities. If he blows me off, it's probably for whoever this other person is. If he blows me off but accepts your invitation, then maybe it means he's desperate to be with anyone *but* me." She must've realized how that sounded, because she blinked a couple times and added, "No offense."

"None taken. But if he's so desperate not to be with you, then why not break up with you?"

Her shoulders sagged. "I don't know. Every time I think we're getting back to the way we used to be, he shuts down again."

"I hear that." I slurped another noodle. "Do you know why he's so bitter toward your school?"

Kendall shifted in the passenger seat, positioning herself against the door. Something in her demeanor shifted, like a wall had gone up. Her posture went rigid and she avoided my eyes.

"If he's bitter about Templeton, I don't know why. And it has nothing to do with what I asked you to find out." She shoved a forkful of rice and chicken into her mouth and turned to look out the window, chewing in silence.

Well then. Kendall had clammed up the same way TJ did at the mention of his transfer. Were they *both* hiding something? My curiosity got the better of me and I curled a hand around the steering wheel until my knuckles went white, knowing I'd probably regret the next words out of my mouth.

"I'll make it clear that it's not a romantic thing if I invite him to hang out. I'll ask him to teach me how to make leather jewelry."

Kendall turned back to me with a small smile, the wall gone. "He does amazing work, doesn't he?"

I lifted my coat. "Hell yes. He made this out of the leftovers from his belt."

The smile fell from her face. "He made you a belt?"

Oops. I should've known that wouldn't go over well.

"He didn't make it *for* me. He had extra leather and I'd complimented his, so he used the scraps to make one like it. That's all." There. I hoped making it sound like my belt had been a Dumpster dive would keep her jealousy at bay.

Kendall took one look at my waist and let out a loud laugh. "Oh my God, Marisa, I'm so sorry. You don't have to wear that if you don't want to."

I wrinkled my nose in confusion. "What do you mean?"

"I mean you don't have to walk around looking like a dominatrix so you won't hurt TJ's feelings! Really, out of all the beautiful things he is capable of making? All you need is a whip and some thigh-high boots!" She threw her head back and guffawed.

"Um, I like this belt. A lot."

Kendall choked back her laughter and cleared her throat. "Oh. Then by all means, totally forget I said anything."

Okay. I recognized this. This display was nothing more than

her reaction to Mike Kimball all over again. In fourth grade, I'd had a huge crush on him. Kendall constantly stuck up her nose at my lovesick doodling and told me he was ugly and had buckteeth. She made me feel silly for liking him and even sillier for being beside myself with glee when I heard he liked me back. Then Valentine's Day came along, and whaddya know, someone with handwriting exactly like Kendall's left a huge, heart-shaped card on Mike's chair. She never copped to it, but the two of them got in trouble for holding hands during an assembly later that week. She'd gotten me to give up what I wanted by tricking me into thinking I shouldn't want it, and then she'd snatched it for herself.

I wasn't falling for that again.

I pulled my coat down over my belt and smiled. A tiny part of me couldn't help but hope that when Friday came along, I'd be the one TJ chose to spend it with.

17

"MARISA?" MY MOTHER ASKED, LOOKING UP FROM HER MAGAZINE AS I overturned a couch cushion. "What are you doing?"

"I can't find my phone anywhere."

"Did you leave it in the bathroom? I know you've had…a lot on your mind."

In other words, she still felt bad about dropping the Lehigh bomb.

I doubted I'd find my phone in the bathroom, as I wasn't a fan of toilet-texting, but with everything on my mind lately, I wouldn't have put it past me. As I retraced my steps, I heard Nick talking: "Right, because if other kids' grades are going up, then they're getting the answers from somewhere. But where? And who?"

I pushed open the door to his bedroom and mouthed, *Are you talking to Charlie?*

He waved me inside and pressed a button on the phone. "Hey, Char? Marisa's here. I'm putting you on speaker."

"On *my* phone."

"You left it unattended. You're lucky I felt like playing secretary."

"Hey, Marisa." Charlie's tired greeting preempted my sarcastic reply.

"Hey. What's going on?"

"I was telling Nick that I overheard two guys in my chem class talking about drop-off points, like they were comparing. They were whispering, so I couldn't catch their whole conversation. The only other thing I heard was 'What'd you pay?'"

Nick looked at me. "We think whoever hacked the laptop is selling the teacher's answer keys. Mob style, with supersecret drop points and shit. That's why the school hasn't picked up a paper trail."

My eyes bulged. "Holy smokes. Who does something that diabolical in high school? Your parents must be flipping."

A small laugh fluttered from the phone. "You're right—they are. I'm suspended from the cheerleading squad *and* the recruiting team for the honors program. My mom's been threatening defamation lawsuits and every other legal angle she knows. I think it's the only reason I'm still in school."

"Yeah, well, I'm flipping too," Nick said. "What if the asshole who came up to me at the football game thought I was there to buy test answers?" He punched the surface of the desk he was leaning against. "I had him right there and I didn't even know it."

"Nick, you don't know that," Charlie said. "It might've had nothing to do with it."

But it made sense, I had to admit. What didn't make sense was if the person who'd approached Nick and the one I saw TJ talking to in the parking lot were one and the same. TJ didn't go to Templeton anymore, so he had no reason to buy test answers. That still left the questions of who he was talking to and why—and did it even matter?

A scuffling noise came through the phone, followed by Charlie yelling, "Be right there, Mom!" She told us she had to finish her homework, and we hung up.

"So you and Charlie have graduated to phone conversations?" I flopped onto his bed and caught my cell when he threw it at me.

"What does that mean?"

Nick turned his desk chair backward and straddled it. "That we're both capable of dialing a phone and speaking into it."

"More like she's capable of dialing a phone and you're capable of ganking it."

"Nice language skills. Just because a word's in the Urban Dictionary doesn't mean it's real."

"Ever planning to use *your* mad language skills to ask her out?"

"When I'm ready."

"Chickenshit."

Nick grabbed a baseball-patterned stress ball off his desk and winged it at me. "Says the girl who was tearing the house apart looking for her phone so she won't miss the next crack of Shitty Friendall's whip."

I lobbed the ball back and hit him in the shoulder. "Take that, biatch. So maybe it's good if someone is selling the answer keys? There has to be some way to trace the sales, right?"

Nick rubbed where the ball had bounced off him and rotated his shoulder. "It's good because they're letting Charlie stay in school while they investigate. The longer it takes to prove she didn't do it, the more time it buys her."

I rolled onto my back and stared at the ceiling. "Jordan said he'd try to talk to his mother. Something tells me he's not trying very hard."

"You know, Marisa, if you weren't friends with Charlie, I'd think you were a magnet for people who suck."

As if on cue, my cell phone chimed with a text message. I looked at the screen and sure enough, it was from Kendall.

He turned me down for Friday. You're up.

I was way more nervous about asking TJ to hang out than I thought I would be. It still felt wrong to ask, no matter how casually I'd planned it in my mind. What if he thought I was out of line? What if the only person he wanted to hang out with less than Kendall was me? What if—

"Marisa? Did you hear me?"

My pencil stilled where I'd been drumming it against my desk as TJ's voice brought me back to the yearbook classroom.

"Sorry. What?"

TJ smiled. "Off in Narnia?"

I managed a smile back. "Something like that."

"I asked if you wanted to use a different picture next to Mr. Leroche's interview. The one we have looks like a mug shot."

"Oh. If you wouldn't mind getting another one, that would be great."

He slid his chair back to his computer and I turned my attention to my own screen, trying to ignore my racing pulse and the clamminess of my palms. Why did asking him to make plans feel so huge? It wasn't a date. It was so not a big deal.

Screw it.

I scooted my chair over a bit. "Um, TJ?"

He looked up at me.

"Speaking of Narnia...would you mind teaching me how to make some of your stuff? I'd love to make my own, and if you have time one day, I'd like to come back to the barn. Whenever it's good for you, I mean, it doesn't have to be tomorrow or anything, I—"

TJ broke through my babbling with a huge grin. "I'd love to teach you. No one's ever asked before."

My internal organs promptly resumed normal function. "No way. I don't believe that."

"Really. Most people like my work but chalk it up to a weird hobby. I've never had a student." He beamed at me.

Now for the real test.

"Great! Are you free this weekend? Maybe Friday after school?"

For a second, his smile faltered. I waited for the hammer to drop. Then:

"I'm working after school. But I can do Friday night."

The word *okay* came out of my mouth, but in my mind it sounded a hell of a lot more like *oh shit*.

I couldn't believe he'd actually chosen me over his own girlfriend.

18

PART OF ME HAD NEVER REALLY BELIEVED TJ WOULD SAY YES. WHEN HE did, I had to scramble to cover my dumbfoundedness. Then Kendall immediately popped into my mind. How would she take it? What did it mean that he'd accepted my invitation without hesitation after worming out of plans with her? Should I cancel and then show up anyway, hoping to catch him in the act of God-knows-what and get it over with already?

I nixed the last idea for purely selfish reasons, knowing if I busted him too soon, I'd never get my lesson in making leather jewelry.

I'd also received my first assignment from Sara Mendez regarding Jordan: she wanted me to follow him the next time he went to a Templeton football game. I accepted, since it was about the most convenient idea she could've come up with.

As I stared at my phone deciding the best way to break the news about my Friday plans to Kendall, it buzzed in my hand.

Did you ask yet?

Sometimes I swore the girl had my brain tapped.

I wrote back, What did you suggest that he turned down?

Dinner. Why?

With that, my phone started to ring. Before I could even say hello, Kendall greeted me with, "He said yes, didn't he? You're shitting me. You've got to be shitting me."

I sighed. "I'm not shitting you. He told me to come over when he gets off work."

"Damn it, Marisa. I hate him!"

And then she started to cry. Not a drama queen cry, not an I-want-attention cry. Real, heaving, heartbroken sobs. I wanted to crawl into a hole and die.

"Kendall, I'm so sorry. Please don't cry. Listen, I won't go, okay? This is reason enough to break up with him as far as I'm concerned. We can stop right here. Say the word and the investigation is over."

"N-no," she gulped. "I n-need answers. I want to know w-why. I need to know who. I need to make him p-pay for treating me this way."

"Um, now we're getting a little sinister."

"Stop, Marisa. You know what I mean. We have to keep going. I'll never know what happened to our relationship if I break it off now." She sniffled and blew her nose.

"It's your call, but are you sure? I hate seeing you get hurt."

"I'm sure."

If she wasn't sure, she faked it very well. I thought about making an excuse for TJ, pointing out that he didn't get off work until six, but unless he was really a seventy-year-old inside a seventeen-year-old's body, six o'clock was still plenty early for dinner plans. I couldn't come up with a good way to explain his behavior, so I didn't. Instead I said, "I'll let you know what happens."

It didn't make sense to be nervous on my way to TJ's house, but I was anyway. I knew it wasn't a date. Technically, we weren't even friends, but we were hanging out on a Friday night and he'd picked me over Kendall. I hoped he didn't have the wrong impression. Although, that was sort of the point.

When I pulled up to TJ's house, the barn windows were lit from within and I breathed a sigh of relief that he'd spared me the über awkwardness of having to say hello to his family. Then again, he'd probably spared himself too. My parents definitely would've asked questions if I brought a random guy over while dating someone else.

Things only got weirder when I stepped into the barn. TJ greeted me with a warm smile and a "hey." His hair hung in damp curls around his forehead, and he had that wonderful, freshly showered boy smell. The kind that used to make me want to bury my nose in Jordan's neck and bite it and—

My eyes dropped involuntarily to the soft-looking skin near TJ's collar. *Jesus Christ, stop it right now! This is no time to think about neck biting!*

I was mortified at myself. A few months with no action, and a little soap and cologne had me foaming at the mouth. Pathetic.

"Hey," I said weakly. "Thanks for doing this."

"No problem. Come over to the stable before we start, I want to show you something." He started toward the nearest stall and I followed. Then he stepped aside to let me in. On the right wall hung a framed picture of a man and a little boy standing next to a regal-looking brown-and-black horse with a white patch down the center of its nose. The man held the waving boy in his arms and both sported riding boots and matching grins.

I looked back at TJ and smiled. "Is that you?"

"That's me and my dad with Molly, his horse. I was five in that picture. I think she died the year after."

"She's gorgeous. That must've been so sad for both of you."

"Yeah, it was. Shirley, my uncle's horse, died a few months later." He turned and pointed to another picture on the opposite wall. "My dad said I was inconsolable. I sat in the window every day for a month watching the field, waiting for them to come back. I think that's why we only farm trees and pumpkins. We haven't even had a dog since."

He touched the glass over the photo, a far-off look in his eyes, and I let myself watch him for a few beats. I couldn't reconcile the sensitive, nostalgic TJ in front of me with the picture that Kendall had painted of him. The idea that he'd willfully hurt her didn't fit at all.

"You're sure you don't have a talking goat stashed in here?" I said, hoping to lighten the moment.

"I wish! We'd be loaded."

We laughed together and I took one last look at the picture. Next to it hung a shiny plaque engraved with Molly's name beneath an etching of a horse's profile. Below that, in smaller print, it said, "Thomas J. Caruso." Below that, "Jumping."

"So I'm guessing the *T* in TJ stands for Thomas?"

"You guess correctly. Same as my dad."

"And what about the *J*?"

TJ looked at the floor. "My parents have a weird sense of humor."

I couldn't imagine what that meant. "Your middle name's not Jesus, is it?"

He chortled. "No. It's, um, it's Jones."

"Thomas…Jones? Like Tom Jones? As in the old-school singer with the Afro and the camel hump? Oh my God, why would they do that to you?"

TJ looked stricken. "It's my mom's maiden name."

Open mouth, insert foot. "Oh."

A huge grin spread across TJ's face and his shoulders shook with laughter. "Marisa, I'm totally kidding. The J stands for James. I wish you could see your face right now."

If it hadn't been so nice to see him let loose a little, I would've wished for some horse poop and a shovel to fling it at him. I told him as much.

"You're always so serious at school," I said as I took a seat on the stool he pulled up to his worktable for me. "I was almost afraid to talk to you."

He shrugged. "I keep to myself. When you know more about growing trees and tanning leather than you do about football and booze, you learn to keep your mouth shut until you're around the right people."

"So I'm the right people?"

"You wouldn't be here if you weren't."

At that moment, I wanted so badly to ask how he and Kendall wound up together. They seemed like polar opposites, and yet he'd obviously deemed her "the right people" at some point. And she wanted to be with him until she had concrete proof that she shouldn't, which was the reason I was even there. Only I couldn't ask, because TJ had never once mentioned having a girlfriend in front of me.

So I flashed an appreciative smile and said, "Should we get started?"

TJ agreed and went to one of his shelves. When he came back, he had a bracelet-sized strip of cowhide, which he placed on the board in front of me.

"I thought we'd make Charlie's bracelet first, since you know exactly how you want it." He went back to the shelf and grabbed a bottle of purple dye. The same purple we'd talked about in the yearbook classroom, when he'd more or less told me the color looked good on me. I glanced down and stifled a gasp.

I'd worn a purple shirt. Holy hell, I hadn't done that on purpose, had I?

TJ put the bottle down next to me. "The type of dye I use is for vegetable-tanned leather. It can be a little harder to color, but it's a lot more natural than some of the other methods and way better for the environment. I'm all about being eco-friendly." He dragged a hand through his hair and shook his head, revealing red-tinged ears. "Now you know why I keep my mouth shut."

"Because you're ashamed of your ability to carry on an intelligent conversation?"

His lips turned up, embarrassed but grateful. "Thanks. I appreciate that." We smiled at each other for what felt like an awkwardly long time, even though it couldn't have been more than few seconds.

I started to say I didn't know vegetables could be used to tan leather at the same time as he said, "So anyway, this is the color I used for my mother's bracelet." We both stopped and laughed.

"Go ahead," I said. "I'm the student. I should be listening."

"No, it's a good question. Vegetable tanning is one of the oldest methods—the oldest, I think. It's done with extracts from tree bark and plants instead of chemicals, and the leather ends up nice and flexible. You can stamp it with designs too, which reminds me—do you want me to put Charlie's initials on it?"

My face lit up. "You can do that?"

TJ grinned, clearly proud of himself. "Sure. I have the tools and the letter stamps. It'll take two seconds. Unless one of her initials is *P*, then you're SOL. I dropped that one weeks ago and still haven't found it."

I laughed. "She's Charlotte Grace Reiser. Not a *p* in her entire name."

"Excellent. Hey—that reminds me. Did you ever find the rest of your ankle bracelet?"

I frowned and shook my head.

"Damn, that's too bad."

TJ returned to his shelves and came back with a plastic case full of small square letters, a thin metal tool that reminded me of the instrument my dentist used to clean my teeth, and a mallet. He dropped the *C*, *G*, and *R* on the table, then flipped the leather over and lined up the *C* near the edge of the strip closest to him. Leaning in, he placed the tool over the square and positioned the mallet above it. There was an ease to his stance that told me he'd done this a hundred times before but the lines of his profile grew serious with concentration, like he took every time as seriously as the first. His work seemed to put him under a spell. I felt like I shouldn't breathe for fear of messing him up.

I couldn't take my eyes off him.

Without my permission, my gaze roamed from the curls at his temples to the slope of his nose to the curve of his lips and the long, slender lines of his fingers, up his arms, and back again. Watching his hands made me wonder what it would be like to touch them. Which led me to think of them touching me and—

I jumped a mile at the first smack of the mallet.

Suddenly I didn't believe him when he said there were no chemicals in the leather. It was the only explanation for my complete lapse in brain function.

I fidgeted on my stool, while he pounded in the rest of the letters, and tried to purge my mind of the images that had flooded in out of nowhere. I might've been successful too, if not for the next step.

"Now we're ready for the dye," TJ said, unscrewing the cap to the bottle of purple liquid. He brought over a dauber that looked like the one I used to take nail polish off my toes and handed it to me. "Coat this with the coloring and then we'll apply it."

I did as he instructed, holding the dauber above the bottle to let the excess drip off.

That's when he covered my hand with his.

The unexpected warmth startled me, and droplets of dye from

the dauber sprayed all over the table. "Oh! I'm sorry!" I leaped off the stool to inspect my clothes, trying and failing to fight the blush speeding up my neck.

"Did it get on you?" TJ looked me up, down, and sideways, which didn't help my blushing situation. "I don't see any on your clothes. I think we're good." He pulled the stool closer and helped me back on, his hand holding mine the entire time. When I'd gotten comfortable again, or as comfortable as I could be considering I wanted to bolt out of the barn like a bull at a rodeo, he lowered our hands over the leather. "You want to spread the dye over the whole surface using a circular motion, like this." He guided my hand with his own until the entire strip of leather had turned a gorgeous purple hue. When he finally released me, my whole body relaxed.

TJ grinned. "Good work! That wasn't so bad, right?"

I agreed with enthusiasm but thought, *Speak for yourself.*

Somewhere along the line though, I finally started to chill out. By the time we finished the next bracelet—Nick's, which I opted to have embossed with his first name on account of TJ's missing *P*—we were chatting and laughing like there hadn't been any weirdness at all. And maybe there hadn't been. Maybe I'd mistaken my digesting dinner for butterflies in my stomach. That totally had to be it.

Except when TJ walked me to my car, he touched my hand again. It was only once, for the briefest moment—so brief I didn't know if he'd done it by accident or on purpose. I only knew that it felt more like a promise than a parting of ways.

And I didn't like that at all.

As I shut myself inside my car and waved goodbye to TJ, my stomach sank like rock. TJ and I had been together for hours, and I hadn't done a single solitary bit of investigating.

19

I TOSSED AND TURNED ALL NIGHT. I'D BEEN WRONG ABOUT MY DINNER not sitting right; it was all of the stress in my life that was the problem. I couldn't believe I'd spent all that time in TJ's barn just…hanging out. And still no closer to the truth about his relationship with Kendall than I'd ever been. What was I supposed to tell her when she asked what happened? And worse, what was with those crazy thoughts I'd had and the way I'd wigged out? How the hell had I wound up in this mess anyway?

The questions were still floating somewhere in the back of my mind when my mother pranced into my room the next morning and flopped down on my bed.

"Rise and shine! Ready for our annual foray into the wild?"

I pulled the covers over my face. "I am physically incapable of shining today. And what 'foray' are you talking about?"

Mom peeled back the blankets and peered down at me. "We're

going to Maple Acres for our Christmas tree today. Don't you remember? We talked about it last weekend."

"No!" I groaned. "Go without me. Whatever you guys pick is fine." I tried to pull the sheets back over my head, but Mom yanked them down to my waist.

"Come on. We'll stop for coffee on the way. Even Nick is up before you."

She stood with a note of finality, leaving me to rub my eyes and contemplate how much trouble I'd get in if I was still in bed the next time she came looking for me. Until I was sure I had a grip on myself, TJ's farm was the last place I wanted to be. Being there obviously messed with my head, and I needed my brain cells if I was ever going to find out what Kendall wanted me to.

Then again, that was the exact reason I had to go back. I needed to find TJ, block out my fascination with his leatherwork and his barn and his stupid hands, and get what I'd originally gone for: answers.

So when my father called, "Marisa Ann! Fifteen minutes!" I sighed, threw off the covers, and got out of bed.

Less than an hour later, my bundled-up family sat clutching steaming Styrofoam cups as Dad's Explorer treaded over the dirt parking lot. We'd arrived ten minutes after Maple Acres opened, ten minutes later than normal thanks to my dawdling, but still early enough that only a few families were milling around the huge tent at the entrance, where wreaths and cider were sold. To the right, at the bottom of the hill, I spotted TJ in the tree-bundling area. His back was to me, and he and another worker were leaning against the split-rail fence in full lumberjack attire, engrossed in conversation with TJ's uncle, whose hands were pointing every which way. I imagined he was giving their marching orders for another day of pre-Christmas craziness.

When I looked past them, scanning the tree-dotted hills that seem to roll on forever in every direction, my stomach sank. Between finding, agreeing on, and cutting down the tree, we were in for at least an hour-long endeavor. By then, the place would be swarmed, and TJ might not have time to talk to me. It hit me that I could spend the whole morning at Maple Acres and still go back to Kendall empty-handed.

But as the four of us clunked toward the entrance in our snow boots, my gut went from sinking to somersaulting. Because a blond woman stood at a rack of wreaths, her hair twisted into a perfect knot above the furry black collar of her sleek knee-length coat. I would've recognized her anywhere. She was—

"Barbara?" my mother asked, her eyes widening.

Yep. She'd recognized her too.

Barbara, as in Barbara Keene. Kendall's mother. The last person I needed to be seen with.

"Check out Mother of Spaz," Nick whispered in my ear. I elbowed him in the ribs, but he was unfazed. "Think Kendall's got her planting bugs around the farm? I'd be scared to take a crap if I were TJ."

I snorted as Mrs. Keene turned to face us, and my parents shot me dirty looks.

"Elena!" Mrs. Keene said brightly. "How long has it been?"

"Years!" Mom replied as Barbara kissed her on both cheeks. "How is everything?"

"Fine, fine. I've been scouring catalogs for the perfect foyer wreath, and I haven't been able to find one. My daughter recommended"—she looked around the tent, her silver-gloved fingers spread in front of her like she was trying to conjure the right word—"this place. I'd forgotten it was here."

"Marisa told us she's been talking to Kendall again since your family came back from Arizona," Dad said.

At the mention of my name, Mrs. Keene's eyes settled on me. I tried to position myself between Nick and a rack of wreaths, praying they'd hide me if TJ happened to look over. I had no idea how I'd explain chatting up his girlfriend's mother. Except that she threw her arms around me, sending the perfume-laced fuzz of her collar up my nose, and then held me by my shoulders to get a better look at me.

"Marisa." Her smile was warm, but her eyes roved over me from head to foot, like she was taking notes for an assessment she'd share with Kendall later. "You've changed so much! I still remember you as the skinny little girl we took to Myrtle Beach."

"So you're saying she's fat now?" Nick interjected.

Mrs. Keene's face went slack and my father pushed the back of Nick's head, but I wanted to hug him.

"Kidding." Nick flashed his most charming smile and Kendall's mom reciprocated, though she looked a bit like she'd sucked a lemon.

"Did Kendall tell you she's part of the Hartley honors program?" Barbara continued, turning her attention back to me. "I have to say, Marisa, I'm surprised you're not at Templeton with her. You were always so smart. I would've thought you'd gotten into the program too."

"So now you're saying she's stupid?"

Nick ducked before my father could sock him again and came up laughing. "You know I kid. It's my way of saying it's good to see you, Mrs. Keene."

From the corner of my eye, I saw TJ and his coworker walking away from his uncle. And heading for the tent. "It *is* good to see you," I said hurriedly. "But this coffee was a bad idea." I held up my still-full cup. "Sorry, I really need to find a restroom. Text me and I'll catch up with you guys, Nick." I made deliberate eye contact with him, hoping he'd catch the silent *when the coast is clear.* Then I turned and scurried out of the tent, ignoring the looks my parents were giving me. I'd pay for my rudeness later, but I'd cross that bridge when I came to it.

I got about halfway down the hill before TJ spotted me. And

then I practically ran to close the distance between us, not wanting him to see who was inside the tent.

"Marisa," he said, breaking into a warm smile. "Back again?"

"Back again," I panted, coming to a stop in front of him. "My family is here to get our tree." I turned around and relief flooded through me when all I could see from our vantage point was the top of the tent. "They're taking forever picking out a wreath, so I thought I'd come say hi."

"Cool. If they need any help, this is Eli." He clapped the shoulder of the boy at his side. "He's our newest whipping boy."

Eli offered a gloved hand. I studied his face as I shook it. He looked familiar, but I couldn't figure out where I'd seen him before. I racked my brain, trying to place his hazel eyes and his uncertain smile with teeth that overlapped like fallen dominos. I came up blank.

"You look kind of familiar," I said. "Do you go to Herring Cross?"

"Nah." He shook his head and hunched into his coat. "Templeton."

Oh. The word alone formed a new knot in my stomach, and I wished I hadn't asked.

"There's Marvin," TJ said to Eli, motioning into the distance. "Shadow him for the next hour or so, and I'll pick up from there. Okay?"

"You got it, man."

Eli jogged off after the burly guy headed through the trees, leaving me alone with TJ.

"Thanks again for last night," he said. "I had a really nice time."

And there went my brain cells, dropping like freaking flies.

"Me too."

TJ scuffed his work boot against the ground and hitched his thumbs into the pockets of his coat. We stood there, shifting awkwardly for a few seconds before he said, "It's pretty slow right now. Would you, uh, be interested in taking a hayride? Minus the hay?"

"What are you talking about?"

"There's something I want to show you. It'll only take a few minutes. If you want I can tell your parents where we're—"

"No!" I held out my arm to stop him from heading up the hill. "I'll text them. They won't miss me for a few minutes."

I pulled my phone from my pocket and sent a message to Nick: With TJ. Cover for me.

His response came almost immediately: You owe me.

Didn't I know it.

I followed TJ back toward the tree-bundling area, where two tractors hitched to trailers sat waiting outside the fence. In the fall, the trailer beds would've been decorated with hay and pumpkins, but in winter they were used to transport trees from pickup locations after customers cut them down. Not that my dad ever took advantage of the service. He always made us trudge through the snow, carrying the Palmera family tree like a crew of pallbearers.

"Hop in." TJ extended his hand, helping me into the narrow cab next to him. He looked at me with a mischievous twinkle in his eye as the engine roared to life, and once again, I wondered what in the hell I'd gotten myself into.

The tractor bumped and chugged up the hills through the winding dirt paths. I sipped my coffee contentedly, watching the landscape change with each variety of tree. In my head, I kept trying out ways to subtly broach the topic of Templeton. But after the underhanded way Mrs. Keene had thrown my own lack of attendance in my face, what came out of my mouth when TJ killed the engine was the opposite of subtle.

"Do you think you would've been better off staying at Templeton?"

He looked understandably confused. "Why do you ask?"

I sighed. "I tested into the honors program, but my parents couldn't afford to send me. In the back of my mind, I'm always wondering if I screwed myself over by not going."

"As far as what? College?"

"Mhmm. Credits, scholarships. All that stuff."

TJ shook his head. "I wouldn't worry about it, Marisa. Plenty of people get scholarships and college credits without ever setting foot inside Templeton." His face hardened. "It's not the Holy Grail, despite what some people think."

I turned to look him in the eye. "People like who?"

"People who don't have their priorities straight."

"*What people*?" I pressed.

TJ's eyes narrowed. "Wait a minute," he said, regarding me suspiciously. "Are you—did Charlie tell you about my ex-girlfriend?"

His *what*?

"Your *ex*-girlfriend?"

Why would he call Kendall his ex? If they weren't together anymore, she damn sure hadn't gotten the memo. Did this mean he really was the smarmy cheater she suspected him to be? Was he lying to me? A brand-new can of *WTF* had just spewed open like a shaken soda.

"Yeah, *ex*. The prefix that goes before *girlfriend* when you were dating someone but now you're not. And I'm not anymore. File it under 'figuring out my priorities.'"

I couldn't challenge him. Not without giving away my connection to Kendall and the real reason I'd even begun hanging out with him. So, even though I was dying to dig further, I diverted.

"Were your priorities worth the 'change of scenery'?"

He held my gaze without faltering. "I like the scenery just fine." But his eyes stayed locked with mine, telling me he didn't mean the hills or the trees. As my heart began to climb into my throat under the unwavering stare of his gold-brown eyes, the corner of his mouth pulled up, and he cocked his head toward the hood of the tractor. "Check it out."

We'd parked at the top of a hill, overlooking a field with a pond. The pond was smaller than the one next to the barn, which looked like a tiny toy house in the backdrop, and the trees here were sparse and less uniform. In fact, they weren't even Christmas trees. Sunlight shone through bare, regal branches that stretched to the sky and reflected in the water's surface. Frost coated the grass and the spiny, barren bushes surrounding the pond, making the whole place look secret and untouched.

I leaned forward in my seat. "This is beautiful."

"Of every acre on this farm, this is my favorite spot." TJ leaned closer and stretched his arm in front of me, pointing to my right. "See the barn back there? My telescope is trained on this field. When the horses were alive, they loved coming down here in the spring and chewing on the forsythia bushes around the water. I used to stand up there and watch them."

"Horses eat plants?"

"Ours did. They loved strawberries too, so I made my dad plant some back there." He motioned toward the frozen shrubbery, then pointed to the right again. "See those two benches at the edge of the woods?" I followed his finger to two squat stone seats at the rim of the tree line and nodded. "That's where they're buried. My uncle built those as markers so I could still see them from the barn."

"You really took it hard when they died, didn't you?"

TJ shifted, looking embarrassed. "Stuff like that is hard on kids."

"It's hard on anybody. Remember the ankle bracelet you asked me about last night?"

"I do."

I rolled my cup between my hands. "Every year, my grandmother had Christmas Eve dinner at her house. She went all out with the decorations, and she always ordered a bunch of poinsettia plants to line the front walk and the stairs. She called them her 'red carpet.' I used to make her do commentary on my outfits while I walked it." I smiled at the memory. "She passed away on Christmas Eve when I was twelve years old."

TJ touched my shoulder. "I'm sorry to hear that."

"She had a heart attack at some point that morning. But she'd still managed to roll out her red carpet, and I think of her every time I see a poinsettia. I had one on my charm bracelet that my mom had scoured every store in Pennsylvania to find. And now I'll probably never see it again."

"I'm really sorry, Marisa," he said again. "Maybe you could make a new one yourself?"

A sardonic laugh burst from my throat. "I've been too busy making things for other people these days."

If only he knew.

Oblivious to my sarcasm, TJ offered to check with some of his suppliers for me. Then he glanced back at the farm stretched out behind us. "We should get you a real poinsettia from the sales tent.

They're not the best for wearing as jewelry, but maybe you could put it in your hair or something."

He was trying to joke—except that when he mentioned my hair, he brushed a strand behind my ear with his fingers. And then let his fingertips linger at my jaw while the smile melted from his face.

I couldn't move. Every contraction of my heart echoed in my ears as loudly as if it were beating outside my body. TJ's thumb grazed my jawbone ever so gently, and goose bumps sprang up on my skin despite layers of winter clothing.

A loud crackle from the walkie-talkie clipped to TJ's jeans pierced the silence.

We both jumped like we'd been electrocuted. TJ nearly dropped the device as he fumbled it off his pants. My mind raced as he spoke to whomever was on the other end, trying to convince myself that whatever just happened really hadn't.

"Hey. No, I'm at the horse pond. Yeah, sorry. Heading back right now." He shoved the walkie-talkie into his coat pocket and reached for the key in the ignition without looking at me. "It's starting to get busy at the front. We should probably get going."

"Right. Totally. I don't want you to get in trouble, and I'm sure my parents are looking for me." Before I knew what I was doing, I reached out and put my hand on his arm. "But, TJ? Thanks. For bringing me here."

I sat back, taking my hand with me. The corner of his mouth

turned up, and I couldn't tell if it was cold or embarrassment reddening his cheeks.

"Anytime. I...I like hanging out with you."

Is that why it's so important for me to think you're single?

My stomach somersaulted. I'd never had much of a plan when it came to cracking the mystery of TJ, but if I did, this certainly wasn't part of it.

He was never supposed to enjoy spending time with me. And I sure as hell wasn't supposed to like being with him.

20

IF I THOUGHT I'D HAD INSOMNIA THE NIGHT BEFORE WE GOT OUR Christmas tree, it was nothing compared to the night of.

Into the wee hours of the morning, the word *ex-girlfriend* echoed through my head. Someone was being less than honest with me, and if it wasn't Kendall, it was TJ. I didn't understand why TJ would lie about being in a relationship. Until I thought about the trip to the horse pond, the way TJ had touched my hair, my face. Had I imagined it? The whole thing happened in a matter of seconds. I could've totally spaced. Or hallucinated. Or *something*.

Finally, when I couldn't take it anymore, when my sheets were as twisted around my legs as strips of licorice, I threw off my covers and headed into the bathroom. I scraped a comb through my hair and brushed my teeth, then threw on a coat and boots, and left a note for my parents before heading out the front door.

It had snowed overnight. My boots broke through the hardened powder in lopsided ovals as I clomped down the front walk, my nose buried in my collar. Sliding into the driver's seat of my jalopy felt like having an ice cube under my rear end, but it didn't stop me from turning on the car, scraping enough space on each window to be able to see, and reversing out of my driveway as fast as I could.

I had no idea where I was going, but I had a feeling I knew exactly where I'd end up.

Shit!

I cursed silently and then out loud as I drove past TJ's house at the exact moment he approached the edge of his property, obviously headed to the farm for work in cargo pants, his flannel Paul Bunyan coat, and a knit hat that flattened his dark curls against his face. Not only did he see my car, but we also made direct eye contact thanks to the unforgiving winter morning brightness. So much for being on the sly.

Some spy I was.

I waved and flashed an awkward smile as I passed, trying to make it look like I totally meant to be driving by a tree farm in my pajamas at an ungodly hour of morning. Dear God, I was at a tree farm in my pajamas. Pajamas with cupcakes all over them, tucked into my clunky winter boots. And now I had to stop, because there was not an excuse on the planet for why I'd be in TJ's neck of the woods except to be at that farm. I had seriously lost my damn mind.

TJ watched and waved as I made a three-point turn and parked on the opposite side of the street, farther up from where I normally lurked in the shadows, staking out his house. I would've sold my soul for some of those shadows as I emerged from the car, pulling at the hem of my coat to make sure it at least covered the word *sweet* embroidered across my ass.

"Marisa." TJ smiled as he walked toward me. "What brings you back to Maple Acres on this fine subzero morning?"

My teeth chattered as I tried to smile back and think of a halfway decent excuse. There were a hundred reasons I'd come, none of which I could share with him.

Oh hey, TJ. I'm just trying to figure out how you can be so nice and so shady at the same time. Carry on.

Oh, you know, just trying to catch you cheating on the girlfriend you deny having. The usual.

"Um, I think I need to put in an order for one more bracelet. I always forget someone when I try to do my Christmas shopping early." I managed a jittery laugh and TJ beamed.

"No problem. Come over to the barn. I have something I wanted to give you anyway."

He did?

"You do?"

"Uh-huh. I have a few minutes before anyone will be looking for me. Let's go. You look like you're freezing to death."

I followed him, embarrassed and grateful all at once. We trudged through the snow in silence, and the pond came into view, its surface steaming with water vapor. It was so pretty, like ghosts dancing on the surface. I whipped out my phone and snapped a picture. Since I'd already started the day embarrassing myself, I might as well go all the way and give drawing the barn another go.

When TJ pushed open the wooden barn door, much to my dismay, it was only about half a degree warmer inside. He pulled a stool up against his worktable and patted the seat.

"Here. Sit down. I'll get you some hot chocolate."

And then tell me again how single you are?

"That sounds amazing."

I sat and curled into myself as much as I could, huffing hot air into my gloveless hands and rubbing them together. TJ flipped on the space heaters and the coffee machine before turning back to me with a laugh.

"You're not even wearing real pants! There're still a couple weeks until Christmas. What was your rush?"

"I-I don't know. I wanted to get it done while I was thinking about it, I guess."

"I hear that." He picked up a small box from the end of the long, wood table and brought it over to me. "I could wait to give this to you, but I really don't want to."

I looked at him and then at the box.

"That's for me?"

He nodded. "Open it up."

I clamped my frozen fingers around the box and lifted the lid. I gasped. "TJ! This is *gorgeous*!"

He jammed his hands in his pockets and looked at the floor. "You like it?"

I lifted the bracelet out of the box. He'd stained the leather a deep caramel and dotted the edges with tiny, clear crystals. Woven down the center were thin strips of brilliant gray blue, white, and green. I rotated it around and around on my fingers, studying the design from every angle.

"I *love* it. You didn't have to do this."

He hunched into his coat, embarrassed at my praise. "You told me that you tried to draw the barn and the pond but couldn't quite capture the scene. So I started wondering, what would it look like if I tried to capture it for her with something I can make?" He looked sheepish again. "And that's what I came up with."

I kept looking from the bracelet to him, my mouth hanging open but nothing intelligible coming out. He'd even put *crystals* on it for me. "Thank you" was the best I could do.

"Open the clasp. There's something on the flip side I think you'll like."

I did what he asked, and for a second, I forgot how to breathe.

On the underside of the leather, he'd stamped the letter *M*. And next to that, he'd painted a poinsettia.

I ran my thumb over the delicate red and black brushstrokes, at a total loss for words. There was so much artistry, so much care in that one tiny flower. He'd made this for me, without me asking him to. And it was perfect.

"It was the best I could do on short notice," he said. When I could do nothing but gape at him, TJ laughed. "Here, put it on." He slipped the bracelet onto my wrist and after he clasped it, he squeezed my fingers. "Marisa, your hands are freezing!" He placed both my hands together in a praying position, sandwiched them between his own, and rubbed vigorously. He paused to blow a warm breath against my palms, then smiled at me as he started to rub again.

And then something very strange happened. A warmth that had nothing to do with the space heater and everything to do with his grin and his hands on mine and the cinnamon-and-chamomile scent of his breath spread through me, flooding me so quickly that I snatched my hands away, startling even myself.

"Thanks," I fumbled. "I forgot my gloves." *And my clothes, and my mind, but who is keeping track?*

"And your hat too." Apparently, he was. He gave me a teasing smile.

TJ lifted the knit cap from his head and mussed his hair before shimmying the thick wool down over my forehead and around my ears. His lips curled in a faint smile, but my own muscles were paralyzed. I was all too aware of the distinct lack of distance between us and the fact that it was making me uncomfortable for all the wrong reasons—one, because I couldn't seem to pull my eyes away from his lips. I'd never noticed how beautifully shaped they were, with a deep *V* in his top lip and a slight pout to the bottom one.

Why was I noticing now?

His hands were the second thing making my heart flail around in my chest. Again. They lingered at the edges of the cap he'd placed on my head while his eyes grew darker and the smile faded from his face. We were only inches apart and I could no longer tell where the frozen puffs of my rapidly increasing breath ended and his began. His fingertips gently traced the line of my jaw, and I knew without a doubt that I hadn't imagined them there yesterday.

Then the distance between us closed completely, and I only felt hands in my hair and the most amazing softness against my lips.

That was the moment I should've pulled back. But something inside me erupted like a volcano, and I shot off the stool, pressing myself against him. He pulled the hat from my head and threw it to the ground, threading his strong fingers deeper into my hair and sliding his tongue into my mouth. My hands found their way inside his coat and my fists curled so tightly into his thermal shirt that soon my thumbs were touching the bare, cool skin at his waist where I'd pulled the material free from his pants.

I didn't even know how I wound up sitting on the table, gripping his neck as our lips met again and again. When we broke apart, panting and wide-eyed, it was clear that neither of us had a clue how this had happened. We stared at each other, not saying a word.

I raised my fingertips to my cheek. Not a single part of me, inside or out, felt close to cold anymore.

TJ stepped back and scooped his hat off the floor. He jammed it back on his head, looking at the ground, the walls, the stables, anything but me. "Marisa, I'm really sorry. I—"

I couldn't let him finish. I jumped down from the table. "I have to go." I ran out of the barn, barely hearing him call after me as I sped to my car without stopping.

I didn't need him to tell me we'd made a mistake. I already knew.

21

I SPENT SUNDAY AFTERNOON AND EVENING PACING THE FLOOR OF MY room, trying to figure out how I'd ended up in this world of shit and, more importantly, how to get myself out. I didn't know how I'd look TJ in the face again, and I sure as hell couldn't face Kendall. I'd kissed her boyfriend. Whether he copped to the title or not didn't matter. My loyalty was supposed to be to Kendall, and TJ was off-limits. Yet I'd not just kissed him—I'd full-on made out with him and groped him. And I loved it. Oh God.

I flopped onto my bed and clamped my hands over my forehead. What had I done? What was I going to do? How had I let myself go from cheater buster to cheating participant?

My cell phone rang and my stomach cramped like it was trying to digest an anvil. When I saw Kendall's name on the screen, I almost heaved. I ignored the call and shoved my phone under my pillow. A minute later, it rang again. And then again, and then again.

Did she know?

I sat up with a very real fear that I might have to dive for my garbage can and vomit. The ping of my voicemail notification distracted me, keeping the chunks at bay. I slid a clammy hand beneath my pillow and retrieved the phone. When I played the message, Kendall's small, defeated voice met my ears. She sounded as if she was either holding back tears, or had already spent the morning crying and had none left.

Oh God.

"Marisa, it's Kendall. Can you call me as soon as you get this? I… could really use a friend right now."

I lowered the phone. Something was wrong, but she didn't know about TJ and me. If she did, I'd be the last person on earth she'd call when she needed a friend. Not that I'd call myself anything close to a friend right now.

I picked up the phone and hit her number.

"Marisa?"

"Kendall? What happened?"

For a few seconds, quiet sobs and sniffles were all I heard. Then: "TJ broke up with me."

I pulled into the Keenes' circular driveway about a half an hour later. Kendall had asked me to come over, and I didn't have the heart to say no, even though a thousand questions were swirling through my mind like whirlpools.

Why had TJ lied to me about being broken up with Kendall? Had he been planning to dump her? And if he'd been cheating on her all along, then why wait until he kissed *me* to cut her loose?

She opened the door sporting yoga pants, a Juicy Couture sweatshirt, and puffy, red eyes that burned holes of guilt in my soul.

"Come on in," she sniffled. "I'm watching movies in my room."

I followed her up the winding staircase to a sizeable room decorated in pink and green accents. Frilly curtains were drawn over the windows, and most of the light came from the TV at the foot of the queen-size bed. A corner of the blankets had been pulled back, revealing pink-and-white flowered sheets and rumpled pillows. Kendall dragged a white armchair up next to the headboard, then promptly climbed under the sheets, curling herself around one of the pillows.

"So," I said, dropping into the chair and eyeing the TV. "*Dirty Dancing?*"

"I needed something old and cheesy."

We were quiet for a minute. "Do you want to talk?"

She looked over at me with watery eyes. "Can you just keep me company for a little bit?"

"Yeah. Definitely." I leaned back, trying to get comfortable, which was impossible, considering the chair had nothing to do with my discomfort.

The more time that passed with only the sounds from the television and Kendall's intermittent sniffling, the more terrified I became that I might leap up, shout, "I kissed TJ!" and bolt from the room like the flames of Hell were licking my feet.

When I couldn't take it anymore, I fumbled for my purse and blurted, "I have something I want to give you."

I reached into my bag and pulled out the heart pin I'd been working on since Kendall first commissioned my help. I held it out in the palm of my hand. The right half was a swirl of tiny pink, yellow, and ocean-blue crystals. The left half—

Kendall gasped. "Marisa! Are those shells?"

I nodded. "It's actually one of the shells you and I collected in Myrtle Beach that year." I'd crushed it up and arranged the fragments mosaic style on the left side of the pin.

Kendall's eyes welled up as she took the pin and cupped it in her hand. "I can't believe you kept those. It was such a long time ago."

"And here we are again." *After I made out with your boyfriend.*

A wistful smile came over her face. "Remember the night we had an ice-cream-eating contest?"

"How could I forget? We were both sick as dogs."

Kendall laughed. "You threw up in the bathtub."

"Ugh. And you tried to cover and tell your parents it was you, but I had regurgitated peanut butter sauce stuck in my hair."

We were both giggling at that point, but as she ran her finger over the shell pieces, she bit her lip. "I have to tell you, Marisa, I said and did a lot of things when we were younger that I'm not proud of. I've always been competitive, and all the reasons I liked you were reasons I was jealous of you. I wasn't a very good friend." She sniffled and a tear slipped over each cheek. "Can you forgive me?"

Forget salt. This was salt soaked in alcohol soaked in arsenic rubbed in my wound.

"Kendall, why would you be jealous of me? You were pretty and popular and smart. What's left?"

She wiped her eyes with the back of her hand. "You were all those things too, but people liked you in spite of it, not because of it. They liked *who* you were, not what you were. And the grades and the friends and all those things, they came so easily for you. It got to the point where I spent so much time trying to be better than you that I forgot how much I liked being your friend. And by that time, I didn't really know how to be anyone's friend."

I sat back in my chair, not believing my ears. "Whoa. I never knew you felt that way."

Kendall nodded. "It's the same thing that happened with TJ. I never expected someone as good as him to go for someone like me. Everyone at Templeton thought I was shallow and fake, and the only person who gave me the time of day turned out to be this amazing guy I never dreamed I'd fall for." She hung her head. "Now I've lost him too."

I reached for her hand, not sure what to say but knowing I wanted to spill my guts all over her bedroom. Kendall and I had history together, and while it wasn't always harmonious, we'd still meant something to each other. TJ was a guy I'd developed an ill-timed attraction to.

If Kendall and I were going to be friends again, I'd have to forget about him.

I slid into my seat in the yearbook classroom, doing everything in my power to avoid looking in TJ's direction. It didn't matter, because the moment he saw me, he shifted toward me in his chair.

"Marisa, can we talk? You've been avoiding me."

I stared at my computer screen. "I don't have anything to say."

"I think we should talk. There are some things I need to get out in the open."

Now? *Now* he wanted to get things out in the open? I didn't respond.

"Listen, when I said I was sorry I kissed you—"

My hands slammed down on my desk. "*Shh!*"

He looked around and lowered his voice. "I didn't mean I was sorry it happened. I mean, I was, but not for the reasons you're probably thinking." Ellen Horowitz chose that moment to plop down in the seat in front of TJ's, and by the way he clenched his jaw and gave her the evil eye, her presence had effectively ended our conversation. "Can we please talk later?" he whispered.

Little did he know, I knew exactly why he was sorry. But I wasn't ready to face him. I felt too guilty, too conflicted, and I was angry with him for lying. Letting him think he'd offended me with his remorse over kissing me served as the perfect cover.

"I'm not ready to talk, and I don't know when I will be."

"You're wearing my bracelet."

I looked down at my wrist. "What does that have to do with anything? I like the bracelet."

A hint of a smile appeared. "I know you like it, but you wouldn't wear it if you hated the person who made it for you, right?"

I fingered the bracelet, letting his question hang between us. I wasn't entirely sure of the answer.

He waited, his jaw muscles twitching like he couldn't decide whether or not to let the point go. "Okay," he said finally. "Can we at least talk business then?"

I turned toward him, trying my best to make it look like I'd pushed all things personal aside. "Sure. What's up?"

"So I heard a bunch of senior and junior guys are planning this elaborate promposal together to ask girls to the winter formal."

"They know it's not the prom, right?"

I didn't know why I'd said that. I wasn't surprised. At Herring

Cross, prom lived in the shadow of the winter formal. For whatever reason, that was the dance the school went all out for, with a fancy venue and elaborate holiday decorations and a sit-down dinner. Prom was a paper-streamers-and-hand-made-banners blip on the radar and was held in our stuffy, badly lit gym. Still, I had to be sarcastic. Being a bitch kept me from staring at his lips and reliving our kiss again.

In theory.

"Right," TJ said, "but if they do it for the real prom, it's too late to get it in the yearbook. It's supposed to be huge. They're filming it to post online and everything. I talked to Mr. C, and he wants me to cover it for the student life section. Except I can't, because I have to work."

"Work? When is this thing happening?"

"After school on Friday, in the parking lot at Waterside Pizza. I already asked Ellen if she could cover it, and she can't." He side-eyed Ellen's back. "Do you think you can go?"

Friday was actually the next Templeton football game, the night I needed to stalk Jordan for Sara. If the promposal happened right after school, I should have plenty of time to do both. Not to mention Kendall wanted to get together. We'd been doing that a lot since TJ broke up with her. If I asked her to have pizza with me, I could kill two birds with one stone. Not that my answer was anywhere near as civil or logical as my thought process.

"Why not? I don't have a life or anything."

TJ frowned. "If you can't do it, I can talk to my uncle about going in late. But it's Christmas season and we're really busy and—"

"I'll do it. Don't be a martyr."

He slumped in his chair and nodded before turning back to his computer. Cue Marisa feeling awful for being such a raging bitch. I sighed. "TJ?"

He looked at me.

"Maybe we can talk next week, okay?"

His hopeful smile melted my heart, and I didn't know who I should smack first—him or myself.

22

AFTER OUR CONVERSATION ABOUT THE PROMPOSAL ENDED, I WALKED toward my locker to find a commotion in one of the junior halls. Girls were clustered near a row of lockers, squee-ing and OMG-ing and being generally shrill and annoying.

"Who did it?" one of them squealed.

"It's so pretty!" cooed another.

I craned my neck to see what they were talking about. At the center of the fuss stood Sara Mendez, grinning from ear to ear. Her locker door had been wrapped in shimmery, white wrapping paper and dotted with silky, red bows. White rose petals were scattered all over the floor, and inside the door, a single white rose had been taped up next to diagonal green and red letters that spelled out *Winter Formal?*

The crowd buzzed louder and grew larger with each passing second. A moment later, they let up a collective shriek as one of the girls gasped and pointed down the hall. There at the end stood Jordan, holding a white rose that matched the one in Sara's locker and wearing a cocky, self-satisfied grin on his face.

"What do you say?" he asked Sara.

Only he could barely be heard over the screaming and clapping of what seemed like every junior girl in the school. You would've thought they'd discovered a freaking boy band concert in the middle of the hall. I actually had to cover my ears to protect my hearing, which was probably why TJ tapped me on the shoulder.

"What's going on?" he yelled.

I pointed to Sara's locker, knowing it was pointless to try and make myself heard.

She moved through the crowd, nodding her head, her hands covering her cheeks, though I didn't know why. From where I stood, I didn't see a trace of blushing. If she wasn't relishing every bit of this attention, I'd eat my own foot.

When she reached Jordan, Sara nodded again and said yes. He wrapped his arms around her in a big bear hug. That's when I noticed one of Jordan's friends in the corner, recording the whole thing.

TJ leaned closer to my ear. "Guess Jordan couldn't wait for Friday."

I shook my head. Apparently, whatever the senior and junior guys had planned for Friday wasn't good enough for Jordan. He'd had to find a way to top it, to beat them to the punch. I wasn't surprised.

Sometimes he reminded me a lot of Kendall.

It took a little nudging to persuade Kendall that it didn't matter if we were seen together now that she and TJ were broken up. She only agreed when I pointed out that TJ would be nowhere near Waterside, and it no longer mattered if anyone else recognized her while we were together.

Still, I'm sure she was as disappointed as I was surprised when the restaurant door opened, bringing with it a blast of cold air and a pink-cheeked Charlie. I scooted out of the red vinyl booth that Kendall and I were sharing while we waited for our pizza.

"Hey! What are you doing here?"

"What are you talking about?" She knitted her brow as she took off her gloves. "Your brother told me to meet you guys here."

"He did? But he's not—"

I cut myself off as I realized what was happening. Nick had told me he was "hanging out with some kids" after school and didn't need a ride. When I'd tried to get more details, he'd mumbled unintelligibly and walked off.

Now I understood. Nick was part of the promposal. Charlie was about to get asked to the Herring Cross winter formal.

And I was covering it for the yearbook.

"Um, he's not here yet. One of his friends should be dropping him off any minute. They had...some after-school thing. Anyway, sit down." I motioned toward the booth, ignoring the fact that she was looking at me like I had an extra limb growing out of my head. Her expression hardened when she spotted Kendall, and under my breath, I added, "Be nice."

"Hey," Charlie said, shooting a stiff smile at Kendall.

Kendall sat on her hands. "Hey. Sorry I've been taking up so much of Marisa's time lately. I'm not trying to steal her from you, I swear." Her gaze shifted over to me and she grinned warmly. "Hopefully we can share."

"I'm sorry to hear about you and TJ," Charlie said. "What happened?"

Kendall squirmed in her seat and I fought the urge to do the same. I hadn't breathed a word about kissing TJ, not even to Charlie. I couldn't bring myself to say what had happened out loud. It would only raise questions I didn't have answers to.

"I don't know exactly." Kendall picked at her napkin. "I mean, I know our relationship wasn't perfect, or I wouldn't have needed Marisa's help, but I thought we could fix it. He told me he didn't want to see me anymore."

"Sorry. That sucks."

I cringed. Charlie's genuine sensitivity was top notch, but her phony stuff needed a buttload of work. I almost couldn't blame Kendall for seizing the opportunity to hit below the belt.

"Yeah, I'm sorry to hear about your drama too. I hope you don't get kicked out of school."

Charlie glared at me. My jaw dropped in indignation. "I didn't say a word!"

Our waitress came with our pizza then, and Kendall picked a long string of cheese off a slice and dropped it into her mouth. "Everybody in the honors program knows."

"For the record, I didn't steal those answer sheets, which anybody who knows me would never question. And I'm not getting kicked out of school." Charlie snatched her napkin from her lap and threw it on the table. "Excuse me, I have to go to the bathroom."

"I probably shouldn't have said that if I want her to stop hating me," Kendall said as Charlie cleared hearing range.

"She doesn't hate you. It's a sore subject, that's all. She's really upset about it."

"Of course she is. It's a huge accusation. No one expects someone like her to go rogue."

"Um, right. Because she didn't." Kendall shrugged and I couldn't believe I had to defend something as obvious as Charlie's innocence for the second time in less than two weeks. It irked me, but I didn't have the right to be angry with Kendall at the moment. Not after what I'd done.

I knew if I ever wanted to have a clear conscience again, I needed to tell Kendall about what happened between me and TJ. I couldn't stand keeping the secret inside for one more second.

My heart thundered. My mouth opened. And then the sound

of blaring horns, hoots, and hollers sounded in the distance, growing louder and louder. I looked out the window. A line of cars zigzagged into the parking lot, swerving through the empty spaces with boys from school hanging out windows, waving their arms and yelping. Silver, red, and green tinsel and paint decorated their cars, and the words *WINTER FORMAL?* were written on every windshield. The same hip-hop song blasted from every car, slightly out of sync, but not enough to muddle the lyrics: *I want you to say yes/And I'm gonna say yes/I want you to say yes*. Squeals rose up around us.

Charlie came out of the bathroom looking bewildered. "What's going on?"

I scooted out of the booth with yearbook's expensive camera and my purse and grabbed the sleeve of her coat. "Come on. You're about to find out."

We made our way onto the sidewalk with the rest of the crowd, and I elbowed my way to the front to get some pictures for yearbook. The cars parked in a *V* formation, like a flock of decorated metal birds, and in each corner of the lot stood someone with a cell phone. When all the cars had parked, one person got out of each car holding white poster board in his hands. They climbed atop the roof of their cars and laid the poster board down.

One of the guys was my brother. I'd always known Nick was a good dancer, but two seconds later when they broke into a choreographed dance number, I discovered the boy could *move*.

The fact that only a couple of the other guys didn't look like bumbling idiots had no bearing on the level of copious screaming and squealing and clapping around me. Even Kendall had a big smile on her face. It was kind of hard not to. Especially when the song reached its last chorus, and the rest of the boys emerged from the cars and climbed onto the hoods and roofs. They shook their asses to the final notes, and then everyone grabbed their pieces of poster board and held it high in the air. Each card had a name written on it with a question mark. With their other hands, they pointed to the words *WINTER FORMAL?* on their cars' windshields.

Nick's card, of course, said *CHARLOTTE?*

She jumped up and down, laughing and clapping. I had to laugh too—until she turned to me and her face fell. "What?" I asked, suddenly afraid she was about to embarrass my brother by saying no. "Do you not want to—" But she wasn't looking at me. She was looking past me. I followed her horrified gaze over my shoulder. It was trained on Kendall.

And Kendall's dumbfounded stare was fixed on the back of the formation of cars, where TJ stood atop the roof of a Nissan, holding a piece of poster board with my name on it.

23

THE RUCKUS CONTINUED AROUND US, BUT I COULD HAVE SWORN THE whole world went silent.

TJ lowered his sign in slow motion, his lips parted in bewilderment as he looked at Kendall and me standing next to each other. Kendall's fists balled at her sides as she turned to face me.

"You. Fucking. Bitch," she said through clenched teeth. And then the floodgates released. "You *bitch*! Did you bring me here to see this? Did you *know* this was going to happen?" She shoved me into Charlie, and I'm pretty sure she would've punched me, if Charlie hadn't leaped between us, throwing Kendall off balance and causing her to land hard on her backside.

"Kendall, are you okay?" I asked.

She sat on the sidewalk, cheeks flaming, chest heaving with furious breaths. "I can't believe I apologized to you," she growled. She scrambled to her feet, snatching her bag off the ground.

"Kendall, I swear I didn't know—"

"SHUT UP. You are the worst friend ever! Funny how you didn't bother to admit you've always been jealous of me too, huh, Marisa? You've always wanted the things I had, whether you say it or not. Your life is full of stupid, useless shit like this." She yanked my heart pin off her bag and threw it at me. "Keep it. And keep him." She jerked her head in TJ's direction. "Enjoy my leftovers like you've been doing your whole fucking life."

With that Kendall turned and stormed off to her car, leaving every eye in the parking lot on me. Everyone's eyes except for TJ's, who leaped off the car and took off after her.

"Are you sure you're okay?" Charlie asked again. She'd driven her own car to Waterside but wouldn't leave my front seat until I could convince her I wasn't about to drive off a cliff.

"Let's see. Kendall hates me, my cover with TJ is blown, half the senior and junior class witnessed one of the worst moments of my entire life, and at least four people caught it on video. I'm awesome."

"She was pretty harsh."

I looked out the window. "I deserved it," I said quietly. "I made out with her boyfriend."

"You *what*?" Charlie yelped loud enough to make me wince. A grin spread across her face. "You nasty whore! TJ is hot!" She gave my arm a way-to-go punch but composed herself when she saw I wasn't amused. "I mean, how did that happen? Are you into him?"

"I don't know." But the squirm in my stomach told me I did know. "The more I got to know him, the more I liked him, and then all of a sudden I was noticing things I shouldn't have noticed and looking at parts of him I had no business looking at, and he makes leather jewelry, and oh my God, that kiss was amazing." I draped myself over the steering wheel and banged my head against it a few times.

"He makes jewelry? Jesus Christ, you're soul mates."

"You're not helping."

"I'm sorry. One more inappropriate question and then I'll grow up. Tongue or no tongue?"

"Tongue."

"Did he feel you up? Did you feel him up? I bet lifting all those pumpkins and Christmas trees makes for some nice upper body strength."

"Charlie! Do *you* want to go to the dance with him?"

She waved her mittened hands in the air. "Sorry, sorry. I got a little carried away." She tapped her hand against the dashboard and looked thoughtful. "What do you think you'll do? Are you going to say yes?"

I leaned back against my headrest. "Who knows if he even wants to take me anymore? You'll notice he's not here." I buried my face in the steering wheel again. "Now I'm the girl who got asked to the dance by the guy who took off after his ex-girlfriend. And she is going to tell him why I started spending time with him, and he's going to hate me."

Charlie stroked my hair. "It's his own fault, you know. If he'd had the balls to break up with her, Kendall never would've asked you to spy on him. Do you really want to date a guy who doesn't even tell people he has a girlfriend?"

"According to him, he *didn't* have a girlfriend."

"According to him before or after he kissed you?"

"Before."

"Oh." Charlie nodded slowly. "That changes things."

"It doesn't change anything now. Everything is still a disaster and that promposal video is still going to be all over the internet." I closed my eyes. "Do me a favor. Do not let me watch it."

"Unless there's a way I can put locks on your eyelids, you know you're gonna do it." She twisted her lips. "What else can I do to help?"

I sighed. "Come with me to the Templeton game tonight?" She looked away, but I'd already seen the hesitation in her eyes. Being suspended from the cheerleading squad was embarrassing enough without having to sit in the stands among the people making her life hell with false accusations. But I couldn't do this alone. "Please, Char?"

"Why are you still going?"

"I told Sara I would. She doesn't know Reverse Cupid and me are the same person. How can I get out of it?"

Charlie fake coughed. "I think the flu is going around."

"I can't. One, she already paid me. Two, I need this for the Story Break essay. And three…I'm too curious not to go. But I need you with me. To be my bodyguard if Kendall is there."

"You don't think I'm in the same boat, Palmera? She and half the school are hoping I get expelled."

"We can protect each other?" I offered weakly.

Charlie smiled a mischievous, Cheshire cat grin. "Not gonna lie. Knocking that wench to the ground when she came at you felt damn good, even if it was an accident. Next time, I'm drop-kicking her in the face."

We both laughed. My world might've been going to hell in a handbasket, but at least I had Charlie along for the ride.

24

I MUST'VE BEEN A GLUTTON FOR PUNISHMENT GOING TO THAT GAME. I guess I figured it wouldn't be that bad, going someplace where everyone's focus would be on football and only a handful of people knew me. I should've stayed home with a warm blanket wrapped around me. Preferably over my head.

I felt eyes following me as soon as Charlie and I started our ascent up the hill from the Templeton parking lot.

"Everyone's looking at me," I whispered under my breath.

"They're looking at me, dumbass," she whispered back. "It's like Kendall said. Everybody knows."

I stopped in my tracks. "God, Char, I'm sorry. Do you want to leave? I never should've made you come here." I turned on my heels. "Let's go get ice cream and find a mov—"

She yanked my coat and spun me around, linking her arm through mine and propelling me forward. "I'm not chickening out and neither are you. Whatever these jerks think they know about me, it doesn't even scratch the surface."

I freed my arm and slung it around her shoulders. "Damn straight. And at least you won't be going viral for all the wrong reasons, right?"

Charlie waved off the comment. "Marisa, people were taking videos at the promposal, and yes, every girl there had a cell phone. But why would any of them have been pointed at you and not the ridiculous display of winter formal enthusiasm?"

"Because I almost got knocked on my ass by a cute blond, who then literally got knocked on her ass by you. Oh wait," I said wryly. "I take it back. You might be breaking the internet after all."

She rolled her eyes. "That all happened while everyone's attention was on the main event. You're totally overthinking this."

I didn't agree, but I squeezed her arm anyway. "Have I told you lately that I love you?"

She squeezed back. "Have I told you lately that you need a new hobby? This detective gig has been nothing but trouble."

I laughed a little. "After tonight, my cheater-buster days are over. I'm telling Kendall to take down the—" A brick of worry dropped in my stomach. "Oh God. What if she won't take down the site now? She probably won't even take my calls, let alone do me any favors."

"Simple. If anyone emails you, email them back and say you're no longer in business. You said you changed the password on the account, right?"

Yes, and thank all things holy that I had. For the first time since the promposal, my insides uncoiled a little. Charlie had a point: even if someone *had* caught my and Kendall's fight on video, it was probably an afterthought. And Kendall being unable to access or keep tabs on me through the Busted emails—or worse, reply to them herself with lies and slander—was a huge load off my chest. I inhaled deeply, the first easy breath I'd taken in hours.

Maybe I could even enjoy the last bust of my so-called investigative career tonight, just a little bit.

The thought made me smile. As Charlie got in line for coffee at the Snack Shack, I almost didn't notice the bare legs covered in blond hair angled toward me until I saw the person attached to them was smiling back at me. Then he waved.

"Damn it!" I said under my breath, averting my eyes from the Californian teleporter who, as evidenced by his shorts, had still not figured out that he was in Pennsylvania in the dead of winter. I hurried past him and attempted a casual lean against a telephone pole until I spotted Charlie heading in my direction.

"How many times can I accidentally make eye contact with that kid back there before he mistakes it as an invitation?" I said, nodding toward surfer boy.

Charlie snorted. "He's a dude. He already took it that way. All the more reason for you to not leave my side again tonight."

We made our way up the bleachers, waving at Mindy on the

track. "I still can't believe they suspended you from the squad," I said.

"I can't believe your brother asked me to the dance. And to a movie."

"What?" I stopped midclimb.

"Yep. Somewhere in the world, pigs are shitting rainbows. Come on, you're holding up traffic."

We kept moving to a free space in the nosebleeds. I wanted a spot where I could watch the goings-on below inconspicuously. With any luck, Jordan wouldn't know I was there until it was too late. But the higher we climbed, the more I felt like a sea of heads turned in our wake. There were far too many snickers, knowing looks, and exchanged whispers for my liking. Whether they were directed at Charlie or me—or both—didn't matter. My skin crawled with the sense that we'd wandered into the belly of the beast.

"I mean, obviously I know about the dance, but when is this movie thing happening?" I asked as soon as we sat down, trying to focus on something other than my discomfort.

Charlie looked at her hands. "Um, he wanted to go tonight."

"He did? Then what are you doing here?"

She gave a small shrug. "You needed me. Hos before bros. Literally."

"Is...that how you think of him? Because you know he didn't ask you to the dance as a 'bro,' right?"

She picked at the lid on her coffee cup, avoiding my eyes. "I like hanging out with him, even if I've only ever done it with you around. He's funny, he's loyal, and he's definitely not torture to look at." She nudged me. "Plus, I already know I like his family. I guess I'm willing to see where it goes." She snuck a glance at me out of the corner of her eye. "Are you cool with that?"

"My brain is, but maybe not so much my stomach?"

We both laughed until Charlie stopped abruptly and smacked my arm. "There's Jordan." She tilted her head toward where Jordan stood against the chain-link fence.

"He's alone."

I spoke too soon. Even before I'd finished my sentence, his mother and another woman ambled up to his side.

"He's with his *mother*," Charlie growled. She started to stand. "Let me at her. I swear I'm going to impale their asses on that fence, kabob style, and let crows peck out their eyes."

"Shh!" I yanked her arm and forced her to sit. "Making death threats against a teacher on school property is a great way to make sure you get expelled, Einstein."

Charlie's lips pinched together. "Fine. I won't say it, but I'm thinking it."

As I watched Jordan schmooze with his mom and her colleague, an idea started to form. He'd told me he'd try to talk to his mother about Charlie's situation, to defend her. I didn't trust him to do it after the way our conversation had ended. But...

"Should I go talk to them?"

Charlie's eyebrows shot up, wordlessly asking if I'd lost my mind. "It's not spying if he knows you're here, *Einstein*."

"I know, but what if I can convince his mother to drop the accusations against you? She always liked me—at least, I think she did. And he said himself that she feels terrible about it."

"She might like you, and she might've liked me before all this happened, but it's not going to change the fact that I was the last person to touch her computer before her tests got leaked. We need proof, not character witnesses."

It didn't matter. I already knew I was going to do it. My fingers curled around my purse as I gathered my nerve. I stood up.

That's when one of the guys sitting with the giggles-and-whispers crew stood up too. He lifted his arms above his head and grinned at me. In the split second it took for me to wonder why a complete stranger would be smiling at me, I also realized it wasn't the kind of smile anyone would want directed at them. It was condescending. Bullying. Like he was ready to attack and proud of it. It was the smile of someone who knew he had the upper hand and wanted everyone else to know it too.

Another second later, the entire campus did know it when he shouted, "Hey, it's the Busted bitch!"

And just to be sure there was no confusion, he pointed at me with both raised hands.

My heart fell right out of my ass. At least that's what it felt like. Shouts and catcalls rose around me as all heads turned to witness my horror. Time slowed until every second felt like eternity.

They knew. They all knew.

How did they all know?

"I hear you like leftovers!" one of the girls cackled.

That's how. Someone's camera had been trained on me after all.

My gaze floated down the bleachers in a daze until my eyes locked on Jordan's. For a second, everything when silent. Then the world came roaring back in a deafening blast, and I bolted down the concrete steps and ran.

25

I RAN UNTIL I REACHED THE SCHOOL'S FRONT STEPS, PANTING FOR breath and crying. I sat down hard and sobbed into my knees, barely registering the sound of footfalls hot on my heels.

"Marisa? What happened?"

My head snapped up at the sound of Jordan's voice. I'd expected Charlie to be on my trail, but there he stood, blue eyes wide with concern, chest heaving slightly from running to keep up with me. I put my head back down, pressing my knees against my eyelids to block everything out.

"Like you don't know."

He sat down next to me. "I really don't. Is this about Charlie?"

I rounded on him. "Would you care if it was? Seems to me you haven't done a damn thing to get her name cleared." I stuffed my mittens in my pockets and produced a tissue to wipe my face.

"You really think it's that easy? Marisa, I want to help. I do. But believe me when I tell you I can't. I don't go to school here and it's in the school board's hands now. I have zero clout with them. You're being unfair."

I rubbed at my eyes. Maybe it *was* unfair to expect Jordan to pull strings for me, for Charlie. But I needed to be angry at someone, and it was much easier to believe that he'd knowingly let me down yet again.

"If anyone knows how to be unfair, it's you."

I waited for the inevitable storm-off, his standard reaction when I copped an attitude. I wanted to be alone, to find Charlie and get the hell out of there, and I couldn't do it with him breathing bullshit down my neck.

Not only did he not leave, he gathered my hands in his. The sheer shock of it stopped my tears in their tracks. He rubbed his thumbs over my knuckles.

"Listen. I never wanted to break up with you."

My heart stuttered. I didn't know why he'd chosen now to talk about this, but I wanted answers as badly as ever. "Then why did you?"

He looked down at the steps, still kneading my fingers in his surprisingly warm hands. "I kind of met someone."

The lump rose in my throat again and I pulled my hands away. "So you did cheat on me."

"No, I..." He rubbed the back of his neck. "I broke up with you before anything happened. It was the one time in my life I tried to do the right thing, except I guess there was no right thing, because you would've been hurt either way."

"So then you *wanted* to cheat on me, but in order to keep your conscience clean, you dumped me instead?"

He fidgeted and ran a hand back and forth over his hair. "Doesn't sound so noble when you put it that way."

"Forgive me if I don't nominate you for sainthood." We sat in silence, Jordan's leg bouncing against the step, me wiping tears and snot from my face. And then something really strange happened. A giggle bubbled up in my throat. And then another. I looked at Jordan. We both cracked up laughing.

Sure, it stung to finally hear the truth, but not as much or as long as I'd expected it to. Somewhere in the midst of my obsessing over why we'd broken up, I'd failed to notice that it didn't really matter anymore.

As our chuckles died down, Jordan and I looked at each other and cracked up all over again.

"So who was she?" I asked, wiping away tears of laughter this time. "Sara?"

Jordan shook his head. "No, no one you'd know. If it helps, she sort of broke my heart."

"Well, I'm not going to send you flowers or anything, but I can empathize. It sucks."

He took my hands again. "I meant it when I said our breakup

had nothing to do with you. You didn't do anything wrong. You were a good girlfriend. A great girlfriend."

We looked at each other, half smiles playing on our lips. For the first time in months, I saw a spark in Jordan's eyes that told me the person I'd fallen for was still in there. And that beneath his indifferent swagger, he had real regret for what he'd put me through. I squeezed his hands. My smile froze in place when he responded by rotating his palms and threading his fingers through mine. The smile faded from his lips and he leaned in.

I don't know what would've happened if I hadn't heard Charlie's voice right then. But if she hadn't chosen that exact second to come running down the hill, I never would've looked up. Or across the street, where TJ stood next to his open car door, watching Jordan and me.

"Marisa!" Charlie called. I yanked my hands away from Jordan's, my eyes darting from her rapidly approaching figure to TJ's car pulling away from the curb. Charlie's eyes were huge and panicked as she skidded to a stop in front of the steps. "I'll be straight with you: it's bad." She doubled over to catch her breath, resting her hands on her knees. Her right hand held her cell phone. "It's really bad. Forget drop-kicking her. I'm pulling every last hair out of her stupid precious head." She looked at Jordan as if she'd just noticed him. "And while I'm on a roll, you'll want to go ahead and back up off Marisa, before this phone ends up down your throat."

Jordan scowled. "Jesus, Reiser, do you ever have anything nice to say?"

"Sure, when I'm not talking to douchebags."

I shot to my feet and stood between them. "Enough, guys." I turned to Charlie. "What do you mean it's bad?"

She held up her phone and tapped the screen a few times. When she turned it toward me, she said, "Your website underwent, uh, a few changes."

The glittery red background of the Busted website loaded on her phone. Only it didn't say Busted anymore. A giant black *X* flashed over the old heading, and from its center, the word *BITCH* appeared like a train emerging from a tunnel, starting off small and growing larger until it swallowed the entire foreground of the fissured heart pin. Her corny tagline about not hating the player had been replaced with CAN'T BE TRUSTED in smaller but still capitalized letters.

Jordan stood behind me. "'Busted bitch can't be trusted,'" he read over my shoulder. "What the fuck does that mean?"

I barely heard him. I was too busy reading what Kendall had written about me, with my full name in prominent bold letters.

Marisa Ann Palmera will pretend to be your friend. She'll pretend to want to help. And she won't stop until she's taken

what's yours. The website went on to talk about how I'd betrayed her to the point where her boyfriend asked me to the dance. She'd laid on the martyrdom thick and juicy.

Beneath the blurb, the icing on the cake, she'd inserted the video of the promposal. The thumbnail displayed the frozen image of Kendall's face, haunted and hurt, as I looked on in horror. The perfect snapshot of disaster.

"What the hell?" Jordan murmured. He reached over my shoulder and pressed play before I could stop him.

"Hey!" Charlie grabbed for the phone, but Jordan snatched it out of my hand and put his arm out to ward her off. I closed my eyes as the familiar sounds blared from the phone, seeing the whole event unfold in my mind all over again.

Charlie smacked and kicked Jordan, but it was like pummeling a statue. His eyebrows were two slanted lines as he stared at the screen, his jaw muscles locked tight. It didn't make sense that he seemed angry as the footage played out, yet he continued to hold Charlie at bay like an adrenaline-fueled King Kong. I pulled her arms to her sides, knowing her rage on my behalf was sweet but useless. If he didn't watch it now, he'd see the video later. No sense in delaying the inevitable.

Only when Jordan's own cell phone rang did he let his guard down. He kept Charlie's phone in one hand and answered his with the other, taking long, quick strides away from us, as if he didn't want us to hear his conversation.

"What were you two doing?" Charlie hissed.

"Nothing."

"It didn't look like nothing."

"*Nothing*, Char. Drop it. This night is shitty enough."

Charlie pressed her lips together and wisely heeded my warning.

"Reiser!" Jordan shouted. We both looked up in time to see Charlie's phone flying at us. She caught it, fumbling it between her mittened hands before getting a secure grip.

"Ass! You would've been in deep shit if you broke my phone!" Charlie called at his retreating back.

He still had his own phone pressed against his ear. Without looking back, he raised an arm in more of a salute than a wave and replied, "I'm out of here."

Charlie's face contorted with disgust. "What crawled up his ass and died?"

I didn't respond. I scooped my purse off the steps and started to go after him. Charlie grabbed my arm.

"Where are you going?"

"I'm following him."

"Are you nuts? Following people is what got you into this mess. You don't owe Sara Mendez anything." She clung to my arm and dug her heels into the ground as I tried to walk away.

"Sara thinks I'm the one Jordan is cheating with, remember? This 'mess' probably has her firing up the wood chipper as we speak.

My name is shit, Char. I have to do something about it." I strained to keep moving, but she locked her boots against the concrete.

"Catching Jordan with someone other than Sara only proves he's a whore. It won't make all the crap that came from spying go away. And as for the damn essay, make something up. I'm sorry I ever gave you that flyer."

"Easy for you to say. We wouldn't be here if you had parents like mine."

Her hands fell to her sides and her mouth drooped. "A lot of good it did me."

I felt a stab of guilt, but apologies would have to wait. "You're either with me or you're not. Decide fast, because I'm leaving."

I watched her pupils dart from side to side as she warred with herself. Then her grip on my arm loosened. "Come on," she said. "Our douchebag's getting away."

26

"LOOK AWAY. I'M GOING TO TALK ON THE PHONE WHILE DRIVING," I TOLD Charlie as I manned the wheel with one hand and one eye, trailing Jordan's car, and searched for TJ's number with the others.

She snorted and ripped the phone out of my hand. "Who are you calling?"

"TJ. I saw him across from the school while I was talking to Jordan."

"What was he doing there?"

"Who knows? Looking for Kendall?"

Charlie whistled as she scrolled through my contacts. "Damn. If he saw what I saw, it really does suck to be you tonight."

She pressed the ringing phone against my ear as I shot her a stink eye. "Don't remind me. He's not answer—TJ?" I almost drove off the road when his voice met my ear. I would've bet money he'd send me to voicemail. "Hi, it's Marisa. Listen—"

"So all this time you've been pretending to be my friend because you were spying on me?"

Maybe calling from the car hadn't been such a great idea. "I wasn't pretending to be your friend, TJ, I—"

"Then Kendall was right about one thing. You're a pretty lousy friend if you think this is what friendship is."

My fingers clenched my phone. "You're one to talk! She never would've had to ask me for help if you'd opened your mouth and broke it off sooner! What kind of boyfriend breaks plans with his girlfriend to meet up with strange people in parking lots and make bracelets with another girl? What the hell is your deal anyway?"

TJ took a breath, like he needed to calm himself. "My situation with Kendall is a lot more complicated than it seems."

"Well, now's your chance. Explain."

"If you'd given me a little more time, I would've opened up to you on my own. But I'm glad I didn't. I obviously misjudged the kind of person you are. Besides, it looks like you have your hands full with Jordan Pace."

With that, he hung up.

I swore under my breath and threw the phone into the cup holder. "It's official. He hates me."

"Please tell me you have enough sense to let sleeping dogs lie and you're not going to keep up the investigation."

"Of course I am! If TJ wants nothing to do with me, I at least have to make things right with Kendall. I have to prove I didn't try to steal her boyfriend."

Charlie gaped at me. "After she told you your life and your work are shit, and blasted you on the internet? Marisa, I'm seriously starting to wonder if you're deaf, because you can't possibly hear how ridiculous you sound."

"She said and did those things because she thinks I betrayed her."

"You did!"

"No, I didn't! Not intentionally, anyway."

"And if she were really your friend, she'd know that."

We fell silent as Jordan's car made a left up ahead. Then I sighed. "I at least need to get her to take the site down."

Charlie didn't comment. She stared out the windshield, an unusual seriousness in her expression. "Tell me the truth," she finally said. "Are we following Jordan because you're still clinging to the idea of getting back together?"

I looked from the road to her and back again, words choking my throat even though I felt sure of my answer. "No. I swear to you."

She turned to me. "Do you want to be with TJ?"

I shrank in my seat, keeping my eyes trained on Jordan's car. It was true that I liked TJ a lot more than I should have. I definitely enjoyed kissing him way more than I should have. But I'd never stopped to think about what would happen between us if the situation were different. Or even if it wasn't. Trying to come up with an answer now made me feel like my tongue had been swapped out for a cement block.

A smirk formed on Charlie's lips. "Your silence is answer enough."

I only half heard her. My eyes narrowed as we passed a house adorned with colored Christmas lights and an inflatable snowman in the front yard. I could've sworn I'd seen it before.

"Does this neighborhood look familiar to you?" I asked.

Charlie sat up straighter and looked out the window. "Now that you mention it, it kind of does. Where are we?"

"Monroe, I think."

The déjà vu only grew stronger as Jordan made another left turn.

"Oh my God," Charlie said. "I know where we are."

A second later, I did too. Not that I believed my eyes, because it should've been the last place on earth we'd end up.

But unless the stress of my night had caused me to hallucinate, Jordan had just pulled up the long, circular driveway to Kendall Keene's house.

27

CHARLIE AND I STARED IN DISBELIEF FROM WHERE WE WERE PARKED on the street.

"How do Jordan and Kendall know each other?" Charlie asked.

"Maybe they don't. Maybe he's using her driveway to turn around."

Nope. Jordan's headlights cut off and his car door opened. I must've been on autopilot, because I grabbed the yearbook camera from my back seat and snapped a picture. Charlie looked as confused as I felt.

"Does Kendall know you dated Jordan?"

"I don't think so. I've never had a reason to bring him up."

"So this isn't some sort of revenge booty call she orchestrated to get back at you?"

That sounded right up Kendall's alley, with the exception that she knew nothing of my history with Jordan. Yet Kendall herself opened the door for him. We were too far and it was too dark to see her face when she found Jordan on her front step, but she didn't hesitate to let him in. I snapped another picture before the door closed.

"Was that for you or for Sara?" Charlie asked. "Or TJ?"

I pulled up the grainy image on my screen and zoomed in on Kendall. It was dark and blurry, but there was no mistaking the smile on her face. I frowned at Charlie. "Whichever one of us needs it most."

A few seconds later, a light came on in one of the turreted windows on the upper level. A window with frilly, pink-and-green curtains.

"I think they're in her bedroom," Charlie said, reading my mind. No sooner had she finished her sentence than the light went out. "No way. Do you think they're doing it?"

The sour taste of betrayal lingered in my mouth. If Kendall and Jordan were hooking up, why had she been so focused on TJ's extracurricular activities? And how dare she accuse me of stealing something she'd already thrown away? Maybe I was jumping to conclusions, but something was very wrong here and I had to figure out what.

I held up my phone and waited, watching for the light to go back on. When it didn't, I hit TJ's number and sent him a text.

Any reason why Jordan Pace would be at Kendall's house right now?

A long, loaded pause followed before my phone buzzed with his response:

I might have an idea.

I lay in bed that night with my mind reeling. I'd been humiliated by my ex–best friend, comforted and almost kissed by my ex-boyfriend, and then discovered the two of them were possibly hooking up behind everyone's backs. It had been a hell of a twenty-four hours.

On top of it, I'd gone into the Busted email account to find it littered with hate mail. Complete strangers had gone out of their way to tell me how horrible I was, and one of them even used the word *unprofessional*.

Unprofessional. Like this private eye crap was real.

The email I *didn't* receive bothered me most though. For all the overly brave anonymous venom, the one eff-you I expected never materialized: Sara's. When I finally drifted off for a few minutes, I dreamed that she and her friends snuck up behind me at my locker with baseball bats, pounding away until my limbs snapped like tree branches and fell onto the linoleum in sharp right angles.

I woke with a start and launched myself at my computer, taking half of my bedding with me. I didn't need another person plotting revenge against me. I opened an email and addressed it to SaraCat42.

Hi, Sara,

You probably know who Reverse Cupid is already, but in case you haven't heard, it's me, Marisa Palmera. I know you think there's something going on between Jordan and me, but I can assure you there's not. I went to the Templeton game last night like you asked me to, and I saw him there. He didn't have a girl with him, but did he tell you where he went afterward?

Marisa

I left it at that. Mentioning the video seemed like a stupid move. If she'd seen it, she'd draw her own conclusions, and if she hadn't, there was no sense in pointing a giant flashing sign at it.

I looked at the clock—4:00 a.m. All I could do was wait for the ax to fall. And figure out what to say to TJ when I saw him. I'd responded to his **I might have an idea** text message with **Care to elaborate?** But he hadn't answered.

While I was on a roll, I unplugged my phone from its charger and clicked on Kendall's name. I started to type and deleted my message three times. Finally, I wrote **I think we both have some explaining to** do and hit send. At that point, I couldn't see the harm in adding one more knot to my intestines.

An eternity of silence passed while I alternately checked my phone and email. Nothing appeared in either one.

I looked at the clock again—4:15. This was going to be a long night.

I pulled out the chair at my craft table, knowing I'd never get back to sleep. I needed a way to occupy my mind, to remember that I was good at something. My fingers wandered over to the box at the far edge of the table, one that I hadn't opened in quite a while, and an idea started to form. I set to work. Gradually, some of the tension faded from my shoulders. My plan might not get me anywhere, but for once, I felt like I was doing something right.

28

THE FIRST THING I BECAME AWARE OF WAS A SHARP PAIN IN MY forehead. For a second, I wondered if my run-in with Sara and her baseball bat had been real. I peeled my face from the sticky surface it had congealed to and rubbed the stinging spot on my head. A tiny blue crystal came off on my fingertip.

I'd fallen asleep at my craft table. Not just fallen asleep—face-planted into a crystal and passed out cold.

I groaned as I massaged the dented spot on my head and the night before came rushing back. Before I could grab for my phone to see if anyone had acknowledged me, my bedroom door opened slightly. Nick's eye appeared in the crack.

"Hey," he said. "You okay?"

"Well, in one night, I became the laughingstock of Monroe County, made more enemies than I have in my entire life, and almost gave myself a lobotomy with a bead. So yeah, I'm stellar."

Nick leaned against the door frame with his hands in the pockets of his sweatpants. "Charlie says she's making you cookies today."

"Aw, she's the best."

His face instantly went all moony. "Yeah, she is." He caught himself and stood up straighter. "She knows what you're going through."

I rubbed my eyes, finally starting to wake up a little. "I guess at this point it can't get much worse, right?" I reached for where I'd left my phone the night before, but my hand came in contact with an empty table. I leaned down to see if it had fallen on the floor. Not there either.

"Where's my phone?" I stood up to look around and noticed an empty space where my computer had been too. "What happened to my—" I whipped around to face my brother. "What's going on?"

Nick ducked out of my room, trying and failing to shut the door before I started chasing him. I threw it open and reached his door right before he could close it, hurling all my weight against it and yelling that I'd shave off his eyebrows in his sleep if he didn't give my stuff back. The door gave way and Nick leaped over his bed, half laughing and half hovering behind it like it wasn't the least effective barricade on the planet. "Trust me," he said, "you don't want to look at the internet right now. I'm doing you a favor."

I charged at him. He tried to roll over his bed, but I dove on top of him and shoved his face into the comforter so that only one eye stared up at me. "Tell me what's going on right now or I send

Charlie my video of you cleaning our bathroom in your underwear and singing with your headphones on."

"No!" He stuck his tongue out and tried to lick my hand. I relocated my grip to his forehead and pushed harder.

"*Dream on*," I sang in my best screechy falsetto, imitating Nick in the video I'd shot on the sly a couple months ago. He'd threatened my life if I ever posted it anywhere, but at this point, nothing he did could be much worse than what had already happened to me. "*Dream on, aaaahhhahaha!*"

"Okay!" He pushed himself up like Gulliver breaking away from Lilliputian restraints, and I rolled backward off the bed and onto the floor. When I looked up, Nick was peering over the edge and holding out his hand to help me up. "Don't say I didn't warn you." He rubbed the side of his face as he headed to his closet. "Shit, I think some of Kendall's spaz rubbed off on you. You are freakishly strong." He pulled my laptop from beneath a pile of crap on his closet floor and opened it. When he turned it toward me, the Busted-turned-Bitch website lit up the screen.

I didn't reach for it. "Oh God. What now?"

Nick proffered the computer. "Do you want to know or not?"

I took it from him, and the way my stomach lurched made me grateful I hadn't eaten breakfast yet.

At first glance, nothing seemed different. The bitch headline still came screaming out of the old Busted one, and the video of the promposal still showcased the same god-awful thumbnail.

And then I scrolled a little further.

The blood drained from my face. A photo from last year's bonfire stared back at me. The picture had been taken from Kevin's deck, looking down into the backyard. Kevin and two of his friends stood in front of the fire with their arms around each other's shoulders, beers held high in their free hands. But off to the side sat two people unaware that their picture was being taken. Jordan had his arm wrapped around my shoulder and my hand rested on his knee. We were looking at each other, lost in our own little world. The caption below read Marisa gets cozy with the boyfriend of another client.

"*What?* This picture is old! Where did she even get it?"

My mind raced. Could Jordan have done this? Was this the reason he'd gone to Kendall's house? It didn't make any sense. Why would he implicate himself as part of Kendall's disgusting need for revenge?

I scrolled down again to read the testimonial that went along with the picture.

> I wanted to make sure my boyfriend was only into me, so I asked Marisa for help. All she needed to do was catch him with another girl, and instead she was the one in his face all the time. She may have proved my boyfriend doesn't deserve me, but she did it by being as big a slut as he is.

My throat constricted. *In his face all the time* were the exact words Sara had used in her original email to me. Kendall might've seen it before I changed the password, but how could she possibly have known who'd written it? Not only that, if Kendall and Jordan were friends—or friends with benefits—why would she let Sara call him out this way?

The misery didn't stop there. Beneath Sara's lovely little blurb, Kendall had added another photo. Jordan and me at our lockers, talking. My back faced the camera and Jordan's eyes were trained on my face. My green shirt, black flats, and TJ's black belt around my waist told me it was the day Jordan had asked me to the bonfire.

Apparently, Sara Cat had done a little spy work of her own.

I looked at Nick. "I don't even know what to say anymore."

"Say the word and I'll make Pace a eunuch."

"He didn't get me into this mess. I did. I did this all by my own stupid self." I stared at the screen again, watching the word *Bitch* blare into view over and over.

I'd made some seriously dumb decisions in my life, but the dumbest was letting Kendall Keene back into it.

29

A VERY BIG PART OF ME WANTED TO FAKE SICK ON MONDAY MORNING. Especially when I woke up to the sound of my cell phone ringing instead of my alarm. I jumped for it, too sleepy to fully register that the screen said *Private Call*.

"Marisa Palmera?" The voice was male and barely concealing snickers.

"Who is this? How did you get my number?"

"Do you like leftover sausage?"

"Leftover sausage? I don't get it."

Whoever was on the line couldn't contain himself anymore and burst into laughter before hanging up the phone.

Oh. Leftover sausage. I got it now.

I slunk back to bed and pulled the covers over my head, tempted to turn off my alarm altogether and "accidentally" oversleep. But I didn't. And by the time I showered, ate breakfast, and kissed my parents goodbye, something happened.

I got rip-roaring mad.

I was angry at Kendall for asking me to help her and then selling me out, angry at TJ for kissing me, angry at myself for liking it. I was angry at Sara for being such a ginormous bitch and angry at Jordan for the domino effect he'd started when he had broken my heart. Truthfully, I was angry at myself for that part too. He might've dumped me, but I was the one who'd allowed my insecurities to take over my life.

By the time I stormed through the glass doors of Herring Cross High, I was determined that my days of being trampled and discarded were over, website or no website. I stomped through the maze of hallways to the junior lockers until I caught a glimpse of long, dark hair and big boobs.

"I need to talk to you."

Sara looked me up and down, coating me with disgust. "What for? It's not like I'll believe a word out of your mouth."

I don't know where my bravery came from, but I grabbed her arm and threw a curt "excuse us" over my shoulder as I dragged her into an exit alcove. But one of her little friends decided to get cute with me. Big mistake.

"Take your skanky hands off her," a tiny blond with sparkly clips in her hair demanded. "Haven't you done enough already?"

I whipped around. "Aren't you dating Evan Salinger?" Her petite nostrils flared and her lips parted, but before she could answer, I added, "You're not the only one. Check his phone sometime."

I turned my back on her gaping mouth and addressed Sara. "I never lied to you. In fact, I never did anything to you except follow Jordan like you asked me to. Whatever you think is going on between him and me is a figment of your imagination."

She folded her arms across her chest. "Bullshit, Marisa. I see the way you throw yourself at him. I should've known you were Reverse Cupid, because you're the only one obsessed enough to do something so lame."

"You didn't think Busted was lame when you asked for my help, and you definitely didn't think it was lame when you were trying to be like me."

Her face puckered like she'd eaten the world's most potent Sour Patch Kid. "What are you talking about? I'd never try to be like you."

"I'm talking about the picture you took of Jordan and me at my locker that Kendall put on the Busted site. You must be pretty obsessed yourself if you're stalking the goddamn halls to catch us *talking*."

Her face scrunched up even more. "Who is Kendall?"

"Oh, spare me, 'Who's Kendall?' She's the one you sold me and Jordan out to when I came clean about being Reverse Cupid. I saw the pictures. Don't bother to play dumb."

Sara's arms dropped to her sides and her fingers curled into fists. I thought she might punch me. "I don't know anyone named Kendall," she growled. "And I don't know what pictures you're talking about. The only thing I saw on that stupid website is the video of you stealing another girl's boyfriend."

The rage zipping through my veins stilled as if I'd been zapped with a stun gun. Standing six inches from her face and looking her dead in the eye, I had an awful suspicion Sara might be telling the truth.

"Kendall *is* the girl in the video. The one whose boyfriend asked me to the Winter Formal. Ex. Ex-boyfriend."

"And why the hell would I know who she is?"

"Then who gave her those pictures?"

"*What fucking pictures?*"

Oh shit. She really didn't know. Which meant she didn't know where Jordan had gone after the Templeton game, which meant she probably didn't know he even knew Kendall. Which meant I couldn't tell her without throwing him under the bus.

Thinking fast, I shifted my bag onto my hip and took out my phone. "Here," I said, pulling up the website and handing her the phone. "You're really going to tell me you didn't take these pictures?"

Sara's face paled, then flushed as she looked at the screen. If I could've taken a picture of her, the perfect caption would've been "Busted."

"How did you get these? Did you go through Jordan's phone?"

Or not.

"I didn't get them from anywhere. I'm Reverse Cupid, but

Kendall runs the website. She's the one who posted these. Why would Jordan have them on his phone?"

Sara rolled her eyes. "Like you don't know that's where they came from. Quit playing innocent, Marisa. If you think I believe for a second that you didn't have something to do with this, then you're as stupid as you are desperate."

My blood boiled. Sheer willpower kept me from shoving her into the cinderblock wall behind her. "You're pretty brave, throwing around the word *stupid* if you honestly believe I'd make a website trashing *myself*, or that Jordan somehow took pictures that he's fucking *in*. So here's your last chance to tell me where they came from, or I promise, you will be sorry."

I braced myself in case she lunged at me. An image of Sara and me clawing at each other on the linoleum floor flashed through my mind, and I realized too late that I might've set myself up to be the laughingstock of the internet yet again.

But she didn't lunge. She didn't even move. She stood rooted to the floor, breathing hard through flared nostrils like she couldn't decide between beating me to a pulp or some other option that involved my death and dismemberment. When she yanked her messenger bag toward her abdomen, I figured she'd chosen plan B. She unsnapped her bag and lifted the flap that covered the opening.

That's when I saw it.

The brilliant, heart-shaped collage of colors I'd left in the cubby of Jordan's locker not so long ago. He'd given Sara my pin. The pin inspired by our first kiss.

Jordan Pace was a douchebag of epic proportions.

Before she could notice my thunderstruck stare, Sara whipped her phone out of her bag and started to scroll through it. "They're my pictures," she said. "I sent them to Jordan—"

"What's going on here?"

We looked up at the same time. Jordan stood in the hall, books against his hip and questions in his eyes.

"You," Sara spat before I could react. I never knew one syllable could ooze so much venom. "Do you know how my pictures wound up on that website?"

Jordan's Adam's apple bobbed with a labored swallow. "What website?"

"The one you hijacked Charlie's phone to look at before you bolted from the Templeton game on Friday night," I said.

Sara's head whipped in my direction. She narrowed her eyes. "Where did he go later that night? You asked me if I knew."

Before I could answer, Jordan took her arm. "Sara, let's go somewhere and talk."

She jerked free of his grip. "Keep your hands off me. I'm not listening to another word of your horseshit or hers." Her glare fixed on me. "You can have him if you want him. You losers deserve each other."

With that, she pushed past Jordan and stormed down the hall.

Jordan glowered at me, enough ice in his eyes to frost the alcove's glass door if the cold hadn't already taken care of it. "Thanks," he spat.

Thanks? Like I'd ruined his life instead of the other way around?

And somehow, the mountain of questions and ever-growing confusion in my brain only allowed me proper indignation over one thing:

"You gave her my pin."

He sputtered a few unintelligible syllables and looked around like he had no idea what to do with that response. "You left it in my locker. What was I supposed to do with it? What the hell is going on here, Marisa?"

"That pin meant something to me. I made it because *you* meant something to me. I would rather you throw it away than give it to someone you don't even care about." I didn't bother to acknowledge the second half of his question.

"Who says I don't care about Sara? Christ, Marisa, that's not your call. You'd think with the number of people who hate you right now you'd learn to mind your own business."

No, he didn't.

I exhaled, both shocked and proud at the lack of sting that resulted from his words. I wanted nothing more than to be done with him, once and for all. And it felt damn good.

My voice was even despite the anger that edged my words when

I spoke again. "You don't get it, Jordan. You never will. When you care about someone, you don't sneak around and do things that would hurt her if you did them to her face. You care about how your actions affect her." I took a step toward him. "You don't worry that the grass is greener in every goddamn yard but your own. You put her first once in a while instead of thinking about yourself all. The fucking. Time." I broke eye contact in order to dig through the front pocket of my bag but kept right on talking. "You know what? I'm glad you gave my pin to Sara. You're over me, and I've never been happier to be over you. Someone who appreciates the pin might as well keep it." My hand closed over what I'd been looking for. I pulled my fist out of my bag and slammed my hand against Jordan's chest. "And while you're at it, give this back to Kendall for me."

I walked away, leaving him fumbling to catch the blue, pink, and yellow mosaic pin Kendall had thrown at me the day of the promposal. A few feet away, I spun around, smug and satisfied when I took in Jordan staring bug-eyed at the pin in his palm, looking like he might retch.

"That's right," I said, smirking from ear to ear. "I know all about the two of you. And it seems she's got a bone to pick with you too, or your face wouldn't be splashed all over that website next to mine. Maybe next time you should take your own advice and think about keeping your business a little closer to home."

I turned and stalked off, indifferent to the stares and snickers following me down the hall. It didn't matter what anyone else thought of me at that moment. I felt better than I had in a very long time.

30

I DIDN'T SEE SARA OR JORDAN FOR THE REST OF THE DAY, BUT I DIDN'T see TJ either. Apparently, he wasn't as brave as I was.

When I realized he hadn't come to school, I sent him a text. **Thanks for letting me face the firing squad alone.**

He wrote back, **Sick last night, better now. Can you come to the barn to talk after school?**

Sick. A likely story. Still, I agreed to meet him.

My foot pressed hard against the brake when I turned onto the street between the Carusos' house and the farm. Parked off to the side, in the same spot as the night Charlie and I first spied on TJ, sat the car with the Templeton decal.

I parked my car and got out, circling the other vehicle slowly, like I expected it to come to life and shout *boo* in my face. There was nothing remarkable about it: older model Honda, drab blue color, relatively clean interior. Nothing noteworthy except the heart pendant hanging from the rearview mirror.

Yep, it was definitely the same car. I leaned closer to the driver's side window to take a better look. Undecorated, the hearts were silver and almost industrial looking, identical to the one suspended from a chain of silver beads, like a dog tag necklace. As much as I wanted to believe it was a weird coincidence, I had a nagging feeling it was more weird, less coincidence.

I headed across the street, ready to find out.

"You don't look sick," I said when the barn door swung open, revealing TJ in jeans, a thermal Henley, and a knit cap. He looked pretty freaking hot, actually. Charlie hadn't been off base with her comment about the effects of lifting trees on his upper body. I had to look away before a full-body blush won out over the frigid temperature.

"I'm not anymore. I had a stomach thing, but it must've been one of those twenty-four-hour viruses. I'm fine now."

"I've heard of that virus." I stepped inside, unwinding my scarf from my neck. "It's called 'utter humiliation and dread.' Supposed to be a bitch and half—" I stopped when I saw the tall, thin boy sitting on TJ's worktable. "Um, hi."

He scooted off the table and nodded at me. "Hey. What's up?"

"I could ask you the same thing."

"Marisa, you remember Eli," TJ said. His expression hardened. "You've, uh, seen me with him before."

"Right." I nodded and turned to Eli. "You work on the farm."

But something told me that had nothing to do with why he was currently sitting in TJ's barn.

I glanced from TJ to Eli and back again. When no one said anything, I broke the silence. "What's going on here?"

TJ's eyes locked with mine, his expression unreadable. Finally, he nodded in the direction of the loft. "Come upstairs. It's kind of complicated."

I followed them up, wishing TJ'd knock off the drawn-out suspense. Being in the dark had gotten old about a hundred years ago. Eli sank into the armchair while TJ collapsed onto the faded sofa and hugged one of the throw pillows against his chest, calling my attention to his dumb, stupid arms again and making my mind replay the way it felt to have them around me. I didn't want to be attracted to him. I didn't need another distraction in the form of warm skin and soft lips and strong hands and—

UGH!

I was so busy trying not to notice all the things I couldn't stop noticing that I hadn't realized TJ was looking at me, waiting for me to sit down. Next to him. On that impossibly small couch. I perched at the edge of the cushion, trying not to look as uncomfortable as I felt.

"All right, here's the story." He curled his hands around the corners of the pillow and tucked them under his arms. "Kendall moved back from Arizona in the middle of junior year, and to say she was unpopular when she started at Templeton is an understatement. She got wait-listed for the Hartley program, and she and her mother made a huge deal, complaining that it was unfair. I probably don't need to tell you that Kendall's not great at taking no for an answer."

I nodded, feeling a little queasy. This was a very different story from the one Kendall had told me. I specifically remembered her bragging that the slots had been full, and they'd let her in anyway.

So if TJ was telling the truth, then what else had Kendall lied to me about?

"Making waves right off the bat didn't sit well with a lot of people, especially the girls who felt like she was trying to take their place at the top of the food chain," TJ continued. "In their minds, she needed to work her way up from the bottom. But Kendall had ranked in the top ten at her school in Arizona, and she saw being left out of the honors program as a demotion that was going to sabotage all her hard work. She wouldn't let it go. So the top brass fought back by making her life hell. I'm talking pranks, bullying, the works."

"One time they stole her car keys and left a dead mouse in her trunk," Eli added.

My eyebrows floated toward my hairline as they spoke. Any pretty, popular girl was bound to have her enemies. Add in a strong personality like Kendall's and it wasn't hard to believe she'd had her share. But an entire fleet of students turning on her and torturing her sounded straight out of a nightmare.

And just like that, the ever-precarious scales that measured my love-hate relationship with Kendall tipped violently in her favor.

"She was in my math class and I was one of the few people who'd talk to her without an ulterior motive," TJ continued. "Eventually we started doing homework together and hanging out after school. I realized that yeah, she was super-driven, but it was mostly because the girl is *terrified* of failing. Not only at school-related stuff, but everything. She wanted people to like her, and I think, in her mind, that meant she had to be the best at everything. Once I understood that, it was easy to overlook what everyone else saw as her flaws. And then one day, one thing led to another and..." He shifted in his seat and my stomach clenched. He wasn't telling me anything I didn't already know, but that didn't mean I wanted to hear it.

"Uh-huh. Got it."

"Anyway, she was different than I thought. She lives in this fancy house with fancy cars, but she never cared that I didn't. She had a sense of humor and she cared about her grades."

TJ snorted and threw a glance at Eli, who nodded ever so slightly.

"Not long after Kendall and I got together, our math teacher asked me to stay after class," TJ continued. "He'd been giving me extra credit for tutoring other kids, including Kendall, while he was busy coaching track, and so he'd given me the keys to his classroom. All of a sudden he's asking me if I went through his desk drawers, telling me I need to level with him. I had no idea what he was talking about." He grabbed a loose thread from the bottom of the pillow and twisted it around his finger. "Supposedly the test scores from all his classes had shot up with the last exam. Only he didn't think my tutoring had anything to with it."

I sat up straighter. "Wait a minute. Are you saying the same thing that's happening to Charlie happened to you?"

TJ looked at Eli, then at me. "I'm saying I was set up. And I think Kendall might be the person who did it."

"You—what?" It took me a second to digest his statement. "Then what are you still doing with her? Were. Why were you still with her?"

"Marisa, I broke up with Kendall months ago. She wouldn't accept it, so maybe in her mind, we were still together, but whatever she *hired* you to catch me doing, it wasn't cheating. Up until the other day, we were still hanging out, trying to make it work as friends. Because I didn't have proof that she took advantage of me or swiped the keys, and I didn't want to completely cut her out of my life. I do care about her, despite what you think."

My posture stiffened. I wanted to ask, *Then why did you kiss me?* But I wasn't about to do it in front of Eli.

So even though his statement sat rotting in my stomach, I didn't touch it.

I said, "Kendall called me the morning after…the morning after you gave me my bracelet." His eyes held mine, acknowledging what else happened that day. "And she told me you broke up with her."

"I did, in a way. I told her I didn't think we should see each other at all anymore. She kept making it clear that she wanted to get back together, even though I kept making it clear that wasn't happening. How could I, without knowing if she's been lying to my face?"

"No," I said, more to myself than to him. "She's competitive, but she's not desperate. She'd die if she got caught doing something like that."

TJ's lips thinned and his jaw hardened. "She hasn't been caught."

"Yet," Eli said pointedly.

"Are you telling me you're trying to trap her?" My eyes widened as something finally clicked. "Holy crap, you're Hood Boy!"

Eli laughed and flipped the hood of his sweatshirt up over his baseball cap. "At your service."

I spun back to TJ, trying to ignore the flutter in my belly when he looked at me through those dark lashes. Now was not the time to get all hot and bothered—not that it had ever been.

"After Mr. Katz accused me of tampering with his tests, Eli told me he saw Kendall coming out of his classroom after school," TJ said. "I was at work and Mr. Katz was at track, so the room should have been locked. When Eli mentioned it in front of Kendall, she said she'd been taking a makeup test but she got so…weird. I don't even know if I can explain it, but we've been suspicious ever since. The more I thought about it, the more I think she took my keys, stole the data, and put the keys back before I ever noticed. I think she wanted me to take the fall. Eli's been trying to prove it."

"Prove it how?"

Eli's heel bounced against the floor. "I'm trying to find people who cheated and get them to talk, which is a lot harder than it sounds."

"But don't you go to Templeton?"

He and TJ exchanged a look. "I'm not what you'd call the most popular kid in school. I only transferred there because my mom remarried."

"And his stepbrother is a jackass. Another jerk who can't handle new people on his turf. So it's not exactly shocking that Eli got framed too."

I turned back to Eli. "You did?"

"Not for cheating," Eli said. "My asshole stepbrother set me up. Took me to the school one night with a few cans of spray paint like we were gonna bond writing graffiti or some shit, then calls the cops and takes off laughing like a little bitch."

"And so…you and TJ bonded over your false accusations?"

His chin jutted in TJ's direction. "T covered for me. Told the cops I was there to meet him about a project and the paint was part of it. He had my back, and now I've got his."

I looked at TJ, slightly dizzy from the back-and-forth. "What were you doing at the school then?"

He'd wound the pillow thread so tightly around his pointer finger that the tip had turned purple. "I *was* working on a project. I used to write for the school paper, and I'd borrowed the digital media department's camera to take pictures of the campus earlier for this big story about Templeton's fiftieth anniversary. After I got home, I realized I'd lost one of the lenses, and there was no way I was blowing my money to replace it. So I went back to find it. Guess I was in the right place at the right time." Coming from TJ, it didn't surprise me at all that he'd refer to accidental involvement in vandalism as a good thing. "It was bad enough that the teachers all looked at me like I should've had a giant scarlet *C* on my chest for *cheater*. I didn't want to see Eli get blamed for something he didn't do."

"Okay." I nodded, trying to process everything they'd told me. "I guess my next question is, why all the secret meetings? Don't you two believe in cell phones?"

As if on cue, Eli's phone rang in the pocket of his jeans. He pulled it out and, looking at the screen, announced, "I gotta jet." He rose from his chair and put the phone back in his pocket without answering it. "I'm supposed to be grounded and Mom's gonna kill me if I'm not doing homework when she gets home."

"All right, man." TJ extended his hand, which Eli grasped for a bro handshake.

"Later, Marisa. Nice meeting you." Eli stopped to shake my hand too. He held it a beat too long, and half his mouth quirked up into a grateful, crooked-toothed grin. "I'm glad TJ has someone else in his corner."

With that, he let go and bounded down the stairs.

"To answer your question," TJ said, "Eli's mom keeps tight reins on his internet and cell phone usage. He's spent some time with the wrong crowds, and even though he's cleaned up his act, it's her way of making sure it stays clean. Meeting in person eliminates a lot of prying ears and eyes." He looked at me and snorted. "Or so we thought."

I sat back, letting all this information sink in. My head spun with it. So much so that I hadn't even asked Eli about the heart in his car. But it didn't seem important anymore, not compared to what they'd told me about Kendall. She'd flat-out lied to me, and she'd possibly driven TJ out of Templeton. The Kendall I knew was competitive and, yes, a little manipulative. But I didn't want to believe she was capable of something as awful as this, because if she was, then that meant...

It all came together in my head and I couldn't believe I hadn't made the connection sooner.

"Oh my God," I said. "Kendall's the one who stole the information from Mrs. Pace's laptop." I looked at TJ, expecting him to appear angry at Kendall's deceit or even smug at my blindness.

What I didn't expect was the look of total disgust on his face.

"Or maybe someone *gave* it to her?" he leered.

I blinked. "You think Jordan is in on this?"

"Don't you think it's a little convenient that she's rubbing elbows with the chemistry teacher's son? Kendall's very good at getting what she wants from people."

"You really think Jordan would just hand over his mother's lesson plans?"

TJ stuffed the pillow into the corner of the couch. "God, Marisa, you really have no clue when it comes to him, do you? It didn't occur to you for one second that he might have something to do with it, did it?" He stood up and threw his hands in the air. "Why would it? You're never going to be over him."

I sat there shell-shocked, tripping over my own tongue. "I *am* over him," I finally managed. "And—and you're one to talk, keeping Kendall in your back pocket on the off chance that you might be wrong about her."

TJ looked at the floor and scraped the toe of his boot against it. "All things considered, it didn't seem important," he mumbled.

"Ugh! You're just like the rest of those guys, aren't you? She's a person, not a minor freaking detail."

I hadn't realized how much I wanted him to be different from other guys I was asked to investigate. How much I needed him to be the exception to the rule. Because if he wasn't, then maybe one didn't exist.

"I broke up with Kendall long before I asked you to the dance, and things were rocky between us a long time before that. I didn't do anything wrong." TJ's eyebrows drew together. "Whose side are you on here?"

I massaged my temples, suddenly exhausted. "I don't know. Not Jordan's."

"I saw the two of you at the Templeton game. I was there meeting Eli, and I saw you." He pushed his hands into his pockets and turned away from me, but not quickly enough to hide the darkness in his eyes and the disappointed set of his lips. He was hurt.

Because he liked me. A lot.

"Nothing happened between us at the Templeton game."

He turned back to me, his forehead creased with indignation. "We both know where it was going if Charlie hadn't interrupted."

White-hot embarrassment flushed through me. My mouth opened and closed. I knew what Jordan had intended to do, but he hadn't done it. I'd never stopped to think about an alternate ending.

"That's not fair. You're making assumptions about something that never happened."

"What if it had?" His eyes bored into mine. "Tell me the truth. What would you have done if Jordan kissed you that night?"

I pressed my lips together, feeling heat climb up my neck. Could I honestly say I would've pulled away? Would I have kissed back? Would I have fallen into his trap again, or would I have realized he wasn't the one I wanted to kiss anymore? It didn't matter, because it hadn't happened.

And I'd come to that realization on my own.

I stood up, moving closer to TJ until I stood right in front of him. I looked up at him and lifted my hands to let my fingertips linger at his rib cage. "I don't know what I would've done if he kissed me that night," I murmured, gently tugging his shirt around my fingers. "But I know what I'd do if you kissed me right now."

His hands came up to wrap around mine, enveloping them in warmth. His thumbs slid against my palms, gently massaging the insides of my hands, and he exhaled that delicious cinnamon-and-chamomile scent that turned my insides to pudding.

Detaching me from his shirt, he pressed my fingertips against his bottom lip. "I'm not going to," he said softly. "I think we both have some things to figure out before this goes any further."

"But I—"

The sound of the barn door banging open interrupted my protest. Our heads turned at the same time and in two seconds flat, six feet of space had grown between us. Too late though.

Kendall looked up at us from the main floor, her arms folded across the chest of her camel-colored coat, making its white, furry collar bunch up against her jawline.

"What are you doing here?" she sneered at me.

"What are *you* doing here?" TJ countered.

She kept her eyes on me as if he hadn't even spoken. "I have no idea why I'm surprised that you decided not to take me up on my offer. It's not like I expect you to care about my side of the story after what you did to me."

I had no idea what offer she meant, and I didn't care. I gripped the loft railing and glared down at her. "What I did to *you*?" My knuckles turned white with the effort of restraining myself from saying more. There were so many accusations I wanted to throw at her, so much venom I wanted to spew until her honey-golden locks dripped with it. But I knew if I ever planned to get to the bottom of her deception once and for all, I had to control myself. I gritted my teeth. "And what offer are you talking about?"

This time, it was me she ignored. Giving both of us a derisive once-over, she told TJ, "I hope she's worth it." Then she turned and stormed out of the barn.

31

SOMETHING INSIDE ME SNAPPED AS I WATCHED HER SELF-RIGHTEOUS ass flounce out the door. The nerve of her, talking about what I'd done to *her* after she'd spearheaded a worldwide smear campaign against me, for crying out loud. She'd tried to ruin my life, and possibly TJ's and Charlie's lives too. Who the hell did she think she was?

I took off like a racehorse out of the gate, bolting down the stairs so fast that they shook. Pure adrenaline pumped my legs and I shot out of the door seconds behind Kendall.

"Kendall!"

She didn't turn around. "Fuck off, Marisa."

That did it. I launched myself at her back with kung fu skills I never knew I had, and we landed in the snow with a thud and a yelp.

"Get off me!" Kendall screeched, wriggling onto her back like a wild animal beneath my weight. I shoved her shoulders into the ground, not caring that the snow seeped through the knees of my jeans as I pinned her.

"Where did you get those pictures of Jordan and me?" I yelled in her face.

"Get off me, you bitch!"

She flailed an arm free and smacked me in the face, catching fingerfuls of hair and knocking my knit cap cockeyed in the process. I grabbed her wrist and rammed it back to the ground. Two red streaks appeared on her cheek when she scratched her own face trying to fight it.

"Tell me where you got them! And then tell me you're taking that site down or I swear to God, you're going to regret it!"

"Stop!" The sound of pounding footfalls met my ears seconds before hands swooped down and pulled me off Kendall like a bird snatching a fish out of water.

"Let go of me!" I shouted at TJ, bucking and flinging myself in every direction, but he wrapped his arms around me and held fast. "Did you have something to do with Charlie being framed?" I demanded as Kendall scrambled to her feet. "Did you?"

"You are insane!" She smacked at the snow on her clothes and tried to flip her matted hair away from her face, but it stuck to her cheeks in wet, dirty clumps.

"If you had anything to do with it, I swear to God I'll find out. I'll ruin you, Kendall, I swear it." I made one more attempt to lunge at her, but TJ's arms stayed locked around my shoulders.

"Go ahead and try, Marisa." She clawed at the snow by her feet, then hurled a snowball at my face. "You're already fucking ruined."

Then she turned and stomped toward her car, leaving the remains of our friendship to melt away with the snow.

~

TJ didn't let go of me until Kendall had revved her engine and sped away.

"What the hell were you thinking?" He dropped my arms. I hadn't stopped squirming and promptly fell on my butt. For a moment, we stared at each other, breathing hard. He leaned down and picked up my hat, which had fallen off sometime after Kendall'd whacked me, and held out his other hand to help me up.

"I'm sorry," I said, reaching for his hand and brushing myself off. "I couldn't help it. I can't believe how selfish she is."

"We still don't know how much of what we talked about is true. Thank God you didn't say more. I don't want her to know I'm looking for answers about what happened to me."

"Not that I'd throw you under the bus, but what difference does it make now?"

TJ frowned. "I already broke up with her and hooked up with her friend. If it turns out she's innocent, why add insult to injury?"

I snatched my hat back and jammed it on my head, dirt, wetness, and all. "We didn't hook up. We kissed. And unless you blabbed, she doesn't even know about that part. I'm done protecting her, and you should be too."

He hooked his thumbs into his belt loops and hunched his shoulders. Whether it was the cold or a gesture of apology, I couldn't tell.

"You of all people should understand wanting to give someone the benefit of the doubt."

So we were back to Jordan again. I rolled my eyes. "Do I have to remind you that you *and* Jordan are on that website right next to me?"

"Of course not." He scratched his head and dug the heel of his work boot into the snow. "What offer was she talking about?"

"I don't know," I said as I rolled my sleeves back to keep the moisture off my skin. "I was more interested in beating the crap out of her than finding out."

To my surprise, TJ smiled. And then chuckled. "I'll deny saying this later, but that was kind of hot."

I couldn't not smile back. Except when I did, his eyes dropped to the ground and the grin dropped off his face. So much for that.

"Yeah, well, it doesn't feel so hot right now," I said. "I'd better get home and wash these clothes."

I started toward my car, but TJ called after me. "Marisa?"

I turned around.

"I'll keep you posted if Eli finds anything, okay?"

"Sounds good." I resumed crunching through the snow, but only took a few steps before I turned again. "TJ?"

"Yeah?"

"I'm assuming your invitation to the winter formal is recalled?"

He rocked on his heels. "It's not that I don't want to go with you, Marisa, but I don't think—"

I cut him off. "Don't worry about it. I just realized I never gave you an answer. For the record, it would've been yes."

I didn't wait for a response before finishing the trek to my car. I had bigger fish to fry at the moment. I understood that TJ still felt some twisted tether of loyalty to Kendall, but I'd had enough. It was one thing to mess with me, but if she thought she could mess with my friends and get away with it, she had another thing coming.

I took out my phone and went to text Kendall, but found she'd beaten me to it. When I looked at her message, I finally knew what "offer" she'd been talking about:

Stay away from TJ and I'll explain everything.

I snorted. That sounded more like a threat than an offer, and I wasn't impressed. I hit reply. The message was short and not so sweet:

Take down the website or I'm taking you down.

32

I'D GONE TO BED THAT NIGHT WITH MY MIND RACING, TRYING TO FIGURE out how I could put my so-called PI skills to use for a purpose other than catching cheaters. I was missing an important detail, something that should've been jumping out at me but wasn't.

Until it did.

I sat bolt upright in bed and sent a text to TJ asking the name of Eli's stepbrother. But I got no response and I fell asleep waiting for his answer.

The next morning, my arm reached outside my sheets for my phone before I even opened my eyes. My text chain with Kendall had gone silent after I'd threatened her. Either she'd dismissed me, or I'd made her angrier and this was the calm before the storm. I was too afraid to pull up the Busted website and find out.

When I looked at the screen, I had a reply from TJ: Jason Carvalho.

I knew it. It had finally hit me why Eli looked so familiar—I'd seen him walking behind Charlie's ex the night he'd shown up at the Templeton game with his new girlfriend.

My heart started to pound. I scrolled through my phone, needing an answer faster than a text message could get it to me. When I called Charlie, she didn't answer. Unsurprising, since she slept like the dead. I hit another number and soon, a groggy-sounding Mindy greeted me.

"Marisa? It's six thirty in the morning. Did someone die?"

"Geez, no. No one died. Sorry for the early call but I need to know what Charlie's ex-boyfriend's last name is."

"You need his name? Why didn't you ask Charlie?"

I waved my fist at the phone. "Long story. Do you know what it is?"

"It's Carvello or Asswad or something like that."

I couldn't help but laugh. "Carvalho?"

"That's it. Why?"

"I think our boy Greggie-George might be able to help me clear Charlie's name."

"Greggie-huh?"

I smiled and shook my head. "Go back to sleep, Mindy. I'll explain everything later, but let me talk to Charlie before you say anything to her."

"You're speaking Chinese to me right now. I don't even know what you're saying."

"Perfect. Sweet dreams."

I hung up and tapped my phone against my lips. With one eye half-open, I pulled up the Busted site.

It was still there. The video, the pictures, all of it.

Was Kendall trying to tell me she wasn't scared? Was she taunting me? Did she not realize she'd messed with the wrong person?

I tried to pretend it didn't bother me that she'd blatantly ignored my warning. If my plan for today went off the way I wanted it to, it wouldn't be long until I had Kendall eating out of my hand.

"Honey?" My mother poked her head into my room. Perfect timing. "Were you talking to someone?"

"I was asking someone to bring me my calc homework today. My stomach isn't feeling so great and I don't think I should go to school."

Mom's forehead creased with worry and she came over to kiss my temple. "You don't have a fever, but you do look a little pale." Ha. I'll bet I did. "There's a bug going around. I'll make you some tea before I leave for work."

"Sounds awesome." *Especially the part where you leave.*

But as she reached my bedroom door, her shoulders tensed, like she was bracing herself to say something she didn't want to. "Honey," she began, "Is there anything I need to speak to Mrs. Keene about?"

Oh no. What did that mean? Did my mother know what was going on? My defenses flared.

"Like what?"

"I don't know. Is Kendall—bothering you at all?"

Mom was definitely up to something. She definitely knew *something*.

"Who told you? Did Nick tell you?"

"You ran off when we bumped into Barbara at the tree farm." She fiddled with the doorknob. "And then Mrs. Horowitz came to pick up her son from school yesterday, and we were chatting. Her daughter Ellen is in some of your classes."

I groaned. Why did the world have to be so damn small? Between my parents' technological ineptitude and the fact that my mother taught kids who weren't old enough to read, I thought they'd remain blissfully ignorant of my situation. Damn Ellen Horowitz. Damn her straight to hell.

I rubbed my eyes. "Did she show you the video?"

Mom's nostrils flared. "What video? There's a video? Sweetheart, what kind of trouble are you in?"

"Oh my God, Mom, not that kind of video!" I blanched, then took a breath to calm myself. If I acted like it was no biggie, maybe she'd believe me. "This isn't kindergarten, Mom. You can't fix what's going on between Kendall and me by sitting her mother down for a chat. I can handle it myself."

"You're a smart girl. You can handle anything. But be warned, if I think someone is hurting my daughter, I'm going to step in."

I managed a weak smile. "I know, Mom. I'm fine, I promise." I put my hand on my stomach and whimpered a little, to let her know I wasn't all *that* fine.

She smiled back. "I'll go get your tea."

The minute she shut the door behind her, I got up to find my car keys. I'd need them once the house was empty. Then I picked up my phone and hit Charlie's number again.

Sleep had almost cocooned me in its wondrous bliss when the sound of horrific retching coming from the bathroom in the hall made me sit up in bed. A few seconds later, the toilet flushed and Nick appeared in my doorway.

"Holy hell, are you okay?"

He smirked and scratched at his stomach. "I knew you were up to something when Mom told me you were staying home, so I faked sick too. That was a little added touch. How'd I do?"

"Pretty freaking disgusting."

He leaped onto the foot of my bed. "So what are we doing today?"

"*We're* not doing anything. I'm having breakfast with Charlie before school starts."

Nick balked. "Why do you get to have breakfast with Charlie without me?"

I threw off my covers and headed to my closet. "Aren't you dating? You can see her whenever you want."

The silence that followed told me something wasn't right. I stopped mid-closet rifle and turned around. Nick stared at the wall, drumming his fingers against my comforter.

"Have you even talked to her since the promposal?"

"Shut up."

"Have you kissed her yet?"

"Shut up."

I dropped the hanger I'd been holding and put my hands on my hips. "Nick! Are you kidding me? For someone who talks such a big game, you have none!"

"Kiss my ass. I haven't figured out the right time yet."

"Well, it's not this morning, I can tell you that."

Nick jumped up and trotted toward the door. "Meet you downstairs in half an hour," he called on his way out. "You're driving."

Nick was none too pleased when he found out my whole plan, but I still couldn't get him to stay out of it. If anything, he attached himself to me like a barnacle once he found out Charlie's ex would be at breakfast.

She and Jason were already sitting next to each other in a

booth when Nick and I arrived at the diner about a half mile off the Templeton campus. Since I hadn't noticed Charlie's car in the lot, I assumed Jason had picked her up. They looked uncomfortable as hell, but it didn't stop Nick from grumbling under his breath at the sight of them seated side by side.

"Hey," I said as Nick and I slid into the booth. I stuck my hand across the table at Jason. "Hi, Jason. Marisa. How's that vanilla ice cream treating you?"

Jason looked at Charlie and then back at me, ignoring my hand. "Am I supposed to know what that means?"

"Maybe you should ask Kelly," Charlie muttered to the table.

"Why do we care if he asks Kelly?" Nick asked.

Jason looked even more bewildered. "You told me we were here to call a truce," he said to Charlie.

"Not quite." I pulled my phone out of my purse.

Charlie folded her arms. "Did Kelly know you already had a girlfriend when she became your girlfriend?"

"Not that it matters now," Nick piped up, an edge of defensiveness in his voice.

"Actually, that's a good question," I cut in. "Did Kelly know about Charlie when you started dating?"

Jason folded and unfolded his hands on the table. "No. What's going on here? What does this have to do with anything?"

I started to scroll through my phone. "Maybe a better question is, how did Charlie find out you were cheating with Kelly?" I held my phone up to his face. "And the answer is, I told her."

He squinted at the picture that started everything. His face turned every conceivable shade of red. "Where the fuck did you get that?"

I dropped the phone into my purse and folded my hands in front of me on the table. "That's irrelevant. What's important is that if you value your relationship with Kelly, at least more than you valued your relationship with Charlie, then you'll help us."

"Help you? I don't even know you!"

"Also irrelevant. Because if you feel even a little bad about what you did, you'll want to do this."

"Do *what*?"

Before I could answer, Charlie turned to Jason. "Did you even like me?"

"Of course I did."

"Pff. Clearly," Nick scoffed.

Charlie shot a *butt out* look across the table at the same time as Jason said, "Hey, who are you, her fucking bodyguard?" She put her hand on Jason's arm and Nick stiffened.

"Listen," Charlie said. "I'm not mad at you anymore, but you know you hurt me. I think you owe me one, Jay."

Jason sat back against the booth. "I'm still waiting for someone to tell me what you all want from me."

"To drop dead?" Nick volunteered.

I kicked him under the table. Hard.

"Eli Jasper is your stepbrother, right?" I continued.

"What of it? Eli and I live under the same roof, but that's about it. We're not exactly the Brady Bunch."

"I know. He tells me you're quite the artist. It's a shame you don't want to take credit for your work." Jason's mouth opened and closed like that of a goldfish. Before he could respond, I forged ahead. "Luckily, I'm not asking you to tell each other bedtime stories. I'm asking you to help him so we can help Charlie."

"And how am I supposed to do that?"

Charlie turned to him. "Be honest. Do you know anyone in Mrs. Pace's class who cheated?"

Jason swallowed and squirmed like a worm on a hook. "I can't say for sure. I have my suspicions."

Nick opened his big mouth again. "Wow, way to let her take the fall."

"*Nick!*" Charlie and I both rounded on him as Jason's hand slammed down on the table.

"Fuck you! I keep hearing that you want my help, but what you're really asking is for a chair jammed up your ass."

"Guys!" Charlie cut in sharply before things could escalate. "Can I talk to Jason alone, please?" She gave Nick an ice-cold look and if I hadn't wanted to yank his hair out myself, I would've had to resist the urge to tell him to dress warmly on his way to the doghouse.

I pulled Nick's sleeve. "Come on. We'll go get some coffee at the counter." He must've figured out I'd unravel his entire shirt if I had to, because he slid out of the booth after me with one last dirty look at Jason.

"You're ruining everything," I whispered through gritted teeth as we slid onto stools at the diner counter. "This is exactly why you're not supposed to be here."

Nick scowled. "You think I like watching this? Why does it still bother her so much that this kid cheated on her? She has me now."

"Because his cheating isn't about you. And since she's not a mind reader and you haven't made a move since the promposal, how is she supposed to know she has you?"

Nick glared in the direction of Charlie's booth like he hadn't heard me. "Look at him. He's practically sitting on top of her."

"Coffee?" A waitress with a pencil behind her ear asked.

"Yes," I replied. "And maybe put some vodka in his."

I got a stony stare in response. "How old are you?"

"I was kidding."

"You'd better be."

I stuck out my tongue out at her backside as she retreated to the shelf for our coffee cups, then turned my attention to Nick.

"You are in so much trouble if you ruined this for us."

"I don't understand why you need his help. If he can get names of people who cheated, why can't he give them to this Eli kid and let him handle it?"

"Because they don't get along. If it were that easy, we wouldn't be here."

"And you didn't know whether to guilt him over Charlie or blackmail him, so you thought you'd try both?"

"Basically."

Nick shook his head. "This is getting ridiculous."

The waitress returned with our coffee, and not long after, Jason came up behind us. "I'll help," he said, yanking up the zipper to his coat. "As long as you delete those pictures right now."

"Great!" I whipped out my phone with exaggerated cheer. I had no problem deleting the pictures, because I'd already emailed them to myself. Dude must not have been the sharpest tool in the shed. "So we'll need you to get us the names of anyone you know or suspect has cheated. Then we need to find out where they're getting the information and who they're getting it from. We'll probably need to rig a fake purchase—"

"I know," Jason said, holding up his hand. "Charlie told me everything." He started for the door. "And I would've helped without the fucking extortion, just so you know."

"That's not what Eli said."

"Fuck Eli. Watch me prove in two minutes what that dumbass has been trying to do for two semesters."

Wow, this kid liked to drop f-bombs. With that last detonation, he turned and pushed through the doorway. Meanwhile, Charlie sat at the table fishing money out of her purse for the milkshake she'd ordered.

"I'll get that, Char." Nick leaped off his stool and scooted into the booth next to her, reaching for his wallet in his back pocket.

"I've got it." She didn't look at him.

"Put your money away. I'll—"

"*I've. Got. It.*"

Oh, snap. I turned away and tried to pretend I wasn't eavesdropping and peeking out of the corner of my eye.

"You're mad at me, aren't you?" Nick stopped tugging at his wallet and tentatively reached for her hand. She pulled it away.

"What were you thinking, Nick? My whole life depends on Jason helping Marisa and me right now, and if you don't like that, that's too bad!"

"I know, Char. I'm sorry—"

"It's nice that you're mad about what he did to me, but that's my battle, not yours."

"You're right. It's not, but—"

"It was hard enough for me to be nice to him without you goading him and making him angry. I know you did it because you're my friend, but asking me to the dance doesn't give you the right to treat me like your propert—"

He kissed her then. Dove right in and silenced her, midlecture.

I almost choked on my coffee. Apparently Charlie's f-bomb—*friend*—had finally catapulted him into action.

Nick pulled away and Charlie sat there, lips parted in stunned silence, searching his face. Nick wasted no time sliding his hand behind her neck and going in again. Despite my stomach's violent protest at watching my brother kiss my friend, I couldn't look away. Part of me was terrified she'd slap him and throw her milkshake in his face.

She didn't though.

She closed her eyes and melted into him, wrapping her hand around the forearm that held her. A second later, she threw all caution to the wind and slid both arms around him. Nick pulled her close against him with his other arm. It was the kind of kiss girls dreamed about: spontaneous and tender and passionate.

And completely disgusting, because it was my brother and my best friend.

The sound of our waitress slamming a bill on the table made them jump apart.

"Are we done here?"

Nick's shoulders shook with barely stifled laughter as Charlie ducked and giggled a "yes." The moment the waitress walked away, they fell on top of each other laughing like little kids.

I had to smile too. At least someone had their act together where relationships were concerned.

33

AS MUCH AS HE PROTESTED, I WOULDN'T LET NICK COME WITH ME FOR part two of my plan. It was something I had to do alone, and he'd almost foiled me once already. Luckily he was on such a high from his touchdown with Charlie that he gave up more easily than normal.

My next stop was Templeton High. If I was ever going to get to the bottom of all the drama, I had to infiltrate enemy camp. Knowing I couldn't keep it a secret much longer, I finally filled Charlie in on my suspicions about Kendall's role in the cheating scandal. I had to threaten to strand her at my house with Nick—who liked the idea just fine—before she calmed herself enough to promise not to hunt down Kendall and do anything rash. Like, say, dive-bomb Kendall into the snow and try to rip her hair out.

My palms were sweating against the steering wheel as I pulled into the Templeton parking lot. Charlie and I had called Mindy during the car ride and came up with an excuse to get me into Jordan's mother's classroom. But I hadn't thought much about what I'd do once I got there. It wasn't the best-laid plan, but I hoped my knack for thriving under pressure would kick in when I needed it most.

Phase One, the only phase that existed so far, was getting Mrs. Pace out of her classroom. I shuddered as Charlie and I headed up the steps where Jordan had almost kissed me the night of the football game, and then we pushed through the main doors. Charlie wished me luck as she slipped into an adjacent hall. With her head already on the chopping block, we'd decided against involving her in my scheme. Which was why Mindy stood on the other side of the vestibule waiting for me, like we'd planned. She made eye contact, then looked outside with no outward acknowledgment of me. I veered left into the main office, where a secretary with frizzy hair and an expression of boredom sat at the front desk.

"Hi, I'm here to see Mrs. Pace," I said.

"And you are?"

"I'm a friend of her son's. He asked me to drop this off to her." I held up the manila envelope stuffed with blank paper that I'd brought.

She propped her elbow up on the desk and opened her hand. "I'll put it in her mailbox."

Uh-oh.

"Um, I'd like to see her if that's okay. She's a friend of the family and Jordan made it sound important." I indicated the envelope again.

She picked up the phone like it weighed a thousand pounds and hit a button with the pen she'd been seesawing against the desk. "Mrs. Pace to the front office, please. You have a visitor."

Right on cue, Mindy walked past the glass frame of the office, spotted me, and doubled back, waving. She opened the door and poked her head inside. "Oh hey! You're the one looking for Mrs. Pace, right?" She turned to the woman at the desk. "She's talking to someone at the end of the hall, Judy. I'll escort her down if you want."

Judy made a twirling motion with her finger. "Follow Miss Kishore, please."

Phew. So far so good. I gave Mindy a thumbs-up near my abdomen as the office door closed behind me. Mrs. Pace wasn't really standing at the end of the hall, of course. That had been a ploy to make sure Judy didn't cancel the page. Now, if everything went the way it was supposed to, Jordan's mother should be on her way to the office while Mindy took me in the opposite direction to her classroom.

"Oh my God, Marisa, I'm seriously peeing myself. Do you really think you can do this without getting caught?"

I blew out a nervous breath and scanned the hall. At that point, I would've rather run head-on into Mrs. Pace than to happen upon Kendall. Only because I couldn't guarantee that I wouldn't finish what I started at TJ's farm.

At which point, I did run into someone. Or he ran into me. I couldn't tell. I only knew that my shoulder jostled and a second later, a guy was apologizing to me.

“I’m so sor—” He tilted his head in puzzlement. “Marisa?”

“Eli. Um, hi.”

“What are you—?”

“Get back under your toadstool, Jasper,” Mindy spat. I was shocked to hear the venom in her voice.

“—doing here?” he asked, ignoring her.

“Marisa doesn’t have all morning, and neither do I.” Mindy folded her arms across her chest.

Eli’s body tensed, like he was willing himself to keep cool in the face of Mindy’s rudeness. She’d heckled him at the football game, but I thought that had been for Jason’s benefit. In all honesty, she was embarrassing me.

“Long story.” I made my expression as apologetic as I could. “I’m sure you’ll hear about it later.”

He nodded. “Cool.” With an icy glance at Mindy, he started away. “Catch you later.”

“Mindy!” I said when there was some distance between us and Eli. “Why were you so rude to him?”

“He’s a shady little toad, Marisa. Do you know how many times he’s been caught lurking outside the girls’ locker room? Because it’s more than once. Don’t tell him anything about what we’re doing. He’ll probably muck it all up with his creep slime.”

“Geez, Greggie-George really buried that poor guy’s reputation, didn’t he?” It made me seriously reconsider whether or not it was wise to have Jason on our team. Although I supposed it was too late now.

"Who the hell is Greggie-George?"

"Never mind." I took her arm and started down the hall again. "If I can get my hands on Mrs. Pace's grade chart, that'll point me in the direction of the cheaters. I know I can figure out who's behind this."

I didn't dare tell her who I suspected. The fewer people who knew all the details, the better.

We stopped at the end of a long hall. It was quiet, save for the handful of early arrivals gathering books at their lockers. In another fifteen minutes or so, the school would be swarmed.

"Okay," Mindy said. "Her room is 302. I'll walk by and make sure it's empty, and then I'll give you the signal."

"And you'll text me if you see anyone coming?"

"You know the service here sucks. I'll do it, but you might be staring that bitch in the face by the time you get it."

I shrugged. "If that happens, I'll wing it. I've always thought I might be able to talk some sense into her anyway."

Mindy nodded. "All right. Good luck." She sauntered down the hall, slowing in front of room 302. After a quick scan, she glanced at me and gave a slight nod.

I hurried inside the classroom. It looked like any other chem class, with a whiteboard at the front and a tall desk that doubled as a podium. Oversized storage closets were on the side wall, windows at the back, and desks in between. I zeroed in on the podium.

Jackpot.

You'd think someone who'd had information stolen from her laptop wouldn't leave it sitting out in an empty classroom, but she had. It made me even angrier that she'd accuse Charlie of hacking it. If she did this regularly, anyone could come in and help themselves. Especially since the computer hadn't been idle long enough for the screen to go dark.

A pile of papers sat next to the computer, and a flicker of hope swelled in my chest. If she'd been entering grades before we interrupted then maybe…I maximized a tab at the bottom of the screen. A huge smile spread across my face. Right there before my eyes was the very information I'd been looking for: a spreadsheet of assignments labeled CHEM I PERIOD TWO and the grades each student had received. I whipped out my phone and took a picture, then skimmed the list for Charlie's name. It wasn't there. I tried the tab labeled PERIOD THREE and, finding nothing, moved on to PERIOD FIVE.

Zilch.

Crap, crap, crap. This wasn't Charlie's class. Precious minutes were slipping away and all I had were names of students from a course Charlie didn't even take. I minimized the page and hope sparked again when I saw another spreadsheet on the desktop labeled CHEM II. I clicked on it. And groaned when a box popped up asking me for a password. Unfortunately, Mrs. Pace was smarter than I gave her credit for.

I thought about typing in *Jordan* and saying a Hail Mary, but I didn't have time. My phone vibrated and I heard voices approaching, voices I recognized. I froze, then frantically looked around for somewhere to hide. The first storage cabinet I tried was locked.

Shit!

I yanked at the next one and found it not only unlocked, but with enough empty space to squeeze and contort my way inside. My body bent at angles that no one except a Cirque du Soleil performer should ever attempt, something hard and unyielding dug into my shin, and a nasty chemical smell went straight to my brain, but I managed to conceal myself behind the mostly closed door. I heard the classroom door slam shut.

"What are you doing here? Why aren't you at school?" Kendall's voice asked. From my hiding place, I saw a paper-thin slice of her profile.

"How am I supposed to go to school?" Jordan answered. "You put my picture all over your goddamn website and made me look like an idiot, and now you won't return my calls or texts. What did I ever do to you?"

"Ask your girlfriend."

"Girlfriend? Who? Marisa?"

Kendall bristled and even from my hiding place, I felt the tension crackling in the pause that followed. "No," she growled. "Sara. Or who knows? Maybe it *is* Marisa. Sara obviously thought so when she sent you those pictures."

"First of all, one of those pictures is fucking ancient, and second, how do you know about Sara?" I couldn't see Jordan, but the increasing volume of his voice told me he might lose his grip any second.

"You should know better than to leave your phone unattended, Jordan, especially if there's evidence on it."

"Evidence? It's called my goddamn life! And you know what, Kendall? I don't have a girlfriend at all, thanks to you. Marisa and I broke up months ago, the minute I knew I wanted to be with you."

I gasped. And then clamped my hand over my mouth and squeezed my eyes shut, praying they hadn't heard. I couldn't believe my ears. Jordan had left me for Kendall. She was the girl who'd broken his heart?

"I told you I loved you, and not only did you pick that toolbox over me, but now you're ruining my chances with anyone else!" Jordan continued.

"All I did was go through your phone because it was there, because you were stupid enough to leave it in my room. And what do I find but all these texts from *Sara*, some girl you never even told me about, accusing you of cheating with my best friend and sending you pictures to back it up."

I almost retched hearing Kendall call me her best friend. What a liar. But now I understood why Sara hadn't known about the pictures on the Busted website—Kendall had stolen them from Jordan's phone.

"I don't have to tell you about anyone!" Jordan's voice was shaking, and I knew the veins in his temple must've been bulging the way they did when he got angry. "You led me on, and you used me! Fucking used me! Give me one good reason why I shouldn't go to the—"

My phone vibrated with an audible buzz and I shrank even deeper into the closet.

God, Mindy, not now!

Kendall's head whipped toward the closet. The classroom door opened.

"Jordan? What's going on here?" Mrs. Pace sounded irritated. "What are you two doing in my classroom with the door shut?"

"Sorry, Mom. I had to talk to Kendall."

"Your father and I pay enough for your cell phone plan. How about using it? Kendall, would you excuse us, please?"

"Sure, Mrs. Pace."

Kendall didn't look back at the cabinet before skulking out of the room. A few seconds later, Mrs. Pace spoke again. "Jordan, would you care to explain why I got called down to the office to meet someone who claimed to be dropping off something for you, only to find there's no one there and my son is hiding in my classroom with one of my students when he's supposed to be at school?"

"It's senior skip day, Mom. I don't have to go in."

"Senior skip day in the middle of winter? Do you forget I teach high school? What did I tell you about getting involved with my students?"

"Kendall and I aren't involved, Mom. We're friends."

I heard clicking, followed by, "This isn't what I was working on. Why were you trying to get into my period one spreadsheet? Jordan, tell me what's going on here."

Oh crap. I hadn't closed out of the password-protected screen. Even if TJ was wrong and Jordan hadn't been involved with the cheating scandal, I'd just made things look very bad for him.

"Nothing's going on, Mom. I lied, okay? Kendall and I dated, but we're not anymore. We broke up. Happy now?"

Mrs. Pace sighed. "It's for the best, honey. You have plenty of girls to choose from at your own school."

I stifled a snort. Something about Jordan's mother wanting him to do his dirt on his own turf struck me as hilarious.

"Yeah, but..." Jordan mumbled. "I really liked her."

Oh *vom*. Pathetic.

Mrs. Pace laughed a little. "There are plenty of fish in the sea. Right now you need to worry about getting to school, buddy. Come on. I'll walk you out."

Their voices trailed off and I burst out of the closet, then out the door, nearly knocking over a pair of girls who were trying to come inside. Mindy appeared out of nowhere.

"Oh my God, Marisa," she said, wringing her hands. "Did they see you? I tried to warn you but it happened so fast!"

"I don't think they saw me, but I didn't find much. Get me out of here, Mindy."

I had to move fast. Wherever Jordan went next, I wanted to be right on his tail.

34

MINDY USHERED ME TO THE CLOSEST EXIT, WHICH, UNFORTUNATELY, was nowhere near the main exit, where Mrs. Pace had taken Jordan. By the time I made it back to my car, I knew I'd lost him. Not that it was going to stop me.

I turned on my car and pulled out my phone to call him.

"Jordan," I said when he picked up. "Where are you?"

"At school."

"Don't bother lying. I saw you. Where are you going?"

He let out an annoyed sigh. "To school. What do you want, Marisa?"

"The truth. Meet me in the woods outside the bio wing when you get there. We need to talk."

With that, I hung up and drove off.

Jordan was leaning against his car when I got to the parking lot. Scratches scarred his driver's-side door handle, what I assumed to be evidence of the break-in he'd been so upset about. Part of me, a huge part, actually, was shocked that he'd waited. I wouldn't have been surprised if he'd gone inside and blown me off, but when I pulled into a space and got out of my car, Jordan nodded wordlessly toward the woods, and I followed him.

We started down the trail used by the bio and geology classes for nature walks and plant and rock identification—and by kids cutting class for various acts of debauchery. Today it provided the perfect backdrop for confronting Jordan.

He brushed the remains of snow off a rock and sat down while I leaned against a tree.

"So tell me about Kendall," I said.

"You first."

"There's not much to tell. She's an old friend who moved away and came back."

Jordan cocked his head. "I'm not coming clean if you don't."

I rolled my eyes. "Fine. She told me TJ might've been cheating on her, so she asked me to find out. In the process, he and I kind of..." I trailed off, not sure how to end that sentence. Had we fallen for each other?

Jordan snorted. "She thought he was cheating on her?" He shook his head and smiled humorlessly.

"And that's funny because—she was cheating on him?" I

prompted. When his stare fixed somewhere around my feet and he didn't answer, I added, "With you?"

A few more seconds of silence followed. Then Jordan sighed. "I met her last year. I was helping my mom pack up her classroom for the summer, and Kendall was in the office trying to work out some issues with her schedule before she switched from regular to honors classes. She was slated to be in my mom's class, so the secretary introduced her. We all started talking, but my mom had some things to finish up, so I showed Kendall around the honors wing."

"Be still my freaking heart."

"Look, I didn't mean for it to happen, okay? I started thinking about her all the time and we exchanged numbers and she was the one who asked me to hang out first. She said she was seeing someone, but she made it sound like things were crap with TJ and it wasn't going to work out. The last time I fell that hard for someone, it was you."

He looked me in the eye when he said it, and his sincerity softened me a little. "Did she know about me?"

"Not specifically. She knew I had a girlfriend, but that was it. I had no idea you two knew each other until I saw that video on Charlie's phone."

"So you broke up with me, but Kendall still wanted to be with TJ," I said.

Jordan nodded.

"Then Sara thought you were still hung up on me, so she

stalked us and sent you pictures accusing you of cheating with me." He nodded again. "And when Kendall found them, she got jealous and posted them on her website." Another affirmation. "Boy, what a tangled web we weave."

He scoffed. "Tell me about it."

I took a breath and perched next to him on the rock. "I need you to be honest with me, Jordan. Did you give Kendall the data from your mother's laptop?"

His mouth dropped open. "W-what—where did you get that idea?" he finally stuttered.

"You said she used you."

"No, I didn't."

Oh crap. He'd said it, but to Kendall in his mother's classroom this morning, not to me. I'd just given myself away, but I didn't have time to worry about covering.

"Please, tell me. The only way to clear Charlie's name is to figure out who's really behind all this. If it's you, then I need you to help us."

Jordan shot to his feet. At the same time, the sound of voices met my ears and the ground crunched under footfalls that weren't mine or Jordan's. I swore under my breath and stood up as Mr. Leroche and his bundled-up bio class headed right for us.

But of course, it wasn't just any bio class. It was TJ's bio class.

He stood at the front of the group, hands deep in the pockets of his Paul Bunyan coat, dark curls framing his temples, and a look in his eyes like his worst suspicions had been confirmed. Like he'd been betrayed.

Damn it! How did this keep happening? I'd been alone with Jordan exactly twice in the past six months, and TJ had caught me both of those times. It was like he had radar or something.

"Mr. Pace, Ms. Palmera," Mr. Leroche called out. "Shouldn't you two be in class?"

"Shouldn't you be inside?" Jordan answered. "It's two degrees out here."

"Perfect weather for experiments on the effects of snow on plants." He flashed a smile. "Now get back to your lessons, or we'll be forced to experiment on the effects of escorting two class-skippers to the principal's office."

"Ha-ha-ha," Jordan deadpanned amid calls of "ooh!" and "burn!" from the bio class.

We shouldered our way through and I squeezed TJ's arm as I passed him. "We need to talk later."

He turned his head in my direction, but it was the only acknowledgment I got as I walked away. That two-second pause was all it took for Jordan to leave me in the dust.

"Wait up," I called. "We're not done."

"I'm done," he said over his shoulder. "I have to get to class."

"Jordan, wait." I jogged to catch up. "I know you could get in a lot of trouble if you're the one who leaked the info, but you can't let

Charlie take the fall. Kendall already sold you out on her website and she'll do it again if she has to. You might as well come clean now."

Jordan spun around as I caught up to him and I nearly bounced off his chest. "Listen," he hissed. "Whether I did or I didn't, I'll deny it no matter what anyone says. That's all you're getting out of me, Marisa. We're done talking about this."

He turned and shoved the school doors open, leaving me alone in the cold.

35

ALL I COULD DO WAS WAIT.

I'd sent Jason the pictures I took in Mrs. Pace's classroom with the hopes that *all* her data had been stolen and sold, not only the information from Charlie's class. In the meantime, I pulled up the Busted website every so often to see if it was still there. It was. I'd decided to give Kendall until 7:00 p.m. before I made her very sorry she'd ever messed with me.

Nick and I made sure to be in our pajamas by the time our parents came home from work. Not that I needed any help making my sick performance convincing when my anxiety levels had me looking as nauseated as I felt. I sat under a blanket with my knees curled to my chest, alternately rotating my bracelet from TJ around my wrist and tapping my thumb against the screen of my phone. Despite my request to talk, TJ hadn't been in touch yet either. I didn't even know if I still wanted to talk to him. How could I tell him Kendall had cheated with Jordan? *Should* I tell him? Did it make any difference at this point?

My phone buzzed in my hand and I jumped. The screen read *Message From Greggie-George*. I opened it.

Looked at your pics. Think I know where to start.

My heart gave a little leap of excitement. I couldn't help it. It was the first good news I'd heard all day. Aside from Jason agreeing to help and Nick finally getting with Charlie, but whatever. I typed in my reply:

Tomorrow, same place, same time?

A few seconds later, my phone buzzed again. Sounds good. Leave the asshole home.

I tried unsuccessfully to stifle a laugh. I was the one who'd shown Jason pictures of himself with his tongue down his girlfriend's throat, pictures I'd climbed his house to take, and it was Nick who'd gotten under his skin. I bit my lip to keep from smiling as I responded.

Might need to bring someone else. Someone less obnoxious.

Someone who'd caught me in one too many precarious situations with Jordan Pace and had no desire to talk to me. Except now I knew I needed to talk to him.

"Mom, I'm going to pick up my homework," I lied as I headed toward the door, coat in hand. I'd reached my limit with TJ's silence and texted him that I'd be at the barn in fifteen.

"You're sick. Can't your friend drop it off?" came the reply from the kitchen.

"I'm feeling better now. Besides, I've been stuck inside all day." I winced a little. Blatantly lying to my mother didn't come without guilt. "I won't be gone long."

My hand had gotten within a millimeter of the doorknob when the bomb dropped.

"Who's the boy in the video, Marisa?"

My arm fell to my side and I turned to see my mother standing in the door frame between the foyer and the kitchen.

"Who showed it to you?"

"I found it. I'm not as out of touch as you think I am."

I sighed and looked at the floor. "He used to be Kendall's boyfriend. He's not anymore."

"Because of what happened on that tape?"

I resisted the urge to point out that calling it a "tape" showed how out of touch she actually was. "No, Mom. They broke up before he asked me to the dance, but Kendall hates me anyway. So I had a date, but now I don't, and that's the end of the story."

"Not if I'm to believe that website."

That made my hackles rise. My grip tightened around my coat

and my teeth clenched. "You know what would be nice? If you *didn't* believe it." I threw the door open and glared at her over my shoulder. "You know me better than that, Mom."

I stormed out the door, wishing I could erase the moment I'd decided to spy on Jason Carvalho as easily as I'd deleted the evidence of it from my phone.

TJ's house was lit from within, but the barn was dark when I parked my car. I opened the door and got out, twirling his bracelet around my wrist while I frowned at the lifeless building.

He's not coming.

I was ready to gather my dejection and go when I heard a click behind me. I turned to see TJ close the front door of the house and head toward me, zipping his jacket. He stopped when he reached my car, staying near the passenger side with his hands shoved in his pockets. Like he didn't want to get too close to me. He didn't look angry. He looked…sad. Like he needed a hug.

So, before I really knew what I was doing, I walked around the car and gave him one.

"What's this all about?" he said as my arms wound around his neck.

"Just because."

"Because what?"

"Because sometimes people need a freaking hug, okay?"

He tucked his head into my shoulder and laughed as his hands settled around my waist, making me wish I didn't have such a bulky coat on. "You're right." The stubble on his jaw tickled my cheek when he spoke. The way my body reacted, it was more like he'd rubbed against me with a face full of electrodes. I closed my eyes, still tingling from the sensation, breathing in the scent of evergreens, freshly cut wood, and winter air that clung to his coat.

"This is nice," he said softly.

"*This* is nice." I pulled back and ran my palm against the growth on his face. "I kind of like you scruffy."

He let me rub his jaw for a moment, exploring his features like a curious child. Until my touch became anything but childlike. My fingers ran over his cheek, traced his chin, grazed his bottom lip. Our mouths were inches apart, and I wanted to know how the grit would feel against my lips and not just my fingertips. I knew that must've been reflected in my eyes from the way he looked at me. I held his face in my hands, and rose up on my toes.

"Marisa," he breathed against my lips. And then he stepped back. "This may be nice, but it's not why you asked me here."

I sank onto my feet, his rejection humming through my whole body. "Right." There was still the matter of that buzzkill. I pulled myself onto the hood of the car and sat on my hands so they couldn't get me in more trouble. "I got Eli's stepbrother to help us out."

"You did? How?"

"Long story. But he's meeting Charlie and me at Galaxy Diner before school tomorrow, and I think you should be there."

"I don't understand. After all this time, now he's willing to help?"

Tiny flurries began to settle in TJ's hair, and I held my palm to the sky. "Honestly, he seemed to like the idea of turning it into a pissing match between him and Eli. Like he wants to one-up him. So I'll leave it up to you to break it to Eli."

TJ shook his head. "Let's see how tomorrow goes first. I'm not sure how happy he'll be that his stepbrother had a change of heart."

"So you'll go?"

"Of course I will. See you then."

He started toward the house and I hopped off the car. "TJ, wait. There's one more thing I should tell you."

When he turned, he studied me for a second. "Why do I get the feeling this is the real reason you came?"

I gripped the hood on either side of me. "I think you were right. About Kendall getting the stolen data from Jordan. I think he gave it to her."

A derisive twitch twisted the corner of his lips. "Did you figure that out while you were sneaking off in the woods together?"

One mention of Jordan and the battlements were up again. It was like our moment ten seconds ago had never even happened.

I pushed off the car and my hands curled in indignation at my sides. "Yes, actually, I did. I followed him this morning to get answers, and I got them. Sort of." I sighed and leaned back. "Kendall and Jordan are a lot more involved than you think."

There. I said it.

TJ cocked an eyebrow. "Involved?"

"Involved. Like the kind of involved he and I used to be, but aren't anymore, no matter what you think. That kind of involved." Afraid I sounded a bit harsh for relaying bad news, I softened my tone and added, "I'm sorry, TJ."

He stared at the ground. "How long?"

"Since this summer. Jordan gave her the guided tour of Templeton and I guess the rest is history." I snorted. "Or maybe I should say chemistry."

He didn't react. He didn't even blink. He stood there, still as a statue, staring at the street. He stayed that way for so long that if he hadn't been standing upright, I would've thought he'd died. I opened my mouth to ask if he was okay, but the sound of laughter cut me off. His laughter. Hollow laughter that told me he didn't find this news funny at all.

"Unreal," he said. "Un-freaking-real. So she sent me up shit creek, hooked up with someone behind my back, and then hired a spy to find out if I was doing the same?"

"Um, allegedly."

He threw his hands in the air and shook his head, still smiling like he'd lost his mind. "Guess you can't make this shit up." He spun on his heels. "I have to go."

And then he was gone.

"Well," I said to no one in particular. "That went well."

36

BY THE TIME I GOT HOME, THE DEADLINE I'D GIVEN KENDALL HAD arrived. I sat in front of my computer and took a breath, praying this would be the time when I'd get the message *Page No Longer Available*.

But no. I was still there. Jordan was still there. Every nasty, untrue thing she'd said about me still glowed black and red on the screen.

That did it.

I grabbed my phone and started a new message to Kendall. To it, I attached the photos I'd taken of her opening the door to Jordan the night Charlie and I followed him to her house. Then I wrote: I think your principal might find these interesting.

Mere seconds later, I felt a buzz in my hand. I had her attention now.

You wouldn't.

A smirk curled on my lips. She'd seen the message between the lines, as clear and obnoxious as the word *Bitch* flashing on her godforsaken website: if I could prove her connection to Jordan, I could create a connection between her and the stolen information. I'd have to sell Jordan out at the same time, but after all the drama he'd caused in my life, I had a hard time feeling overly guilty. I hit the voice activation button on my phone and spoke my reply, hoping the haughty confidence in my words would somehow emanate from the screen when she read them:

"Try me."

Page No Longer Available

The next morning started with the sweet taste of victory. Kendall had texted me in the middle of the night to let me know that her miserable website had finally been stricken from the face of the internet. Unfortunately, it didn't stop the calls from coming, and I still had no idea how the pranksters had gotten my number. Two different blocked calls came in as I headed to the diner before school to meet TJ, Jason, and Charlie. And then a text from Kendall:

Are we good now???

I smirked as I put my phone back in my pocket without answering and headed across the parking lot to the diner. I'd reduced her to spaz-texting. Maybe this day would have lots of good things in store.

Speaking of good things, TJ pulled into the lot. I waved as he stepped out of the car.

"I'm glad you decided to come," I said.

He stepped up onto the sidewalk next to me. "Pretty sure I have more reason than ever to want the truth, right?"

Before I could get another word out, my phone buzzed again.

"You're being paged," TJ said. He held open the door. "Maybe we should get inside."

I followed him in, sneaking a peek at my phone as we walked.

It's not what it looks like with Jordan.

Sure it wasn't. I dropped my phone into my pocket as the hostess led us to our table, rather enjoying the knowledge that I had Kendall squirming.

Charlie and Jason were already seated at the round table in the middle of the dining room. Jason had an empty place setting in front of him, but Charlie was picking at a bagel with cream cheese. The girl needed to be fed every three hours or things got ugly.

"Charlie, Jason, this is TJ," I said as we pulled out our chairs. "You might remember him from his former Templeton status."

"I remember," Jason added, eyeing TJ. "Weren't you banging Kendall Keene?"

"She's my ex," TJ said with a snort.

I looked at Charlie. "And we think Kendall's the one who set up Charlie, and that she did the same to TJ when he went to Templeton."

"Kendall *Keene*?" Jason looked befuddled for a second, then tipped his chair on its hind legs and put his hands behind his head, letting out a low whistle. "Shit, man," he said to TJ. "That's rough."

Kendall's ears must've been ringing, because my phone buzzed again. I slipped it out of my pocket and held it under the table.

You're not answering me.

Holy hell. What Kendall lacked in people skills, she made up for in powers of deduction. Not.

"But I don't get it," Jason said. "Why would Kendall do something like that?"

I set my phone on the table. "That's the part we haven't figured out."

"Yes, we have. Because she's a bitch," Charlie said.

I gave her a look. "We don't know for sure that she's even behind it. All we know is that she and Jordan are apparently closer than we realized, and if anyone could be suckered by a pretty face, it's him." I looked at TJ through the corner of my eye, hoping he cared more about my silent apology for defending Jordan than what I'd implied about the nature of Jordan and Kendall's relationship. He looked down at the table.

"A pretty face and hot body," Jason added. Charlie punched his arm.

"The two of you can't say anything about this," I pressed. "It will never work if she gets wind of it."

Charlie gave a dismissive wave of her hand, having already sworn her silence. "So what next?"

Jason tipped his chair forward and put his phone on the table. "Let me answer that." He pulled up the photo I'd sent him of Mrs. Pace's spreadsheet and enlarged it. "This kid right here." He pointed to a name. "Chris Daly. He plays hockey with me, and he's been benched the last few games for academic probation. Everyone kept saying he's gonna be kicked off the team, and then all of a sudden he's not only playing, he's fucking starting. I heard him bragging about how he got off when they questioned him by memorizing a bunch of shit and making it look like he'd"—he raised his hands near his shoulders and made air quotes that looked more like walrus teeth given his long, lanky fingers—"been taking his studies more seriously."

"So you think he cheated?" I asked.

"Fuck yeah I think he cheated." Jason pushed his phone toward the center of the table and kicked his chair back again, this time with a definite air of irritation. "And I'm out of the starting lineup because of it."

"Perfect." I grinned, and then added, "No offense," when Jason scowled. "Now how do we prove it?"

TJ sat up straighter. "This is all well and good, but I don't see how we can use any of it in our favor. Jason, it doesn't sound like you and this Chris kid are friends, so why would he admit that he cheated, let alone tell you where he got the information?"

Charlie and Jason exchanged a look, then turned their stares on me. "Actually," Charlie said, "this is where Marisa Palmera, private eye, comes in."

"What are you talking about?" I shrank from her gleaming eyes, almost not wanting to know the answer.

Charlie hitched her head toward Jason. "We were talking before you got here, about how Chris…noticed you at some of the football games."

"Noticed me *how*? Like the way the jerks in the bleachers noticed me at the last one?"

"No, no." Jason shook his head and shot TJ a knowing look out of the corner of his eye. "This happened before any of that. It's more like the way T here notices you."

TJ squirmed in my peripheral vision, but I couldn't look at him. I sat forward and gripped the edge of the table. "Where are you going with this?"

"Well…we thought—" Charlie shot a desperate look at Jason and then at me. "Jason was saying the hockey guys go to Fred's Burgers after every game, and there's one tomorrow night, so maybe if we all went together, you wouldn't be alone, but you could still *get* him alone and—"

"No way."

"Yes way!" Charlie shot back. "With the right cover story, this could be exactly what we need."

"Um, this is exactly the worst idea ever. If he's seen me at the football games, he's probably seen me talking to you. And I'm sure he's seen the video of the promposal. Even if I wear a shirt cut down to my belly button and a skirt that skims my ovaries, he'll still realize what I'm playing at if I start chatting him up about hydrogen molecules."

Charlie shrugged. "So what if he's seen us talking? I give—gave—tours for the honors-program hopefuls all the time. So does the princess." She punctuated the word with a disgusted curl of her lip. "Pose as a potential transfer, and boom, there's how you know us." I started to protest, but she talked over me, anticipating my argument. "I was at the promposal because I got asked to the dance. I tossed Kendall's ass because she pushed you. There was an entire crowd of girls around us, and you don't need to explain everyone who brushed up against you that day." She put her hands in the air as if to say, *piece of cake*. "Let your lady parts do the rest."

"You wouldn't be so worried if you knew what Chris was like," Jason added. "He's not cheating in school because he's a fucking scholar. Kid's taken one too many pucks to the head, and the rest of the time, he's stoned."

"That could work," TJ mused. He'd been rubbing his chin—which he still hadn't shaved, and I wondered if it was specifically to drive me crazy—looking lost in thought, but his eyes came alive as he spoke. "You could tell him you're a junior and want to transfer to Templeton for senior year. I'll ask Eli to get—"

"If he's in, I'm out." Jason's chair tipped back and he folded his arms across his chest. "I'm doing this for Charlie, not him."

TJ studied him, like he was trying to decide if it was worth arguing. Then he nodded and turned to me. "Make it sound like you're really worried, because you know you'll have Jordan's mom for chem and you heard her classes are tough. See if he bites."

"And if he doesn't?" I asked.

TJ shrugged. "Show him your ovaries."

"Ha-ha!" Charlie clapped her hands. "Bracelet boy thinks he's a comedian." When I didn't laugh, she cleared her throat and grew serious. "Will you do it, Marisa? The worst that could happen is that he doesn't talk and we end up no closer to solving this than we are right now. We have nothing to lose."

I sank into my chair and rubbed my eyes while three more pairs stared at me, waiting for an answer.

Finally, I sat up. My eyes locked on Charlie's and I hoped she saw the message in them loud and clear: *you'd better appreciate this*.

"So?" she said.

"Guess I'd better polish up my ovaries."

37

IT SEEMED LIKE I BLINKED AND IT WAS TIME FOR THE TEMPLETON hockey game. Nick, Mindy, and Charlie went to the actual game together. I was too afraid of getting called into the Busted Bitch spotlight the way I had at the football game, so TJ and I planned to meet them at Fred's Burgers afterward.

We arrived early, slipping into a booth in the most out-of-the-way corner of the restaurant. Nick would text us when the game let out, and then I'd make my way to the counter at the front, where Mindy would join me and act like we'd met up by some happy accident. Charlie, Nick, and TJ would wait in the back booth until I signaled them to meet me in the parking lot. If Hockey Chris knew Charlie was standing trial for the cheating ring and he really was a part of it, we didn't want to give any indication that Charlie and I were together, let alone friends.

I got one more spaz-text from Kendall as the ice cream sundae I'd ordered arrived: Are you seeing TJ tonight?

I glanced at TJ, who sat across from me in a hooded sweatshirt, sipping a Styrofoam cup of tea. Leave it to him to order tea at a burger joint. I took great pleasure in writing back, yes.

"So," I said as I put my phone away. "You kind of killed the messenger the other day when I told you about Jordan and Kendall."

TJ shifted in his seat. "I didn't mean to. I just needed some time is all."

"I figured. That's why I haven't bothered you since we talked, but I really need to know—what do you think of all this?"

TJ folded his fingers together and ran his thumbs back and forth over his lips. A simple, absent gesture that made my own mouth go dry. "I think," he said, "that you really can't trust anyone."

I deflated. He still didn't trust *me* either. "That's not true. You can't let one bad experience ruin everything."

He raised an eyebrow. "*One* bad experience?"

I fidgeted. "Or two or three."

"If you really believed that, you would've gone to the game tonight instead of holing up at home and you wouldn't be wearing glasses and hiding behind your hair right now."

"Ha! Says the boy channeling the freaking Green Arrow with a hood that's about to swallow his head? I need to look different than I did in the promposal video—the less he associates me with it, the better our chances of getting what we need."

TJ pulled his hood closer to his face. "Exactly."

I sat up straighter. We were talking in circles, but I couldn't let him win this argument. "Fine. After tonight, I'm not going to let the website or anything that happened because of it bother me. No more hiding out like a coward. Kendall Keene is not going to get the better of me, and you shouldn't let her either. From now on, we look forward, not back. What do you think?"

For a second, our eyes locked. Then both our phones buzzed.

"They're on their way," he said, eyeing his screen. "Should be here in ten minutes."

I took a deep breath as my stomach lurched. The ice cream sundae suddenly seemed like a really dumb idea. I set down my spoon. Maybe it was nerves, but I couldn't stop making our conversation as uncomfortable as possible.

"So, the winter formal. I know you're not going with me, but you're still going, right?"

"No way," he said without hesitating. "People will throw eggs at us if we walk in like nothing happened."

"We're on Kendall's turf right now and no one is throwing eggs! She took down the website, you know."

"Yeah, after she got the whole world to believe we freaking victimized her. I can't go from one class to the next without getting dirty looks from at least three girls. And I wasn't going to tell you this, but someone posted your number in one of the boys' bathrooms. I had to black it out with permanent marker."

The blood drained from my face. "What did it say?"

TJ grimaced. "Nothing nice. Or true."

I sank into my seat. No wonder I'd been getting so many prank calls. People really knew how to take things way too far.

A second later though, my resolve returned. "I don't care." I sat up straight. "Like you said, none of it is true. Hiding out is only going to make us look guilty." I took off my glasses and threw them in my purse. "I have nothing to hide."

I picked at the stem of the sundae's cherry, waffling over whether or not I wanted to ask my next question. I decided to go for it. "How did you wind up as part of that promposal anyway? It's so not you."

He slouched in the booth and put his hands in the pockets of his sweatshirt. "Maybe not the dancing part, but that's why I stayed in the car. I wanted to ask you to the dance, but I didn't know how to do it. I've kept a low profile ever since Templeton accused me of cheating, but I was afraid I'd started crossing the line from self-preservation to hermit. So when Kevin asked if I wanted in, I said yes." He forced half his mouth into a smile. "So much for trying to branch out. That's what I get for being social."

"Come on, TJ. Anyone who matters knows you didn't cheat. How long can you let one stupid thing hold you back?"

He raised an eyebrow. "I don't know. How long can you?"

I had a feeling it was another Jordan jab, but I chose not to interpret it that way. I fluffed my hair, purposely pushing it away from my face. "Couldn't tell you. I don't let stupid things get the better of me."

Our phones buzzed again, my cue to get in position. I stood up and shrugged off my jacket with confidence I didn't feel. When TJ's eyes widened at the sight of my tight, low-cut violet shirt and then darted toward the window with a noticeable tightening of his jaw, I felt more than a little pleased.

"Do I look like royalty?" I asked.

He didn't look at me. "You look great. I'm sure he'll appreciate it." He swallowed hard. Then his chin jutted toward the parking lot. "I think I see Charlie's car. You should get going."

I sighed and slung my coat over my arm. "Wish me luck."

Finally, his eyes met mine again. "I appreciate this too. In case I haven't told you."

His sincerity caught me off guard after the defensive tone of our previous conversation, and I could only manage a feeble nod and some weird sound in the back of my throat before heading off.

I settled onto the stool as Nick and Charlie breezed in, Mindy following close behind. Nick and Charlie were holding hands, which was either adorable or gross. I still hadn't decided.

"Look at you, sexy mama." Mindy grinned as she hopped onto the seat next to me.

Nick's eyes bounced off my hint of cleavage—a big hint, admittedly—and he blanched. "Okay. I'm scarred for life now."

"So you know what to do, right?" Charlie whispered. Why she felt the need to lower her voice, I didn't know.

"We've only been over it a thousand times in a twenty-four-hour period, so yeah, I'm good."

She patted me on the back with her free hand as a waitress came over and took our order for sodas. A minute later the restaurant door opened again, bringing with it Jason and a group of whooping, fist-pumping boys wearing hockey jerseys over their clothes.

"They won," Mindy said. "Can you tell?"

"Which one is Chris?"

Just then, a guy with long blond hair jumped in front of the hostess, let out a loud celebratory yell six inches from her face, and picked her up and spun her in a circle.

Dear God in heaven. It was the California teleporter who'd worn shorts to the football game.

"That one," Mindy said wryly. "Lucky you."

"Wait!" I hissed when she started to walk away with her glass of Coke. "Where are you going? You're supposed to stay with me or I'll look like the most obvious plant in the world sitting here by myself!"

She grabbed my coat and draped it over the stool she'd vacated. "Here, say you're saving a seat because you're waiting for someone. We were talking about it in the car, and the fewer Templeton students he sees you with, the better. Sorry!"

She dashed off without another word, leaving me gaping after her. I swiveled back in time to see Jason elbow Hockey Chris in the ribs and nod in my direction. The grin that stretched across Chris's face when he spotted me made my stomach feel like it was being used for a game of cat's cradle. I ducked behind my hair, already abandoning my resolution of bravery. It didn't matter. Jason said something to Chris, and the next thing I knew, he was heading toward me.

"Geez," I muttered. "That didn't take long."

What did last way too long was the handshake Chris and I exchanged when he introduced himself. The touching palms, the eye contact, all of it was drawn out until I'd tripped over my own name and turned red for all the wrong reasons.

"Is this seat taken?" He straddled the stool to my left without waiting for an answer.

"Nope." I gestured to the coat on my other side. "I was supposed to meet a friend, but she's really late. Either she forgot, or I'm being stood up."

"Too bad," he said with a glint in his eyes that indicated he wasn't even a touch sorry. "Are you hungry? We can share some cheese fries, if you want." The waitress must've been hovering, because he looked past me and nodded.

Okay, then. I guess we're sharing cheese fries.

"I've seen you at my school before. But you don't go there." It was both a statement and a question.

"Not yet I don't."

His left eyebrow inched up. "Yet?"

Here was my chance to lay it on thick. "I'm thinking about transferring into the honors program. I've toured the school. I've gone to football games. I've even sat in on some classes." I wrapped a section of hair around my finger and twisted it near my collarbone, pretending not to notice when his gaze fell below my neckline. "But that's the problem. Those classes are *hard*. I'm not sure if I can handle it."

"Which one did you sit in on?"

"Chemistry. Mrs. Pace's class."

"Oof." A paper boat of cheese fries appeared between us and Chris wolfed one down. "She's tough."

"I know. And that class is a *requirement*. I don't know if it's worth having the program on my transcript if I end up with worse grades because of it."

"Tell me about it," he snorted through another mouthful of the fries I still hadn't touched. "Her class almost got me kicked off the hockey team, and I'm not even in the AP version."

"Really?" I made my eyes as big as they could go, hoping I looked superinterested or superhorrified. Or both. I released the piece of hair I'd been playing with, letting my hand trail down the front of my shirt. "Then I guess I'm better off staying where I am."

"Are you sure you're not saying that because you'll miss your boyfriend?"

Crap, crap, crap. Was he baiting me about the video? Had he meant

TJ? There were a thousand wrong ways to answer that question, so I stuck with the one truth I'd probably told him all night:

"I don't have a boyfriend."

"No?"

I held my breath, waiting for the guillotine blade to drop.

"Awesome."

A rush of elated air filled my lungs and I charged ahead, not wanting to get off topic. "Yeah. I really don't want to stay. Good nursing colleges are so hard to get into, and I know I'd be shooting myself in the foot if I don't transfer." I tossed my hair over my shoulder. "So what did you do? Did you get a tutor?"

He studied me for a second—well, parts of me, anyway—until a smile pulled at the corner of his mouth. Then he leaned in and whispered, "If you're that worried about it, I can help you out."

My heart picked up speed.

"You mean you know someone who can tutor me?"

He gave a quick check over both his shoulders and pulled out his cell phone. "Way better than that. I know someone who can get you the answers to all her assignments."

I did my best to look awed, even though my pulse was threatening to asphyxiate me. "You're lying."

"I'm not. Every test, every quiz. All at your fingertips." He held up his phone. "All I need is your phone number. My source will set the price."

I choked back a laugh. I couldn't believe he'd actually said "my source," like he was part of the FBI or something. Or that he didn't seem to think Mrs. Pace would be changing her lesson plans long before I "transferred." Jason had been right when he'd said chem wasn't the only reason Chris was on academic probation.

"There's a price?"

"Very reasonable. Really a small price to pay to guarantee your future." Now he sounded like a smarmy salesman. He leaned in again, holding his phone out to me. "So what's it gonna be? If it makes any difference"—he moved closer, until his breath tickled the crook of my neck—"I know *I'd* really like to see you at Templeton."

I cocked my head, forcing what I hoped was a calm, flirtatious smile. I reached for his phone.

"That makes two of us."

38

"YOU GUYS," I SAID BREATHLESSLY. "WE'RE IN."

Shortly after I'd given Chris my number, Charlie had sent a text telling me to meet them in her car when I finished. I'd hurriedly made an excuse about the "friend" I was supposed to meet having car trouble and said I had to go. A few seconds later I was squeezing into the back seat next to TJ and Mindy, while Nick and Charlie watched from the driver's and passenger's seats.

"Okay, we're all here," Mindy said as the door slammed behind me. "What happened? Did he say anything about the video?"

"If he's seen it, either it didn't connect, or he didn't care."

"He was putty in her effing fingers," Charlie said with a grin. "I can already tell." She held up her hand between the seats for a high five, and I humored her.

"Basically," I said. "Never underestimate the power of lady parts, I guess," I rambled off the condensed version of my encounter with

Chris, finishing with, "I had to give him my number, but I couldn't in case Kendall is his source. So I gave him Nick's instead." I shrugged at my brother. "Sorry, but that's the price of my particular brand of genius this evening. Now you're supposed to get a text from a blocked number telling me what to do next."

"Did you get it yet?" TJ asked.

Nick pulled out his phone. "Not yet."

"Then how do you know it wasn't a ploy to get your number?"

TJ turned to me. For a few seconds, the car went quiet except for the idling of the engine and the faint sound of the radio. Then a loud buzz reverberated through the interior. Nick held up his phone. Charlie leaned in to read.

"Put fifty dollars in an envelope with your cell number written on the outside. Leave it in the mailbox of the abandoned white house on Crabapple Road, #511, no later than nine p.m. Friday. More instructions to follow then."

"Crabapple Road," TJ murmured. "That's the street that borders the east side of the farm. My uncle's been trying to buy that property for almost a year now, but it's in probate. Kendall knew all about it."

We all looked at one another in silence.

"Holy shit," Nick said at last. "This is really happening."

It was happening, and fast. I don't think any of us had actually expected our plan to work, but we jumped into action nonetheless.

"We need to catch whoever picks up the envelope," TJ said. "One of us will have to be staked out at that mailbox at all times until someone comes for it."

"We should probably go in teams," Nick added. "I don't want Charlie sitting outside an abandoned house in the middle of the night all by herself." He caught the indignant look on my face. "Or Marisa."

I shoved his arm. "Nice save."

"Nick and I can take the first shift," Charlie piped up. "I'll put up the money." She held up her hand when the rest of us began to protest. "It's the least I can do. You guys have gone out of your way for me, and you have no idea how much I appreciate it."

"You'd do the same for us," Mindy said.

"Of course I would. I owe all of you so big for this."

"All right, Charlie, so you and Nick will take the first shift," TJ cut in, all business. "Say from nine to midnight? And then either Mindy and Marisa can take over, or I will. We'll rotate until the envelope is gone."

"Wait a minute," I said. "Why should you do a shift alone?"

"Uneven teams," he replied. "What else are we supposed to do?"

At that moment, a knock on the passenger-side window made us all jump out of our skin. I turned, clutching my chest, to see Jason bent outside Charlie's window, his face all but pressed up against the glass. Charlie jammed her finger down on the window button.

"Ass!" she said the minute the glass rolled past his eyes. "You scared the shit out of us!"

He stuck his head into the car. "Did you forget I'm in on this? I want to know what happened."

"We got the lowdown on one of the drop points. We were just saying that TJ needs a partner for his stakeout shift."

TJ's face fell. "No we weren't."

Charlie looked at him. "Yes we—" Her eyes widened as she realized TJ wanted to be alone in a car with Jason only slightly less than Nick did. "Um, I mean Mindy needs a partner. Or Marisa needs a partner." She turned back to Jason. "Either way. Are you in?"

He grinned. "You bet your ass I'm in."

39

CHARLIE MADE HER DROP-OFF AT 8:45 P.M. ON FRIDAY NIGHT. WE'D hoped that if she went as close to the deadline as possible, our "perp" would be waiting in the wings and we'd have an instant-gratification gotcha moment.

No such luck.

Crabapple Road was a dark, narrow, sparsely populated street, and even though the abandoned house sat close to the road, the property was nestled into the woods, which made perfect cover for a stakeout. We'd decided Charlie's car would be the official observation deck for the night. She and Nick drove it to the lookout point, and then the rest of us would meet TJ at his barn prior to our shifts, and he'd drive us over on his tractor. I told my parents I was sleeping at a friend's house, and since Mindy and I catnapped on her couch until my shift started at midnight, it was sort of true.

I'd finagled it—okay, begged, pleaded, and bribed Mindy—so

TJ and I would take the midnight-to-three-in-the-morning shift together, and she'd be with Jason from three to six. It cost me an IOU for three Fudgie's ice cream sundaes and a pair of handmade earrings, but it was well worth it to get some alone time with TJ.

"Hey," he said when he opened the barn door. "Ready for this?"

I put my camera down on his worktable, where a half-sewn piece of cowhide lay open. He must've been working on it for a while, because the space heaters had kicked in enough that I needed to unwind my scarf. "Ready as I'll ever be, I guess."

TJ closed the door, a contemplative look on his face. Like he was about to give me bad news. But then he stepped over and picked up the tasseled ends of my scarf, winding them around his hands. I went completely still.

"Listen, I want to apologize for the other night. I didn't mean to take it out on you when you told me about…you know."

"I—we talked about this. It's fine."

"It wasn't fine." He let the tassels slide through his fingers, then wound them around again. This time, he pulled me closer. "Thanks. For doing all this. It may not change anything for me, but at least I'll have answers."

There were a million ways I wanted to respond, but before I could execute even one, the barn door flew open, and our heads whipped toward it. Jason stood in the door frame, blinking like a doofus.

"Do I have the wrong time?"

"*Yes*," I said, not bothering to hide my annoyance as TJ dropped my scarf and put his hands in his jeans pockets.

Jason ambled inside and closed the door behind him. "That sucks. Now what?"

"Well, I guess you can go home. Your shift doesn't start for another three hours."

His face fell. "I can't go home now! I'm all hopped up on coffee! I'm ready to bust some ass!"

TJ and I exchanged looks. Looks of *dear God, are we really stuck with this overcaffeinated goon for the next three hours?*

"If you stay with us, you still have to do your shift with Mindy," TJ warned. "You're not leaving her in the woods by herself."

Jason rubbed his hands together and looked back and forth from TJ to me, grinning like a Cheshire cat. "Let's do this!"

Yes, we were stuck with him. We really were.

TJ drove us through the winding dirt paths that separated acres of pines from firs as leftover snow crunched beneath the tires and evergreen-scented air chilled our lungs. He must've known the farm like the back of his hand, because the headlights barely illuminated two feet in front of us but he maneuvered through the trails without missing a trick. Or maybe my night vision had suffered on account of hiding behind my glasses so often lately.

He cut the engine a good fifty feet from the road and hopped off the tractor. "Come on," he said. "We'll walk from here in case anyone's coming."

I held my camera with one hand and TJ grabbed the other to help me down. He didn't let go right away when my feet hit the ground, and I wished like anything I could make Jason disappear.

"This place looks like a fucking bomb went off!" Jason said, effectively reminding me that he wasn't going anywhere. TJ dropped my hand.

"Yikes," I said as we approached the overgrown property. "That house is scary."

A dilapidated roof had come into view as we reached the last hill belonging to Maple Acres before it descended into Crabapple Road. The moon glowed full and bright above the house, and while it cast some much-needed light, it also lent it an eerie, horror-movie quality to the scene that made goose bumps rise on my skin. Broken shingles with chipped, peeling paint comprised the rest of the house. Black shutters hung at odd angles around the windows, some of which were broken. The front porch sagged under its own weight. Right near the street stood the black mailbox, looking like it had been on the receiving end of more than a few drunken swats from the baseball bats of bored, moronic teenagers.

"Shit," Jason said. "At least they didn't ask us to bring the envelope inside."

We were crossing the street when Nick and a rumpled-looking

Charlie emerged from the woods. I had to wonder how much time they'd actually spent watching the house.

"Nada," Nick announced. "I think three cars have driven by the entire time we've been here."

"Could you see the car in the woods?" Charlie asked. When we all agreed we couldn't, she squinted at Jason. "What are you doing here?"

"Don't worry. He'll be here for Mindy too," TJ replied. "Let me give you guys a ride back to the barn and we'll take it from here."

Charlie and Nick wished us luck, then disappeared across the street with TJ.

"Ugh, it's freezing in here!" I said as I slid into the passenger seat of the car and Jason hopped into the back. "I hope TJ brings back some hot chocolate."

He poked his head between the seats. "Wanna do some exploring? I bet there's all kinds of neat shit in that house."

"Neat shit like rats and cockroaches. I'll pass."

"Come on! We can't just sit here for three hours!"

"Um, you're sitting here for six. So why don't you stretch out back there and go to sleep, that way you're not totally useless by the time Mindy gets here?"

We continued like that until TJ came back. At one point Jason even got out of the car and tiptoed toward the house, looking back at me and smiling every so often as I furiously hissed his name and demanded he get back inside the car. Apparently caffeine turned him into a damn two-year-old. TJ at least wrangled him into the car with the steaming cups of hot cocoa he'd brought, legitimately having read my mind, but once he did, we both wished he hadn't.

"So," Jason said. "You two…?"

"No," we said in unison.

"Bullshit. I saw the promposal video. That was badass, T. You're a pimp."

TJ leaned against the headrest and closed his eyes, looking like he had a massive headache. "I'm not a pimp."

"So are you two in love? Gonna get married and make babies and shit?"

TJ and I looked at each other. A hint of a smile pulled at his lips. I felt his hand creep closer to mine until our pinkies touched. I hooked my fingers around his and smiled back. He snorted and his face split into a grin. Within seconds, our shoulders shook with uncontrollable snickers.

"Aw, I knew it!" Jason clapped TJ on the shoulder, jostling his hand away from mine. "You guys can't fool me."

Laughing had lightened the mood, and some of the tension eased out of my bones. I shifted to face him. "So what's Kelly doing tonight?"

He leaned back and put his hands behind his head. "Whatever it is, I'm sure she wishes it was me."

I rolled my eyes and laughed again. Jason was something else, and this was going to be a hell of a three hours.

Or ten minutes, as luck would have it. All three of us went still as the rumbling of an approaching car grew louder. We leaned forward in our seats, straining to see through the surrounding overgrowth. Headlights illuminated the clearing around the house for a few breathless seconds. Then they dimmed. I readied my camera.

Through the trees, I saw a car pull up next to the mailbox, the headlights on low. I snapped pictures as fast as my fingers would allow. The driver's side door opened and the interior light went on. Inside our car, TJ gripped the steering wheel. His whole body tensed.

"Can't be," he said under his breath.

"What the…?" Jason shouldered his way between us until he was practically in my lap.

Then I saw it. The hunched, hooded figure that emerged from the car. The familiar slouch of the tall, slim frame.

The silver heart pendant hanging from a chain around the rearview mirror.

I lowered my camera.

Jason squeezed his eyes shut and opened them again, like he wanted to make sure they weren't playing tricks on him. I snapped another picture as proof of the same. It wasn't a trick.

"Shit," he breathed. "It's fucking Eli."

BEFORE I KNEW WHAT HAD HAPPENED, TJ THREW OPEN THE CAR DOOR and bolted.

Jason and I exchanged the briefest look before we did the same. Eli barely had five seconds to react by the time he heard TJ's footsteps pounding toward him. His face still registered surprise and he hadn't yet removed his hand from inside the mailbox when TJ pounced on him.

Eli's hood slipped from his head as TJ grabbed fistfuls of his sweatshirt and shoved him against the car.

"*You're* the one behind this? All this time it was you? You fucking let me blame Kendall?" With each question, he rammed Eli into the car.

"It's not what it looks like, man!" Eli tried to duck away from TJ's grip. TJ slammed him so hard that his head ricocheted off the car.

"It looks to me like you're taking money for stolen information while someone else gets the blame. Sound familiar, Eli?"

In a flash, Jason stood between them, his forearms the only thing preventing TJ from beating Eli to a pulp. "Calm down, T. It's not worth it." He locked an arm against Eli's neck and, with a menacing expression I never would've imagined him capable of, got right in his face. "I always knew you were a fucking weasel," Jason spat.

"Marisa, call the cops," TJ said. I'd been standing there, frozen, terrified, almost like I was watching the scene from someone else's body. When TJ spoke to me, I startled. I was actually here, watching this happen. I snapped one last picture before dropping my camera on its strap around my neck and fumbling for my phone.

"No!" Eli called. "I-I'll go the school board and testify. I'll make them take it off your record. Don't get the cops involved!"

I looked at TJ, phone in hand, waiting for him to tell me what to do.

"All this time you've been letting me think you were trying to help me," TJ seethed. "Making me meet you all over Monroe to give me bogus information and tell me you hit another dead end and making it sound like we couldn't get Jason involved because he hates you."

Jason's glare remained unyielding. "That part is true."

"I'm sorry, man." Eli grimaced against the weight of Jason's arm. "My mother paid good money to make those charges go away. I couldn't let you find out anything else about what happened."

"*What?*" TJ strained and bucked against Jason's arm. "You

were accused too?" He shook his head and corrected his error. "You were *caught*?"

"I *knew* something funny was going on!" Jason said. "You're running a fucking underground cheating ring, and you went running to Mommy about the stupid graffiti prank?" He shoved Eli against the car and pinned him with his elbow. "This kid's mother is like *Mommie Dearest* meets Norma Bates dipped in Judge Judy. Such loving fucking additions to our household."

"I didn't get caught," Eli said, as if Jason hadn't spoken at all. "Someone ratted me out. Someone who still hasn't admitted to it." He threw Jason's elbow off his chest. "I thought I could help myself while I helped you."

TJ rammed his hands through his hair. "Except that you were never helping me. I had my ass handed to me at a hearing, and you were in the clear because your mother shopped you a deal?" Before Eli could get a word out, TJ exploded. "You destroyed my relationship with Kendall, you know that?" As he spoke, a flash of headlights came into view down the road. "You made me think I couldn't trust her and the whole time I shouldn't have trusted *you*."

A sharp twinge pierced my chest. The pained look on TJ's face as he talked about his relationship with Kendall being destroyed stung worse than the winter cold. After all, if his relationship had stayed intact, he never would've met me. I'd never stopped to think he'd been happy with Kendall and wanted to stay that way. Tears pricked my eyes. Maybe he wasn't over her. Maybe I'd stumbled upon the real reason he kept hesitating with me.

Jason loosened his grip as headlights approached, still keeping a hand on the shoulder of each boy but in a less threatening way. He was probably thinking the same thing I was: if the passerby saw them fighting, we might end up with cops on the scene regardless.

Eli straightened his sweatshirt and flipped the hood back over his head. A snakelike smile spread across his face as the car slowed to a stop on the other side of the street. The fact that he looked so smug when the rest of us were so confused made my stomach writhe.

"You give Kendall way more credit than she deserves, man," he said.

The timing couldn't have been more perfect. Because the person who stepped out of the car was none other than Kendall Keene.

She emerged slowly and stood by the door, holding on to it like she thought she might need to use it for protection.

"What's going on here?" she asked, her eyes darting from me to the boys.

"You tell us," I said.

Eli strutted over to Kendall. "She's here to collect her half of the money." He tried to wrap an arm around her shoulders, but she promptly shoved it away, causing the smug smile to drop off his face. “Because God forbid if she’s seen talking to me in school,” he added bitterly.

“You—you two are in this together?” TJ stammered. In the moonlight, he looked pale.

Eli made a sweeping gesture toward Kendall. “Ladies and gentlemen, meet my lovely partner.”

Kendall shut the car door with a weak, defeated click.

“Partner?” TJ spit the word out like a mouthful of blood. He threw his hands up. “Does someone want to tell me what the hell is going on here?”

“TJ,” Kendall whimpered as she crossed the street. “I never meant for you to get involved in this. I swear.”

“And what about Charlie?” I asked.

“She deserved it,” Kendall snapped.

“She *what*?”

Kendall looked at me and then back at TJ. “You know how hard it was for me when I transferred to Templeton.”

TJ jerked his shoulder away from Jason’s hand. “No kidding. I was the one who had your back every time someone made you cry, remember?”

“I know. You were so good to me, but everyone else was awful. Horrible. There were mornings where I made myself sick crying because I didn’t want to go to school and face whatever those jerks were planning to put me through." Her voice cracked and she turned to me. "And your perfect, know-it-all Charlie was one of them."

I clenched my teeth. "I don't believe you."

"Oh, believe it. Ask her about the time her bitch squad took my bathing suit top and my clothes while I was getting changed for swim class. Or the time they stole a dissected cricket from the bio room and left it in my notebook. Or maybe she'd like to tell you about the rotten little present they left in the trunk of my car." Her bottom lip trembled and she took a jagged breath, but I still couldn't believe a word out of her mouth. Wouldn't believe it. "I know she was jealous. My test scores were better than hers for the honors program, but the school still wasn't going to let me in for senior year. They insisted all the spots were full, but I knew they were playing a bullshit game of favorites. Everyone at Templeton was determined to see me fail."

"Why does that matter?" TJ asked. "It evened out in the end. You got in when someone dropped out."

And then it clicked. *I'd* been accepted into the honors program. I'd waited until the last minute to decline my spot in the hopes that my parents would change their mind about sending me to Templeton. Kendall had gotten in because *I* dropped out.

"I got in, but I needed to stay in!" Kendall cried. "I had to prove that I wasn't some squeaky wheel who'd been a waste of grease. But I started having trouble with my schoolwork. I'd never been the best at math or science, but the classes were impossible and I was drowning.

I needed to get back on top somehow, to prove to everyone that they weren't better than me. I was terrified of failing."

Terrified of failing were the exact words TJ had used to describe Kendall. But he didn't appear to have much sympathy as he said, "So you took my keys and stole Mr. Katz's lessons?"

Kendall shook her head. "No. Eli did."

All eyes turned to Eli. He stuck his hands in his pockets and looked at the ground. "I needed the grades," he mumbled. "It was nothing personal, man."

"Nothing per—right. Okay." TJ ran his hand through his hair. "This keeps getting better."

"How did you get one of my hearts?" I broke in, gesturing toward his car. The door was still wide open with the interior light on, and the undecorated heart hung in plain view.

Eli exchanged a look with Kendall. "I found it in the trunk of Pace's car."

"*You* broke into Jordan's car?"

Kendall didn't look at me when she added, "Eli didn't trust me to get what we needed."

"The system wasn't always so complex," Eli said before I could respond. "The first time around, I swiped a list of student phone numbers from the guidance office. I sent blocked texts to a bunch of Mr. Katz's students, anyone with less than a C average. I gave all of them a problem from the next test to prove I was legit and told them they could buy the rest. They'd leave the money in an unused locker in B wing, and I'd drop the answers in theirs."

"I caught Eli making a pickup one day," Kendall continued. "And I told him I wanted in, or I'd rat him out—"

"Which you fucking did anyway," Eli muttered.

"You have no proof of that," Kendall snapped.

A smile slithered across Eli's face. "You know what they say, doll. Keep your friends close..." He didn't need to finish the saying: *keep your enemies closer.*

Kendall turned back to TJ, desperation in her eyes. "I needed the grades for the honors program, and on top of it, my dad had taken a big cut in pay when we transferred back. He wanted me to get a job and start paying for some of my own expenses, but I needed to concentrate on my grades. It seemed like the perfect solution." She twisted her fingers together. "I had no idea you'd end up getting the blame, TJ, I swear."

"But when I did, you never came forward."

Kendall looked at the ground. "I was finally starting to pull myself up from the bottom of the barrel. I couldn't go back. I'm sorry, TJ. I never meant for you to get hurt."

TJ swallowed hard. "Is that what you told yourself when you used Jordan Pace to sleep your way to the top?"

Kendall's head snapped up and she looked at me, wide eyed.

I folded my arms across my chest and glared at her. "Yes, we know all about it, so don't even bother trying to say it wasn't what it looked like. Jordan gave you a tour of the school; you gave him a tour of your pants. Now what we need to know is *why*."

Kendall's face crumpled and she covered it with both hands. Her shoulders shook with great, heaving gasps. "I was s-scared. Scared of being a nobody. I needed something in my back pocket, s-some kind of insurance that I'd still come out on top, even if I was dirt on the bottom of everyone's shoes. I needed to know someone could still love me, because I was so afraid TJ didn't anymore."

I rolled my eyes. "So you pretended to care about Jordan, got him to hack his mother's laptop, and then framed Charlie for the whole thing?"

Jason whistled. "This is fucked *up*."

Kendall dragged her fingertips across her cheeks, leaving mascara-tinged streaks in their wake. "I overheard Charlie saying that she'd fixed Mrs. Pace's computer. Up until she said it, I'd never intended to frame her, but she made it too easy. I didn't want to be the only suspect if things went wrong again. So I told Eli we'd keep splitting the profits if he made the drop-offs. We moved them off-site to keep from getting caught." Her face puckered with a defeated sniffle. "And here we are."

I glared at her. "So when you asked for my help, you never really thought TJ was cheating. You suspected he knew about you stealing the tests and used me to see if he was getting close to the truth."

She nodded. "Yes. I also suspected that Eli was playing both sides of the fence." She shot him a dirty look. "Then you told me someone had shown up at the barn while you were there, and the more I thought about it, the more sense it made. The day you jumped on me like a wild beast and asked if I had anything to do with Charlie getting in trouble, I knew I was right." She punched Eli's shoulder. "You were supposed to keep TJ off our trail, not cover your own ass while you sent him after me."

Eli rubbed his shoulder and cursed at her under his breath.

"Kendall." I said her name in the most condescending tone I could muster, complete with a saccharine smirk. "You can punch whoever you want, point fingers at anyone—whatever makes you happy. It doesn't change the fact that you made your bed and now you'd better change the sheets." I never thought one of Charlie's insane sayings would come in handy, but it fit and I liked it. I held up my camera. "Otherwise, these will be everywhere."

For a second, her mouth formed a stricken O and her pallor grayed. Then she straightened and struck back. Or tried to. "Marisa, you can't. There's no way to undo this, not without getting me *and* Jordan in serious trouble." She mimicked my smirk. "And we both know Jordan holds a very special place in your heart."

"Mmm." I rested my camera on my shoulder and pretended to contemplate her statement. "Yeah, not as special as you think." I focused the camera lens. "So I guess I still have one more question."

Kendall's lips pressed into a thin line and she folded her arms across her chest. "What's that?"

I lined up my shot. "How did it feel to have *my* leftovers?"

The camera clicked, preserving her priceless expression forever.

41

I WAS TOO WIRED TO SLEEP WHEN I GOT HOME THAT NIGHT. NOT TO mention that my phone was chiming every five seconds with texts of disbelief from Charlie, who wanted details, pictures, and my opinion on what our next step should be. I didn't have all the answers for her, though. So I sat down in front of my laptop and started to write instead.

Not even a minute later, the sound of footsteps scuffling down the hall ended with my door being pushed ajar.

"Marisa?" my mother said, her eyes squinty with sleep. "I thought you were staying out tonight. Are you okay?"

"I'm fine, Mom. We figured out who framed Charlie for cheating."

Her eyes went round. "Who? And *how*?"

I grabbed my camera and handed it to her, the screen displaying the last picture I'd snapped of Kendall. "That's who. How is kind of a long story."

Mom's face went from shocked to disgusted over the illuminated screen. “That *troublemaker*,” she spat. She twisted the camera at different angles. “Where were these taken?” Before I could stop her, she jabbed at a button, presumably trying to scroll through the photos. The camera turned off instead.

“Whoa, Mom, hand over the very expensive piece of technology before something gets erased or broken.” I took the camera from her and placed it next to me.

“She was responsible for that video too, wasn’t she?”

“The one where I ‘stole’ her boyfriend? Yeah.”

“Marisa, I hope you know I was only trying to get at the truth when I questioned you. You’ve been distant and secretive, and you were so disappointed about Lehigh—I wanted to know what’s been going through your mind.”

“Don’t worry about Lehigh. If I’m meant to go there, it will all work out. If it doesn’t”—I shrugged—“then it doesn’t. There are plenty of other schools.”

“I know you’ll be amazing no matter where you end up. I’m just sorry we couldn’t make it easier for you.”

I stood up and wrapped her in a bear hug. “Mom, if I’m amazing, I’m pretty sure it’s inherited.” We squeezed each other for a minute, then I dropped back into my desk chair. “Can I tell you the whole story in the morning? It’s been a crazy night.”

“You’d better.” With that she blew me a kiss and closed the door behind her.

I turned to my computer. I needed to get this out while it was still fresh in my mind. All I had was a heading, but I had a feeling the rest would write itself.

For the Love of the News: BUSTED: How Chasing Cheaters Changed My Life.

"Can you believe this?" Charlie clacked into my dining room in her silver high heels and threw a copy of the *Herring Cross Herald*, our town newspaper, onto the table. The headline read: Templeton Chemistry Teacher Drops Charges Against Student.

It was the night of the winter formal and Charlie had come to our house to take pictures before the dance. She and Nick were going to ride together, and I'd insisted on taking my own car in case I wanted to cut out early. Tonight I'd be Marisa Palmera, Big-Ass Third Wheel.

I crossed the room and picked up the paper. I already knew, of course, that Jordan's mom had dropped the charges. I had no idea it had made the paper though.

"'Camilla Pace has issued an apology to Templeton High senior Charlotte Reiser after accusing her of stealing information from her laptop,'" I read aloud. "'A sudden spike in student performance led Pace to believe that Reiser, who'd assisted with removal of a virus from her laptop, had consequently accessed tests and lesson plans, and distributed them to other students on campus. 'I owe Miss Reiser an apology,' Pace stated earlier this week. 'As it turned out, the virus on my laptop caused information I'd saved in email drafts to be disseminated to my list of contacts, some of whom were students. The timing was an unfortunate coincidence, and I'm very sorry for my mistake.'"

"Goodness, Charlie," my mother said. "I can't believe she put you through such an ordeal."

Charlie nodded and gave a shrug. "It's over now."

"Thank God for that." She lifted her camera and pushed the button, but nothing happened. "Girls, I'll be right back. My battery is dead." She winked at me before adding, "No one is going anywhere until I get some pictures of my daughter the detective."

She scurried out of the room and I threw the paper down. "Ugh! Excuse me while I go vomit. I can't believe she lied on record."

"I know." Charlie took the paper and frowned at it, her foot tapping against the floor.

"You're still thinking about what Kendall told me that night, aren't you?"

She looked up at me. "You have no idea how bad I feel, Marisa. I might not have been the one to put the mouse in her car or steal her clothes, but I knew it happened and I knew the people who did it and I did nothing about it. I was too afraid I'd get the blame." Her lips turned down. "Maybe this was fair payback."

"Payback implies you did something wrong, and you didn't," I said.

"I could've done something *right*, and I didn't do that either."

"True. But Kendall told me once that she'd said and done things to me when we were younger that she wasn't proud of. She could've learned from her mistakes, but she continued to trample anyone who got in her way instead. Even people she claimed to care about."

We'd let Kendall and Eli go the night of the confrontation with an ultimatum to turn themselves in by Monday morning or we'd release our pictures to everyone and their mother. By Sunday night, Mrs. Pace had called Charlie at home, begging for forgiveness.

Charlie straightened. "You're right. Kendall can go cry in her effing gold-spun sheets, and *Camilla* can kiss my ass. The lengths she went to for her precious baby are gross. Those asses got away with murder."

"Not surprising," I said. "This is the same woman who doesn't care if her son sleeps with everything that walks, as long as he does it at his own school. I still say we won though. I have the pictures and if we ever need to make their lives miserable, I've got the power."

Charlie perched on the edge of a dining room chair like she was afraid to wrinkle her silky emerald-green dress. "I don't even care that they got away with it. It's not like I expected people to come forward and admit they bought the tests. It's easier for everyone this way, and I got a public apology. We all win, as far as I'm concerned."

"Except for TJ," I said. "He'll never get an apology for what happened to him."

"He's really not coming tonight?" Charlie asked.

I looked down at my sparkly, black stilettos. "I guess not. We haven't talked much since that night." At all, really. Ever since he'd blasted Eli for destroying his relationship with Kendall, I couldn't stop picturing them as a happy couple. Laughing. Holding hands. Kissing. Other things I didn't care to think about. He hadn't wanted to give up on her. Most likely because he hadn't wanted to give her up.

Charlie tapped a manicured nail against her hip. "You know where I stand on this. You're being a baby."

"Let it go, Char."

The sound of the bathroom door being thrown open made our heads turn toward the stairs. Nick came bounding down in his tux, smoothing his hair along the way.

"Two women, both ready before you," I said. "That should tell you something, Nick."

I don't think he heard me. He came to a halt at the bottom of the steps and his jaw dropped. That moony Charlie Face came out in full effect, and I half expected him to start drooling like a Saint Bernard. Charlie stood and smoothed her dress, giving him a suggestive once-over before walking over to him and winding her arms around his waist. You would've thought they were the only two people in the room.

My mother came over to my side. "Are you used to this yet?"

"Nope. I'm still surprised I didn't go into hysterical blindness when I saw them kiss."

"I heard that," Charlie laughed.

Mom leaned in, pretending to fix my earring. "You know I never had anything but faith in you, right?" she whispered.

I nodded.

She gave my cheek a quick kiss before trilling, "Okay, kids! Places, please!"

We obliged my parents with smiles and poses, and then it was time to go.

"Oh crap," I said. "I left my clutch in my room. Nick, can you go get it? I already survived one trip down the stairs in these shoes. I don't want to tempt fate."

"I'll get it." Charlie started toward the steps. "We wouldn't want Nick to slip and fall on his hair gel or anything."

"Hating on my hair won't make it less awesome." Nick grazed the sides of his freshly cut do with his fingertips and grabbed Charlie's shawl off the dining room chair. "I'll bring this out to the car."

A minute or two later, when my bedroom remained suspiciously quiet and I was about to send my mother in after Charlie, I heard, "Hey, Marisa?" I looked up to see Charlie peeking over the stair rail, her hands behind her back. "I can't find your purse. I think you should come up here."

"What are you talking about? It's right on the bed."

"It's not. Can you come up here?"

"Are you blind? Go back in my room and see if it fell between the bed and the wall. I'm telling you, it's there."

Charlie stamped her foot and let out a frustrated grunt. "I wanted to talk to you about *this*." One hand came out from behind her back, brandishing something I'd almost forgotten I made. Something I never intended for anyone else to see. I bit my lip.

I stood up, but she was already clomping down the stairs. Her other hand was curled around my "lost" clutch.

"Come on," she said, cocking her head toward the front door. "Let's go." But when the door opened, her car was no longer sitting beside mine in the driveway. "I texted Nick to say we'd meet him there," she said before I could get out the question. "You and I have a stop to make."

I peered through the window in the passenger seat, thinking how strange it was to have someone else driving my car.

"Why are you making me do this?"

"You need to drop something off to TJ," she said matter-of-factly.

My stomach rolled again as I glanced at the piece of paper in my lap. I'd made it the night I'd been humiliated at the Templeton football game. I didn't know what it was about that night that had possessed me to try drawing the white barn and the pond again, but I had. I'd pushed everything else out of my mind and poured all my energy into that drawing, trying once and for all to the capture everything I'd failed to bring to life before. The next thing I knew, I'd woken up with a crystal in my forehead.

"You said it was TJ's Christmas present." Charlie turned to me and flashed a smile. "He gave you that bracelet. Time to reciprocate."

"It was, Char. I *was* going to give him this. But now I feel stupid. He'll think it's the dumbest thing he's ever seen."

"He will not. That picture screams 'Marisa.'"

"Which is exactly why he'll laugh at it."

"He'll love it."

I stared at the sketch. I loved it, but that didn't mean TJ wouldn't think it was ridiculous. I'd dusted the tufts of snow around the pond with shimmery white powder to make them sparkle the way real snow did in the sun. I'd used a similar gray powder to bring the dancing mist ghosts to life over the pond. In the pond itself, I'd used tiny gray crystals to mimic the reflective parts of the surface. Behind it all stood the white barn, every bit as grand as I saw it in my mind. And next to that, I'd drawn Molly and Shirley, the horses he'd loved so much.

"I made this for me, not him."

"I don't care if you made it for Satan himself, you're giving it to him."

I grabbed the back of her seat and pulled myself up, panicking as we pulled up to TJ's house. "Charlie, turn the car around. What do you want me to do, walk up to the front door? What if his parents answer?"

She threw the car into park and picked up her cell phone from the cup holder. "A problem easily solved." She put the phone to her ear. "TJ? Come to your front door for a second. Marisa has something she wants to give you." With that, she turned to me and smiled.

"I hate you so much right now," I said.

But I got out of the car, picture in hand.

42

"HEY," TJ SAID WHEN HE OPENED THE DOOR. HE CHECKED ME OUT FROM head to toe and promptly redirected his stare to his feet. "You look amazing." In the background, his mother cleared dishes from the dining room table. She waved at me, then disappeared into the kitchen.

"Thanks." I smoothed my slinky black dress, suddenly very glad I'd had the chance to look this good in front of him, even if my shawl did nothing to prevent the goose bumps covering my skin and I was giving myself lockjaw trying not to let my teeth chatter. "I told you I wouldn't let anything stop me anymore. I didn't even bring my glasses."

TJ smiled. "I guess it's too late to get a tux and fix my attitude, huh?"

"It's never too late to fix your attitude."

We grinned at each other for an awkward couple of seconds. "So what's that?" TJ asked, indicating the paper I held against my bosom.

"This…" I looked at it one more time. *Too late to back out now.*

"This is for you." I held it out to him. "My latest attempt at capturing Narnia. Except I replaced the goats with horses."

He took the paper from me, his forehead creased as he studied it. A full minute must've passed before he said, "You made this for me?"

"Well, you made me a bracelet, so…" I studied the concrete step.

"TJ?" His mother called. "Why don't you invite your friend in? You're freezing us out in here!"

"Oh. Um—" He looked at me.

"No, it's okay. I have to get going anyway. Charlie is waiting." I gestured at the car. Charlie was on her cell phone, not looking particularly anxious to be anywhere.

"All right," TJ said. "Thanks for stopping by." He held up my drawing. "This is really great. You did an amazing job."

"I'm glad you like it." I twisted my hands, wanting to say more but not sure what. "Guess I'll see you at school."

I turned and walked away, feeling TJ's eyes on my back as I went. I knew it hadn't gone badly, but it wasn't quite the ending I had in mind. I could only hope he hadn't been completely satisfied either.

The night was every bit as awkward as I imagined it would be, even with, or maybe because of, my friends bending over backward to make sure it wasn't. I was dateless at a dance, and for all my talk about representing modern times and proclaiming myself a non-coward, I still felt like a loser without a date. Even Jordan must've talked his way back into Sara's good graces, because they were hanging all over each other every time I spotted them.

By some miracle, I caught him alone when we were leaving our respective restrooms at the same time. "So," I said. "Have you talked to Kendall lately?"

Jordan shook his head. "Nope. And I don't plan to."

"Me neither. It's probably better this way. And I'm glad your mother apologized to Charlie, even if the story she told the paper wasn't true. You're lucky she protected you."

Jordan sighed. "Listen, Marisa, I talked to Sara and I told her everything. I'm done with screwed-up relationships. I'm sorry I gave away your pin." He reached into the pocket of his jacket. "I got it back for you."

He opened his hand. My heart pin sat in his palm, as shiny and colorful as the day I finished it.

I blinked in surprise. "Jordan! N-no. No, I don't want the pin. I wasn't trying to hassle you."

He took my hand and placed the pin in it, then closed his fingers over mine. "Keep it. So you remember that every once in a while, I do try to do the right thing."

I held the pin against my chest. "I will. Thank you."

Jordan's shoulders relaxed. He looked over at the dance floor, where Sara twirled with one of her friends. Then he smiled at me. "I'm sorry. About everything. You know that, right?"

I nodded. "I know."

"Take care of yourself, okay?"

"I will. You too."

As Jordan turned and walked away, my cell phone vibrated inside my clutch. Who could be texting me now?

I dug the phone out of its impossibly tight confines and let out a little gasp when I saw the message: Outside on the patio. Can you meet me?

It was TJ.

I frantically scanned the windows, trying to spot him outside. It was too dark. So I ran—well, the stiletto-heel version of running—over to our table, snatched my shawl, and dashed out to the patio. Lingering by the door, my gaze darted around. A handful of people had braved the cold, huddled in the corner of the huge stone courtyard to sneak a cigarette or to talk on their phones away from the music. I peered around the massive, acorn-shaped fountain at the center. No TJ in sight.

"*Pssst*, Marisa!"

It came from my right. I headed toward it. "TJ?" I whisper-called. "Is that you?"

"Back here," he said. "In the trees."

"You're in the trees?"

"Not *in* them, in them. I didn't want to get in trouble for being here without a ticket."

Finally, I spotted him. The edge of the patio gave way to a wooded area, and I could just make out his frame leaning against one of the trees. "What are you doing here?"

He stepped toward me. "I owe you an apology."

"For what?"

"For letting you come here alone. I asked you to go to the dance with me, and I should've been here with you."

I wrapped my shawl tighter around my shoulders and looked at my shoes. "I wouldn't want you to take me if it's not really what you wanted. I don't need a pity date." His hands touched my shoulders and I looked up at him.

"It *is* what I wanted. I wouldn't have asked you if it wasn't."

Something about being this close to him, about looking into his eyes, blocked my ability to form a coherent sentence. "Okay. So…" I vaguely registered the muted notes of a slow song pulsating from inside the hall. "Do you want to dance?"

"Actually, I have a better idea." A hint of a smile played on his lips. "How much convincing would it take for you to get out of here with me?"

It didn't take much convincing at all. Within ten minutes, I'd babbled an explanation to Charlie, left my brother with my car keys and a warning to keep his hands where Charlie could see them, and found myself in the front seat of TJ's car, shivering inside my wrap as he aimed the heating vents at me on full blast.

"Where are we going?"

"You'll see," he said with a mischievous glint in his eye.

"I'm a little scared."

"Don't be. You'll like it."

A few minutes later, we were both cracking up laughing as he tried to guide me through his barn with my eyes closed.

"Why can't I look? I'm going to fall on my face!"

"No you won't. I'll let you open your eyes as soon as we get up to the loft."

I planted myself where I stood and stuck out my hand in protest, eyes still squeezed tight. "No way. You cannot bring me up the stairs in these shoes. Not unless you want me to break an ankle."

TJ stepped in front of me, or at least I guessed he did from the movement of the air. "Fair enough. I'll help you take them off. But no peeking." He bent in front of me and took my hand. "Here, hang on to my shoulder." His fingers touched my ankle and he slipped off one shoe, then the other. His hand lingered against my skin, moving up ever so slightly to my calf. Goosebumps that had nothing to do with the cold erupted all over me.

Then, without warning, I felt him near my face again. "Come on," he said softly, the sweetness of his breath touching my lips. "Almost there."

I wanted so badly to open my eyes, to let him see how much I wanted to kiss him, but I forced myself to keep them shut and let him guide me to the loft. Once we reached the top of the stairs, he stood behind me and put his hands on my shoulders.

"Ready?"

I nodded.

"Open your eyes."

I did. And gasped. The soft glow of Christmas lights illuminated the entire space; wrapped around the railing, draped over the coffee table, framing the couch. They cast shadows on paper snowflakes that he'd hung from the ceiling and taped all over the walls. And right there, in the middle of the paper blizzard, he'd hung my drawing.

"It's not the winter formal," he said. "But it was the best I could do on short notice."

"It's beautiful," I breathed. "I can't believe you hung up my picture."

"I can't believe you drew my horses."

"I did it from memory, so I'm sorry if it's not very good."

His hand traveled up my shoulder blade until his thumb grazed the back of my neck. "It's perfect. Thank you." He looked down at me and smiled. "So how about that dance?"

"There's no music."

Really? Really, Marisa?

"We don't need any." He lifted my wrap off my arms and tossed it onto the couch. That's when I noticed he'd traded his usual jeans and Henley for black pants and a white dress shirt. He looked amazing.

We stood facing each other and he put his arms around my waist. I lifted mine around his neck. We only swayed for one or two imaginary beats when I felt words rushing up my throat like a geyser.

"TJ, we should probably talk about Kendall."

He frowned. "There's nothing to talk about. It happened. It's over. End of story."

"I get the feeling you didn't want your relationship with her to be over."

"Marisa." He stilled and rested his hands above my hips. "Did you want it to be over with Jordan when he broke up with you?"

"Not at the time, but—"

"Exactly. It's the same thing with me and Kendall. There are things I'd change about the situation, like having my reputation dragged through the mud, and there are other things I wouldn't. Like breaking up with her."

The perfection of his answer sent warm, sweet relief flooding through me. "Really?"

He nodded.

"So do you believe me when I say I'm not hung up on Jordan anymore?"

He moved his hands to the sides of my face. "I told you," he whispered, leaning in close. "There's nothing to talk about."

As his lips came down on mine, every last thought flew out of my head.

I rose up on my toes and wound my arms tighter around his neck, relishing the smell and taste of him. Pressed up against him, molded into his embrace, I knew that if one worthwhile thing had come out of letting Kendall Keene back into my life, he was it. Her need to be the top dog had caused her to discard one of the best people in her life. And if I got to stand here and thread my fingers through TJ's hair and feel the softness of his lips against mine because of it, then I was more than happy to pick up where she left off.

I didn't even know how we wound up on the couch, limbs tangled around one another. I didn't care. All I knew was that TJ had restored my faith that cheaters didn't have to be the rule and exceptions really did exist. After tonight, I'd no longer be spending my time chasing down other people's problems. I'd be too busy appreciating how perfect life could be, bathed in twinkling lights, surrounded by a swirl of paper snowflakes, and wrapped up in the right pair of arms.

Acknowledgments

This book's journey to publication began four years ago, so if I've forgotten to mention anyone who played a part in bringing it to life, please know that I am truly grateful for your help!

Special thanks to my agent, John M. Cusick, for being the first person to believe in this story, and for your spot-on revision suggestions that made the rest of my edits a breeze. I remain in awe of your awesomeness.

To my editor, Annette Pollert-Morgan, thank you for swooning over this book, for loving the same things that I love about it, and for adding the perfect finishing touches. I am so grateful to you for giving Marisa's story a home.

Hugs to the fabulous readers who suffered through the book's earliest iterations and helped me whip it into shape: Marieke Nijkamp, without whom I would not have written the kissing scene that became the foundation for the entire book. Dahlia Adler (whom we can thank for Marisa's love affair with the word "vom"), Maggie Hall, Jenny Kaczorowski, Erica Chapman, and Katie Mills. Your input and commiseration have been invaluable.

To my husband, thank you for our tradition of cutting down our Christmas tree at Maple Row Tree Farm, the place that inspired TJ and Marisa's "Narnia." The memories I invented for them started with the memories we made for ourselves.

For my mom, mother-in-law, and sister, thank you for the time you took to get me back on my feet during one of the most difficult times of my life. You helped me take the first steps toward light at the end of a long, very dark tunnel. I love you.

And finally, to Aunt Gloria. I will never be able to thank you enough for the five weeks you selflessly spent away from your home and family because you knew how badly I needed you. Thank you for everything you did for my little family, for allowing me the time I needed to finish this story, and for helping me feel like myself again. No matter how many words I write, they will never be adequate enough to express how grateful I am to you.

About the Author

Gina Ciocca graduated from the University of Connecticut with a degree in English, but in her mind, she never left high school. She relocated from Connecticut to Georgia, where she lives with her husband and son. When she's not reading or writing, you can find her taking long walks around the lake in her neighborhood. Gina can also be found online at writersblog-gina.blogspot.com, on Instagram @gmciocca, and Twitter @gmc511.